WITHDRAWN

THE
BACHELORS'
BRIDE

THE BACHELORS' BRIDE

a novel

Stephen Koch

Marion Boyars · New York · London

Published in the United States and Great Britain
in 1986 by Marion Boyars Publishers
262 West 22nd Street, New York, NY 10011 and
24 Lacy Road, London SW15 1NL

Distributed in the United States by
The Scribner Book Companies Inc

Distributed in Canada by
Collier Macmillan Canada Inc

Distributed in Australia by
Wild and Woolley

Library of Congress Cataloging in Publication Data
Koch, Stephen
   The bachelors' bride.
   I. Title.
PS 3561.03B33   1986   813'.54   85-23278

ISBN 0-7145-2856-0 cloth

British Library Cataloguing in Publication Data
Koch, Stephen
   The bachelors' bride: a novel.
   I. Title
813'.54[F]   PS3561.03

Printed and bound in the United States by

for Peter Hujar

I would like to express my gratitude to the Michael Károlyi Memorial Foundation, and especially to the late Madame Catherine Károlyi, for their invaluable assistance in the completion of this novel.

S.K.

PART 1

chapter 1

I first laid eyes on Mel Dworkin during the winter of . . . the Supremes. The scene was one of the great, get-down dancing parties of my youth, wonderful in the sweet, fresh eagerness of its systematic decadence. It was a downtown dancing party, deep in SoHo during SoHo's first phase, raw, real, unrestauranted, before it had even a name. The place was a great grey, grungy, unreconstructed space that shook to the wail of *My World Is Empty Without You, Babe!* and the crowd was frugging itself into abandon in that pounding room. The perfect dancehall of our new energy, our new eros.

It still seems incredible that such a shimmering presence can have become a past. New York was brand new, and the only place in the world. Art, like life, had just begun. We, all of us, had been granted access to some kind of new and potentially endless moment, like nothing that had ever happened before. Youth, and history, had chosen us. The Beatles were at their height and the Supremes were in their wigs. *Baby Love* rang in our ears; just the day before yesterday, Rauschenberg and Johns had been named old masters. The reputation of Mel Dworkin had reached its zenith: he was the painter of the year, our new star. And I was there for it, a very young art historian just about to begin the dissertation that time and a little tragedy would make into *The Bachelors' Bride*.

I admit I was a recent convert to Dworkin's art. When it first started getting all that attention, I had disapproved. I disapproved of its success. Among the younger people at the Institute for Fine Arts, I'd presided over a little faction of *molto serioso* types determined to defend the one true modernism of the School of Paris—a story that so far as I was concerned had come to a happy ending with Jackson Pollock—against these swinging Duchampian showmen. Obscurantists. Panders. Pop artists. Parvenus. Frauds. I proposed to use the searchlight of esthetic orthodoxy to hunt down the heretics and expose them. It makes me smile now. Here I sit, almost twenty years later, an executor of Mel's estate and keeper of the myth. I had not yet had my Damascus experience. That was all before I'd really seen the greatness of Mel's early work, before it had awakened my interest in Duchamp and set me on the path that led to *The Bachelors' Bride*. And before that party.

I suppose the slum where we danced that night must be by now some stockbroker's palace of post-modernism, but in those days lofts south of Houston Street were long colorless halls of superannuated industrial dinge. The single sink, almost the only plumbing, would be an unscrubbable wash-up trough for the wage slaves who'd once burned out their lives in the sweat-shop. The bar that night was no array of French and British bottles glistening before an out-of-work actor pretending to be an art deco icon. It was a sagging card table soppy with spilled cheap wine and beer, melted ice and shattered lemons. I don't remember how I got invited. I don't remember the hosts. I probably crashed. In those days, I spent many hours — when not preparing classes and musing on Duchamp's *The Bride Stripped Bare* — contriving ways to crash parties. For example, I was a regular at Pana Grady's vast, glittering, and utterly crashable bashes at the Dakota. On more than one occasion I had also finagled entrée to Frank O'Hara's much more select assemblies — gatherings of the poet-curator's hundred or two closest friends, across from Grace Church. There crashing took a bit of doing, but I did it, and found myself in very slick company. It was fast-talking, and funny, and a little frightening. I was twice introduced to O'Hara and once even had a real conversation with him. Or rather he chattered happily at me, about *Dark Victory* — "I'll have a large *help*ing of prognosis *neg*-ative." He gasped out the favorite line for what must have been the ten thousandth time, while I caught the fine movements of his eyes looking me over, wondering who, if anyone, I was.

But from the party where I first saw Mel, I remember only the Supremes, bursting through that grimy shouting space

> *Stop! In the name of love!*
> *Be-fore you break my heart!*
> *Stop! In the name of love!*
> *Be-fore we break apart!*

I can also recall . . . no food. Nothing. No dip, no crackers, no cheese. Nothing but empty plastic bowls from which every single potato chip had been snatched away. There were also, so far as I could see, no art world heavies, and I scanned the room in mild disappointment, although a breathless and sweating girl had just told me that Frank Stella had *just* left.

Then suddenly I spotted Mel, instantly recognizable in his fame, and in the flesh.

> *Baby, baby, I'm aware of where you go*
> *Each time you leave my door.*
> *I watch you walk down the street*
> *Knowing your other love you meet . . .*

Mel was dressed entirely in black: black turtle neck, black jeans, black boots, with a belt of hammered silver and turquoise low around his waist. He wasn't dancing, but he was in a state of high excitement, his face in an alcoholic flush. The California looseness of his body, ordinarily so lax and laid back, was tight with sexual intensity working its way out. My man was on the prowl.

I've known of your, your secluded nights
I've even seen her, maybe once or twice.
But is her sweet expression
Worth more than my love and affection?

And of course he didn't notice me at all. Why should he have, in the room-rocking intensity of that moment? Some gawking male intellectual on the sidelines? Mel had very different things on his mind. In the years to come, I learned that Mel drank, among other reasons, to reach desire. It was not always too accessible to him, desire. His myth is that of a cocksman; all the photographs show the lean hungry I-want-it look of a brooding virility. In fact Mel's passions were quite far below the surface. You always could sense their presence, but they were not easily reached. They were visible but inaccessible. A little like his paintings. The old game of present absence that he learned from dear old Duchamp.

The Supremes sang on:

Stop! In the name of love!
Before you break my heart!
Stop! In the name of love!
Before you break my heart!

Dancing made the ancient space shake, and the very slight distinction between invited and uninvited guest vanished in the night. At the edges of the dance floor, the eager, bright-eyed decadence of 1967 had begun to slump and fondle. The night had grown late and loose enough for men to begin to dance with men, something that in 1967 happened only after midnight. And then I spotted Mel again, this time on the sidelines. He was pushing a woman with wonderfully abundant red hair against an unpainted brick wall, both palms spread against the brick above her shoulders, seeming to push himself away from her at the same time he drove in against her, grinding a kiss against her mouth, jabbing his hips against hers, touching and not touching her at once, in a kind of lascivious push-up.

I remember the moment exactly. I stared. I gaped.

Something inside me was seared by the image and it has never left me. It is as though I first saw it five minutes ago. This was the man I myself wished to be. I remember the exact angle of Mel's head as he kissed her; the precise rough rhythm of his movement in and out, self-tantalizing; I remember the exact erotic slant of his neck.

The dancing went on and a few minutes later I saw him again with the red-headed woman, pulling her by the hand as she laughed, and at the far end of the room, shouldering open a room divider our host had set up in the hope of separating the party space from the private regions of their living space back there. They were not going to separate it from Mel. Mel was Mel, and he went where he pleased. Beyond that room divider there was privacy. Beyond that room divider there was a bed. He slipped through it, pulling the redhead by the hand, after him.

Think it over! Think it oh-oh-ver!

My head pounded with the self-permission of the moment, and the Supremes wailed on, ebullient in their latest despair, until Mel re-appeared after the tussle in the back room and was heading with the red-headed girl toward the door.

I danced on, as good as alone in my solitary excitement, picturing their urgent taxi ride back to the cocksman's garçonnière. It was all fantasy, of course: I imagined it all. But in my mind's eyes I orchestrated in detail a squalid and irresistible erotic adventure for him and for her. I pictured their drunken laughing stumble up the stairs that led to his studio. As he dug for his doorkeys I saw their clutching kiss on the landing. I imagined her hand, fingers spread, driving under the waistband of his black jeans. I saw the door swing open; I saw the two of them stumbling into the dark, wide, high workroom. Mel yanked the cord that hung down from the fluorescent light fixtures, and as they made the place flicker into brightness I saw the fixtures sway against the room's dark shadows. I imagined a room that reeked of turpentine and acrylics and work, his work, the half-completed canvasses lining the walls, and I imagined around the couple the whole idiosyncratic private world of junk and dreck and art and objects that Mel used as the starting point for the transformations he worked. As I danced on and on, the fantasy crossed my mind again and again. I saw them engaged in that ecstatic phallic rumpus happening on Mel's mattress on the floor. (I was sure it would be a mattress on the floor. Time proved me right). I saw it, the whole heterosexual ecstasy, all mouth and hunger and self-abandon.

So that was encounter number one — a glimpse, followed by a fantasy in my overheated, celebrity-struck, party-fevered brain. The truth is that I never was in the scuzzy but famous old loft on Bond Street. By the time I had really met Mel and been invited to his house, he was living in his new rich-artist's quarters, with its white on white on white, its marble tables and Corbusier chrome, and its collection of Everybody in that generation, traded for his own work. That place was on Mercer Street and was austere in a way that only money could buy. One did not imagine mad abandoned humping on its glistening floors. But the famous place, the one that fills the reveries of art students the world over is the dump on Bond Street that I imagined that night. That's where the famous photographs of Mel posing by the great early pictures were taken. That's where they got the pictures to make the torn tee-shirt posters of Mel in his paint-spattered jeans that are up in all the dorm rooms; it is from Bond Street that come the images of Mel the seventies created: The James Dean of the plastic arts, Mel the assassinated Orphic hero. I imagined a mattress on the floor that night, and that is exactly what was there. That mattress still can be seen, by the way, in the photograph published on page 67 of my book: *Dworkin: The Anti-Tradition's Heir*. In that picture, Mel stands mugging beside a bemused and staring Andy Warhol. The mattress is almost out of frame on the lower left. I mention it (just in passing) in the chapter on Mel's studio life and the working methods of neo-dada called "The Arena of

Chance." I'm rather proud of that chapter. Starting with purely anecdotal material, I weave one of my better pieces of criticism, I think. In fact, I view it as the last word.

I mentioned a Damascus experience with sixties art, and I should explain. About six months before I first met Mel, right about the time I had passed my orals, Henry Geldzahler had been granted two smallish ground floor rooms in the Metropolitan for the purpose of mounting his selection of contemporary American paintings. It was a very small space for such a purpose — small even for a museum which at that time gave only the most perfunctory attention to that subject. There was room for only a few paintings — in fact one entire wall was glass, floor-to-ceiling windows looking out onto Cleopatra's needle and a parking lot. Geldzahler may not be a figure for whom I am invariably lost in admiration, but it must be conceded that those were great rooms. I discovered them one day on aching legs. I hadn't even any idea they were there. There was the Jasper Johns *White Flag*. There was a large grey and black Stella. There was a Lippold Sunburst. There was also, isolated against one wall (mercifully a wall directly in front of one little bench where one could sit, back to the windows) the very large, now very famous work by Mel painted in 1961, and known as *Chrystie Strut*.

Chrystie Strut. It was a canvas larger than its spectator, eleven feet wide and a little under seven feet high, its surface divided into seven sharply defined pictorial arenas, within which had been silk screened an extraordinarily allusive array of neo-dada detritus. Though some of the images seem to suggest collage, in fact only one image — the picture of Caroline Kennedy on her pony — was torn from a real Daily News and pasted on. Dworkin was very much the master of the silkscreening then so much in vogue, and the work is certainly one of that fashion's most notable examples. The surface is almost busy, an untraceable array of allusions and near allusions, icons and near icons, and some just plain baffles. (For example, the number in the lower left *seems* to be a date. It is not.)

All these images are under a wash of color in a false spectrum, color resting on the surface very much like a stain, which nonetheless sometimes seems to recede into the picture plane and form the ground, an alternation that tends to confound the mounted look of the images spread before us.

Those colors have — and had, then especially, ah, then — a very startling freshness. One had never quite seen them before. God knows I'm no admirer of John Bishop-Martell, or his incompetent monograph on Dworkin. Still, there is a certain impressionistic rightness to Bishop-Martell's aside that *Chrystie Strut* "glows with the light of the sixties."

Anyway. There I sat, now almost twenty years ago, looking at a picture. Let me trace the process of my looking. First, and above all, I tried hard not to look at what was in front of my face. The point is important. The most obviously striking, the by far most notable and commanding aspect of Dworkin's work at this moment was its *presence* — a presence, and a presentness, as immediately perceived as . . . a cry. The cry of *Chrystie Strut*, to be sure, is a cry of joy. Even so, that dimension of triumph, of sudden vision, seemed too strong, too clear . . . too much, in short. My impulse was to evade it. I wanted to look, but I also wanted to look away. I looked away by using the slightly perverse tactic of burying myself in the picture, setting out on in effort to decipher its ravishing web of quotation and allusion, an activity which seemed to me more subtle, and a good deal safer, than the picture's. . . . cry.

I was trying to "figure out" *Chrystie Strut*. I use the phrase advisedly. In fact, I was not understanding anything, but I was being seduced into much. My "readings" — I seem to recall they struck me as wonderfully subtle — were only seducing me deeper and deeper into the picture's dialectic of figure and ground. I did not yet understand how Dworkin's willed illegibility encoded a kind of secret *symbolisme*, a deep closet romanticism — seemingly at odds with the work's immediate, almost brassy vanguardism. (See my "Dilemmas of Literalism in Sixties Painting," and, for that matter, "The Arena of Chance.")

Trying to absorb the details of the picture, I began to notice an effect which one might illustrate by suggesting it is the opposite of that modern-day visual seduction effected by the detail plate in art books and slides, especially of work prior to Cézanne: that easy cropping of Renaissance space which has the effect of making the work look so suddenly *modern*, so suddenly, in a new way . . . *profound*. The hand of the soldier at the foot of the cross becomes so much more arresting, more beautiful, more *ours* than the whole dreary crucifixion. That sort of thing.

Well, as I attempted to cerebrate my way through *Chrystie Strut*, I began to be seduced by an effect exactly opposite. My ability to concentrate on isolated details seemed in a state of continuous dissolution. Try as I might, I was being steadily, hypnotically, irresistibly re-absorbed into the whole surface. I remember thinking it *was* a bit like being high — there was a lot of talk around in those days about the wicked heartless druggy new generation of painters — and the experience *did* rather suggest the sense-isolating aspect of pot. I was trying to escape the picture by cerebrating my way into it. Instead I was lulled into a dissolution of all concentrated attention. Instead of deciphering the surface, I was sinking deeper and deeper into my *absorption*.

In point of fact, I was experiencing for the first time what sixties criticism soon enough would come to adore as the "all-over" experience. *Chrystie Strut* glowed before me in a kind of untimed pulsation, and I slipped into its cool ecstasy as on a drug. I looked, not exactly thoughtlessly, but with my mind awake to a kind of thought-in-general; an extremely alert sensitivity to a complex surface which never exactly produced *a* thought, but something closer to a web of awareness about something not quite there: "an old song," as Wallace Stevens might have put it, "that will not declare itself."

It was an endless moment. I don't know how long I sat on that bench, seeing all of *Chrystie Strut* at once. Probably not long. Ten minutes? Fifteen? I could not have guessed the importance that so soon would be attributed to the experience I was having, and others like it. I had very little sense of the work's historical specifics — for example, I thought not at all about its possible relation to Duchamp, of ways in which *Chrystie Strut* represents a lush, rich, finally romantic vindication of everything that was hateful and mean in the mind of that horrible old man. I knew I was looking at a painting by one Mel Dworkin, but I had no real conception of who Mel Dworkin might be, apart from someone who in my youthful conservatism I'd supposed I disliked.

Nonetheless I was sure — and I am sure still — that I had just passed through an experience not different in quality or kind from ones I'd known in front of Matisse's *Red Studio*, or Picasso's *Night-Fishing at Antibes*, or Pollock's *Blue Poles*, or, for that matter, even the *Demoiselles d'Avignon. Chrystie Strut* was the first, genuine, first-class masterpiece I had seen by an American of my own generation, of my own time, my own place. It enfranchised me.

By the time I stood up from that bench, *my* sixties had begun.

But I didn't actually meet Mel until quite long after, and three months or so after the dancing party. I'd once again rigged an invitation to some soirée, this time very correct, uptown — York Avenue or some such — and rich. It was the home of a collector important enough for graduate students like ourselves to request admission to the sacred precincts. I'd gone with a friend from the institute, my pretext, as I recall. The occasion did not at first seem promising. We had stood unspoken-to for about half an hour, not knowing whether to stare at or ignore the Picabias and Cornells, the Max Ernsts and the Francis Bacons. Boredom had begun to loom large in the solemn social void when with a small enchanted gasp I spotted Mel.

Letting no excitement show, I muttered through rigid lips, "do you see who I see?"

My pretext did.

"*I* am going to talk to him."

Mel sat draped over an easy chair in a small side room, quite alone. The black forelock was in his eyes, and his black horn-rims were slipping down his nose. (I've often thought in some perplexity about the number of things Mel let obscure his vision). His eyes were wandering in undisguised ennui. There was no red-head for him to run after, and he sat talking to nobody, looking in his solitary, vaguely unhappy way quite dignified. I can't imagine why he was at the party at all. Nobody was talking to him. Nobody came near him. It seemed nobody dared.

I dared.

Gripping my drink and swallowing down my fear, I sidled across the room to Mel's half, where he continued to sit gazing around him in abstraction and of course entirely ignoring me. I remember thinking that I never had stood so close to somebody that famous before. I felt the celebrated presence with a special panicky nearness. Mel shifted his weight, weary. My heart was throbbing.

At first I was pretending to be looking through some books on a nearby shelf — a vapid pretext, but the best I could think of for the moment. I was trying to think of something better. I remember thinking it was a bit like looking for a gambit in a pickup. And then I spotted my chance.

Expensively framed on a nearby wall hung one of the most ravishing prints from the notable series of Dworkin lithographs known as *David's Quick Dreams*. I knew my course: I strolled over to the picture, looked it over, took one fortifying slug of my drink and turned to Mel with a big smile.

"That's a pretty terrific picture."

God knows it was not a dazzling gambit, but it was the only thing my nervousness let me find. Mel looked back at me through his black horn-rims. His eyes were hard with all the mistrust of the celebrated. For a moment I was certain he was not going to say anything at all, but simply look away as if I weren't there, as if my foolish compliment never had been turned.

Instead, he finally said, "thanks" . . . still not quite sure.

I think some intellectual variety of grace was handed to me that night. In any case, after I pulled up a footstool and we began to talk, I seemed to be granted almost magical access to everything I wanted to say, exactly as I wanted to say it. I wasn't tongue-tied; I felt no nervousness. My ideas kept popping up, each at the right time and in the right order, and each time I found the right words for them. I even spoke with a certain nervy eloquence. As we went back and forth, I could tell that Mel was interested and even impressed. My confidence grew from that look in his eyes. Conversation locked us together.

Remembering now what we talked about that night, I blush with how much of it was a mere inventory of fashion from Wittgenstein to Ad Reinhardt.But the really magic subject that night was Duchamp. I am afraid I let myself flatter Mel quite shamelessly, but somehow that night flattery was the fuel of inspiration. I knew perfectly well that what I was saying could only be very welcome to Mel. I had managed to guess with considerable accuracy the description of things he was likely to want to hear. Yet I had never felt so sure of myself, it seemed, as then, spinning those off-the-cuff semi-truths that talking to him seemed to make fall into place.

I went on and on about Duchamp. The austere sage of Neuilly and Twelfth Street was, I explained to Mel, the most underrated figure of the great phase of modernism, and the rise of his influence in the sixties was functioning as the return of the modernist, its transforming power. He was destined to preside, like a great, grey, perplexing but benignant ghost, over whatever modernism — that is, whatever serious art — managed to be produced during this century's final half. In this sense he was the pivot for the revaluation of all preceding art that was going on in New York. The Picasso worshippers in the schools were all wrong. Theirs was the new academicism. The mere sensuality of the eye the School of Paris had promoted had become the deadened grip from which any serious new artist would have to release himself to function significantly. The world now, I explained, (and boy, did I harp on the word *now*) yearned for a renovating esthetic of disintegration. The old flaccid sensual unities were finished. Nobody would do serious work based on them ever again. The new re-energizing subversiveness was indeterminacy. Its muse, I said, was dissociation. Its master was Duchamp.

My rapturous seducer's heart flew on sensing how very much Mel wanted to hear all that. I sat on a cassock beside his chair and leaned forward like a lover, explaining how history — and I spoke with the authority of history's appointed spokesman — had dealt a new round. And then I clinched my tirade by clearing my throat and very gently confessing that what had made me see all this with the clarity I now felt had been the experience of coming to understand *Chrystie Strut*.

"Oh yeah," said Mel, trying to keep me from seeing quite how well all this was working with him. "That kind of surprises me. I don't really see much of Duchamp in that picture."

I was quick to contradict. "Oh *I* do."

"Maybe indirectly, kind of," Mel said. "To me, see, Marcel has always been mainly a permission giver. There's no point in making work that looks like his stuff, you know."

"Of *course* not."

"But to me, he gave permission to put into the picture, sort of, what I . . . *really* think." Mel gave me a smile with that last "*really* think."

"But of course. That is Duchamp's role, at least in the first instance. He breaks this paralyzing responsibility of making art somehow . . . live up to what came before."

"Yeah, he did that for me. See, the thing about these guys, especially the really great ones, is that their authority is so strong that it seems as though the only way to do it is their way.

And yet it is really very narrow, what they're doing. Very much their own special thing. It's not so sharable. And once you see that, it suddenly looks . . . limited." Mel gave me the smile again. "You get that the authority comes from a kind of limitation, even for the best, the free-est. Sometimes I look at Picasso or a Pollock and I think, hell, they didn't even see their own possibilities."

I persisted. "Well, for me the question is not at all whether there is some Duchamp in your work, but what the presence of Duchamp has to do with the fact that your work is beautiful. Because after all, your work differs from Duchamp's in all sorts of ways, but most of all in that."

"But Duchamp *is* beautiful."

"In your eyes perhaps, but he never intended the work to be beautiful. Not after 1912, 1913. The notion of the beautiful offended him. Really."

"I know. The thing is he couldn't help it. The stuff is beautiful anyway."

"Well, my theory would be that your work holds its sumptuous surface because it comes from what America has done with Duchamp. Duchamp himself is a perverse figure. He is an essentially mischievous mind, a subversive mind, a withholder, the malicious keeper of a code for self-annihilation. As you sink deeper into Duchamp, the work becomes less accessible. The mystery becomes more arcane, the obscurantism more malicious. Looking at Duchamp is essentially a self-extinguishing process. But not with you. As you look more and more at your work, it becomes more and more gorgeous. It is as though you have been able to make beauty out of Duchamp because you have looked at him through the eyes of Cage."

I had interested him anew. "Hey! Hey, you know, you really may well be right about that. Because you know, when I was back at Berkeley. . . ."

"You *went* to Berkeley?" This fact somehow had never reached my dossier.

"Oh, I didn't really go. I just hung out. You know. Took a course or two. Knew people. So, anyway, I remember I got ahold of a copy of Cage's *Silence*. And I mean . . . *wow*! There is a transforming force. I mean, I really do date something in my life from reading *Silence*. I remember I sat in the backyard of some guy's house in Berkeley and spent the whole day out there reading *Silence*, and when I got to the end I went straight back to the beginning and read it a second time. It was really important for me. Much more important than Marcel. I didn't really know about Marcel until a lot later. He was still classroom stuff, so far as I was concerned."

"You keep calling him Marcel. Do you . . . do you *know* Duchamp? Personally?"

"Uh-huh," Mel nodded, cautious again. He did not seem to like the question, though I'd later learn that his friendship with Duchamp was one of the most important relations in his life. "I know him pretty well." He seemed to withdraw, as if he had opened up too much by showing his enthusiasm for Cage.

Then it dawned on me that we had been talking for a long time and ignoring the party entirely. I was also conscious that we were being left alone in a rather peculiar way. The truth is that, given Mel's preoccupation, nobody dared approach. I saw people glancing at us and pretending not to. For the first time in my life, I was inside the circle of fame. Its isolating glow was all around us. My friend was nowhere to be seen.

Mel wanted to leave. He asked me if I was going his way.

"Downtown?" I jumped at it.

"Downtown."

We shared a taxi, and on the ride south, my eloquence subsided into merely juvenile emotion. *I can't believe it. I am riding downtown in a cab with Mel Dworkin! He's right beside me, here in this cab!*

Conversation vanished. As we rode, Mel was staring out the window at the dark streets sliding by. He was chewing gum. He often chewed gum. *Is he bored? I must be boring him.* The sound of his mouth moving seemed like the sound of Mel looking. The movement of his mouth . . . interested me.

At Seventh Avenue and Perry Street he let me out, refusing my offer of a contribution to the fare and offered instead an old-fashioned he-man handshake.

"Jason, it's been a pleasure." He peered out — I still remember that peering turn of his head. Just like any other American boy, he ended: "See ya", even though, as the cab pulled away, I was absolutely certain I never would see him again.

Except that I did. The very next day.

He called late the next morning to invite me to the Mercer Street loft for drinks with "some people" late that afternoon. I had not known, of course, that Mel had an entourage, but that is precisely what I found that afternoon when I arrived at the appointed place. It was a group of people whom I came to think of as The Bunch. Being surrounded with company was somehow part of Mel's mental processes, and when he retreated into solitude, as he did for example that last winter of his life, it was a pretty sure sign that something was wrong, and that no work was being produced. The Bunch consisted of some fairly classic hangers-on, former studio assistants, sometimes former girlfriends, the occasional rich admirer; here an eager epigone, there a failed contemporary. It also contained some people who later on, during the seventies, became well known. For example, Seymour Kaplan and his wife Iva were really crucial members of The Bunch. A little known fact. Seymour was one of the great slow starters. He was working and working hard all through the sixties, and at that time Mel was one of the few people who were interested, remote though Kaplan is from neo-dada. Then of course there was Jeffrey Hastings. The fatal Jeffrey. Jeffrey too was one of the unknown figures in whom Mel believed, whom Mel admired. Too much. But more of that later. The Bunch had some interesting personnel. Deep in his passive voyeurism, Mel dominated it effortlessly, without seeming even to try. And my success in seducing Mel the night before had led to my being invited — not in so many words of course — to become a member. Once I realized what had happened, and began to think about it, I rationalized the role with the name of Ruskin.

Starfucker!

It was almost as if the choice were not mine. I started going back almost every afternoon for our chats about everything from Wittgenstein to Josef Albers to Tiepolo to the Marquis de Sade. In short order, news of my new friendship began to leak out — I did a great deal of the leaking myself — and with that my whole status in New York began to change. I also became aware of what my fellow teaching assistants at N.Y.U. thought of it and me. It wasn't nice. I ignored them and hurried back to Mercer Street. I had moved beyond them. Unlike them, I had been admitted to the large arena, I was in the real world. I saw no reason to apologize for that. *Sycophant!* I almost could hear them hissing the word in the bitter little masonite cubicles on the third floor of South Hall, as I rushed off for some new encounter on The Scene.

Starfucker!

I was too excited to care.

Often it would be only Mel and me on those afternoons, since chat about Wittgenstein usually cleared the room of the rest of The Bunch. He would take me back to his huge, junk-cluttered, high airy workspace in the Mercer Street place. The work would be covering entire walls, stuck with masking tape to chairs, lying on the floor. The fluorescent lights above us would come flickering on, and he would snap on the radio — Mel seemed unable to look without sound, some junky music in the background. "Look at that. What do you think of that?" He'd point to some new and extravagant Dworkin on the wall.

At this point I would step into my assigned role as exegete and theoretician. What did I think of X? I would look, and then I would tell him exactly what I thought of X. It seemed I always thought something.

"You think so, huh?" he'd say, completely noncommittal, once I was through.

"That's what I think," I would answer, simplicity itself.

"How come?" he would ask.

And so I would proceed to tell him how come. Mel would stand there, chewing his gum, his hands slid into his back pockets, nodding — that nod of comprehension as he shifted his weight made him look like some basketball player listening to a bit of especially subtle advice from the coach. "Riiiight," he would drawl when he got what I was driving at. When I would point, he would look as if for the first time, absorbing my emphasis of his post-modernism like the most dutiful student of all. "Riiight," he would conclude when I pointed out this or that quotation or connection or turn. He would sigh in seeming pleasure. "Cute," he'd say, "that's real cute." He'd nod. He would sip his bourbon.

Then he would pull the cord and the fluorescent lights would die again as we stepped back into what we called "the living space." There was one huge room with glass tables and wicker chairs, the whole space dominated by a bed perched on a high, laddered sleeping platform. "What you say is interesting, Jason. It really is."

Then he would nod, as if to himself, with some deep private gratification.

Sometimes I would stay at the Mercer Street loft half the night talking, and sometimes, once summer had come, we would go to spend the weekend at Mel's wonderful house and studio on a high promontory overlooking the Great Peconic Bay in the town of Springs, out near East Hampton. I remember one night very late with Mel, one of the early summers of our friendship, out at the house in Springs, sitting at the big round butcher-block table he had in the center of his kitchen. I remember the chill salt air coming in from the night and bugs battering against the lamps out on the deck beyond, which was perched on stilts and from which a long flight of wooden stairs led down to Mel's rocky beach on the Bay's shore. I remember Mel standing with a dishtowel in his hand, talking about his work — he always talked about his work — with a quizzical look.

"I'm thinking about fraud," he said. "I think about fraud a lot. People talk about my work being a put-on, and I get mad, and I think, 'those fuckers, the nerve . . .' but then, you know, there used to be times, back when the work was first getting known, and suddenly there was publicity and criticism, and money, and everybody talking — and I would think, 'Well, this has to be some mistake.' I mean, sometimes *I* would think the work was a fraud. I thought, 'This must be part of dada,' you know, part of the inheritance. I'd lay in bed at night, sweaty and amazed, thinking 'What the fuck is going on here? I don't know what to say to these people who tell me all these things.' I would think only, 'I'm scared.' And I was. 'They're all just making a colossal mistake,' I'd say; I mean — I'd been there on Bond Street trying and trying to make these really good pictures, trying to make them look like — really good pictures. I worked and worked and it was just awful, they all looked just awful. And I'd go off to the Cedar Street tavern at night, and there would be all these great men — like de Kooning might be there, or Ad, and they'd be talking and drinking and I'd listen from the sidelines and start again the next morning, trying to be *like* them, you know, but. . . ."

He tossed the towel aside, looked for his drink, and then sat with me. "I just was going crazy with all these ideas, and I couldn't decide which idea to follow. I couldn't decide why to do this instead of that. But I worked. I worked hard — very hard; harder than I worked later, in fact. But all that work and confusion was just making me . . . tired. Tired and bored, and it was so boring to be twenty-three and tired. I just wanted to cry. I'd look at that crap and I'd want to cry. Finally, what I think I did was give up. Forget great men. Forget the Cedar Street. Forget inheritance." He gave me his smile. "Forget importance. Honestly."

The merciful salty air blew in across the kitchen table, and I think it was in this conversation that I noticed how, after he had become famous, Mel had transferred his bar life to his kitchen table. "But I was so bitter," he went on after a minute. "I hurt so much inside . . . and I thought, 'Who gives a damn? It's for damn sure nobody else does, so why should I?' And so I didn't give a damn myself, anymore. There I was, somebody supposed to be making pictures, and *I didn't know how*. I couldn't stand admitting it to myself, but I had no choice — *I didn't know how*. I said to myself, 'I am this little kid who goes out and gets drunk in a barful of famous men and then works himself silly, and I don't know what the fuck I'm doing.' Then something happened, and I think what happened was that I gave up. It was real. Giving up — that part was real."

Mel rubbed his chin. "I kept on doing the work but it was all in bitterness. And stuff started going in that was just crazy, like Caroline Kennedy! You weren't supposed to have *heard* of Caroline Kennedy at the Cedar Street. And you would chop off your hands before you put her in a *picture*. It was nuts. Just nuts. And I saw this picture and I thought, *ponies*. And I put it in."

He paused. "And so I started making those pictures, and I really didn't have the faintest idea of what I was doing. I was just working away, kind of hysterical and then I suddenly thought— Hey. *Hey* now." We both laughed. "I stepped back and I looked and thought: Hmmmmm. It was almost like I was seeing it by giving up, I really felt like this complete failure, but then I guess there was also this still small voice that was saying to me, 'Hey, Mel. Sweetheart. This isn't so bad.' " We laughed again. " 'Don't be so scared.' And I would look at it and I'd think, 'Who gives a shit?' And I would just keep going.

"In those days I was . . . I really was . . . inside something I didn't understand. I really was in the cloud of unknowing. Because it all happened *through unawareness*. All my painting — it was so exciting . . . pretty soon there were these paintings all around the place, and I kept looking at them, and before you know it, I was thinking about it, and even really liking it — I mean, seeing the point. I'm not sure I've gotten all the way to seeing it all *yet*. But it was pretty interesting, sometimes. Still is."

Mel was looking out those open windows, out over the sink, into the night, the dune grass, the mild unsurflike shore of the Great Peconic Bay beyond.

"It was . . . *interesting*. At a certain point I knew that." He rested his chin on his fist. He seemed to be in a reverie. "It was interesting . . . and then there was something else. Slowly, really I can't tell when it happened, I stopped having that feeling that I didn't know how to do it. Instead, I realized that I did know how to make pictures. *My* pictures, at least . . ."

There was silence. "And I am just trying to remember how I knew. And . . . I think I know."

"How?"

"Because . . . because I could imitate it." He turned and looked at me squarely. "That's how I knew. I could imitate it. *I could do it again.*"

I nodded in silence. I felt profoundly privileged. I knew I was being told things Mel would tell nobody else.

He worked in a cloud of unknowing, and I was going to be the voice from that cloud. I would articulate what he had seen. I was chosen.

Starfucker!

chapter 2

Becoming part of Mel's entourage made me feel real, and feeling real produced important changes in my sex life. It was through Mel that I was introduced to Nancy Hopkins, and the truth is that without the new confidence that his friendship gave me, I never would have dared make a move toward her. Nancy was then not yet the grand doyenne of art dealers that she has since become, but she was — as she remains — Mel's dealer, and that gave her great cachet. She was a Connecticut rich girl who'd linked together an inheritance and a divorce settlement and the friendship of a surprising number of rich people to found, in 1966, the Nancy Hopkins Gallery. Those were the days when founding a gallery was not quite the commonplace it has become. She began on 57th Street, but within a year or two she had moved downtown, thereby helping to create the name SoHo was to make for itself. I suppose it must have been in 1967 that Mel made his decision to leave Castelli and be represented by Nancy. The decision was universally regarded as perverse to the point of being suicidal. Instead, it did him no harm and put Nancy on the map overnight. So when I met her, I had the impression of meeting yet another star.

Nancy and I had not one affair but two, the repetition separated by an eight month interlude. Why twice? I suppose so we could test and savor twice the special quality of passionate futility that defined the misalliance. From day one, I regarded Nancy as indescribably glamorous, with her straight, shoulder-length chestnut hair, with her boy-slender body that she was able to transform so quickly, and so athletically, into a sheath of passion. There was something in the way Nancy mingled a kind of straight-jawed nerve with her gentility that I found intensely sexual. I suppose it must be part of my erotic ambiguity, the force that defines so much of this story, that I'm stirred by the hint of something masculine streaking through, ever so lightly, a presence as feminine as hers.

But the affair was certainly futile. I am not sure what, if anything, could possibly have made me into Nancy Hopkins' husband. For one thing, I would have had to grow up a lot, and fast. Reality was still a very new experience for me, and my grip on it was pretty shaky. I also would have had to come across with a lot more dough. As things stood, I must have struck Nancy quite irresistibly as lover, rather than husband, material. For Nancy Hopkins belongs to the breed that marries, and moreover she is one who marries as the rich marry — and don't let anyone fool you, buster, that is different from you and me. On the other hand, I met her during a phase of her life when the prospect of a lover, both real *and* more or less presentable, must have seemed just the ticket. She was still in the process of solidifying her independence from husband number one, Kier Hopkins (AB Yale, 1957, Ll.B 1961; Associate, Debevoise and Plimpton, until 1966; and later partner in a less well-known but more political law firm) whom God, man, and each of the seven sisters had conspired to place beside Nancy at the altar. I've seen pictures of Kier: he is handsome in a dishy kind of collegiate way. On the other hand, Nancy had not yet really gotten to know Tom Cotter, the very charming dilletante and exceptionally successful (i.e. over five million) commodities exchange trader — real husband material there — who replaced me in her affections. But she was interested in a lover, and as a lover I was perfect. I was perfectly presentable, and if I found her attractive, I have to assume the sentiment was returned. Besides that, unlike the husbands, I really knew about art, so I had the lover-like, but not necessarily husbandly trait of being intellectually interesting. And then I was part of the apparatus around Mel, part of the family. Finally, my sexual ambiguity must have helped. It was both a shade piquant and a way of keeping us at a passionate but comfortably palpable distance from one another. There was something nice and safe about it: nothing so *douteux* was likely to get out of hand, go too far, distract Nancy from the really dominating concern of her life just then. That was establishing the gallery. That was Mel. And since I was very new to the game, and still very scared, the safety of an eroticized but unbridgeable distance served me too. It was, for us both, present absence all over again. Dear old Duchamp. Oh, we were experts at it.

We met late one afternoon a month or so after I had joined The Bunch, when I was lounging around with my new hero at Mercer Street. I remember that impression number one was a pang of jealousy and a sense of threat, introduced by the rattle of Nancy's key — for she had her own key; the sign of *real* importance in Mel's life — in the lock. I knew Jeffrey Hastings had one, but Jeffrey was not in town. So this was some new rival at the threshold.

Then the door swung open and in swept Nancy like a country breeze. "Well, hel-lo Mel darling. Welcome me, I am bringing you all kinds of presents," which in practice turned out to be packages from the gallery along with three cheap neckties she'd bought in the 14th Street subway station, each with an exceptionally nuanced color shot through with the most vulgar kind of glittering metallic fiber imaginable.

"Oh hey," Mel draped them over his hand and held them up.

"I *thought* those might strike your fancy." She bent over him where he sat in his chair and he kissed her. "I also have news, some good, some bad, but we can have *that* little conference later. And I have checks, so that helps." She patted a shoulder bag with proprietary satisfaction.

I instantly took the hint that business was about to displace me. I was on my feet. Mel was not.

"Nancy," he said, without getting up, "I don't think you've met a new and very good friend of mine named Jason Phillips, who is a lean and hungry youth from the N.Y.U. Institute, and who turns out to know more about Marcel Duchamp than anybody else I ever met."

"Well," said Nancy, putting out her hand. "That sounds promising. It's a pleasure — a rare pleasure — to meet somebody who understands our Marcel."

As she smiled I could see her reckoning that she had somebody new to deal with here, and without being hostile, there was something reserved deep in her eyes. It was exciting. As the Bachelor met the Bride, a separating look inspired an erotic surge. It would never vanish between Nancy and me until at last it broke us up for good. It was always there, even in our most rapturous sexual moments. I remember for example how Nancy sometimes used to love to ride on top, and when she did she also loved not looking at me, her face turned upward, as if in pain, as if to focus her pleasure, to drive it down and then tease it upward again, in order to get it all, keep it all, for herself. I found that very hot. Of course, that first afternoon I knew nothing about her private relations with Mel. I knew only that she was Nancy Hopkins, and what I saw and felt. What I felt from the moment I shook her hand was that we were going to be lovers, sooner or later.

It was sooner. I had to leave within half an hour of that first meeting — it was plain Mel and Nancy had Important Things to discuss but I've always suspected Nancy thought something very similar herself that day. Anyway, it all happened remarkably easily. We bumped into each other at some opening a week or so later. We went out for a bite. Then we found our way back to Nancy's then apartment in a high-rise on East 89th Street, a place on the thirty-first floor. We ended up on the flocatti on her living-room floor (two of Mel's most splendid recent silk-screens looking down on us) while beyond the windows, and beyond description, mighty Manhattan twinkled in muted vastness. We rolled apart and onto the strewn pile of our clothes. The living-room ceiling came into view.

"That," Nancy said, "was *fun!*"

"*Wasn't* it." I turned to look at her. Just look.

"I *really* enjoyed myself doing *that*," she said.

"Me *too*," I said. Then we pressed our palms together, as if to clinch the deal.

We were an item almost all that winter, and I had entered what seemed a new phase of my life. She and I were together three carefully negotiated nights a week, and on those three nights we invariably made love. The other four nights, we led our overcrowded lives: mine overcrowded with study, hers with the scenic life that was necessarily hers. On those nights we would talk to each other on the telephone at the weary end of the day, when she was home again and I had pushed away from my desk, and we would lay in our separate beds in our separate apartments, telephoning each other to sleep. Those were the moments when my feelings felt like love. That was the luxury of the goodnight hour — that call after midnight that signals sleep in the great secret network of the city's solitaries. The hour for the last gossip of the day. The hour for the intimacies of solitude.

And then, of course, we went out. *Out.* As Nancy's boyfriend, I became what is called "social" for the very first time. It was during that year that I discovered just how presentable it was possible for me to be. After all, I *had* to become "social" — I had a — I had *the*—social girlfriend. Being "social" was one of the things, then as now, that Nancy was best at being. Before or since, whatever it is that Nancy has been or will be, she invariably was and is that. By the time she and I had embarked upon episode number one, Nancy had stopped playing at being one of the heartless. Now she let you know that the once merely beautiful person had grown up at last: she would be table-hopping no more, she had left her girlishly chosen, too-masculine, too-political husband and set herself free for her maturity; she had opened the gallery and was really making it a success. It was true. That dark, sexy, self-possessed allure that used to burn with a slow strong glowing amid the trashy glitter of Max's back room, had now turned into the businesswoman's cool self-possession. It didn't matter: Nancy's transition from art groupie to woman of responsibility left her, if anything, more "social" than ever. There were dinners. There were cocktail parties. There were lunches. There were weekends and quick drinks, there were openings and retrospectives, celebrations and vernissages and auctions and intimate little evenings, and although there seemed never to be a single wedding there was, every now and then, a funeral or two, for while the new generation of the art world seemed never to marry, the older generation, it seemed, was dying.

I don't know what it is about the phenomenon of the year-long love affair — but it does seem to have some intrinsic rhythm which it is dangerous to disregard. If the twelve-month affair is to survive into month thirteen, somewhere around month eight or nine, that first romance had better strike some turbulance. Passion and intensity must assume some form. The danger sign is to have no danger sign, to notice nothing.

Somewhere near the end of month eleven, noticing nothing, I took the subway as usual for one of my week's three nights with Nancy. I had imagined all was well. It was just a June night, and, strange to say, we had no plans for the evening. But when I kissed her at the door, Nancy drew back a bit. There was an imperceptible flicker on her face, a little flinch. When she asked me if I wanted a drink, there was in her voice an ominous level of solemnity.

Of *course* I would like a drink. She poured it with the utmost seriousness, and handed me the glass portentously — a bit as if she were returning some too-precious loan.

She had, she said, something to say.

I sat down in the guest's chair. Nancy sat on the couch across the way. She had my complete attention.

Nancy had been, she explained, thinking. Thinking about us. Very carefully. And in spite of many, many wonderful things, she saw obstacles between us that . . .

I tried to chime in with something. "No, Jason. Please. Let me finish."

She had gone over the whole thing in detail with her therapist and . . . After looking very, very closely at her feelings, she agreed with the therapist that . . . She had many, many conflicting feelings about me and . . . Getting in touch with her deepest feelings had been terribly difficult but . . . She was *fond* of me. Terribly, terribly *fond* of me. Still. She realized she had to make a decision. She had made her decision. In spite of everything between us that decision was . . .

Finally, she was done.

I set down my drink, feeling simultaneously surprised and in the midst of an absolutely familiar scene.

"Well, I guess that doesn't leave much to say."

"I guess not. I am very sorry, Jason."

"So I guess we won't be having dinner after all."

"I think that probably isn't a very good idea."

"All right." I stood up. "Where did I leave my coat?"

She got it for me and handed it to me. Then she stood by the door staring, trying to smile.

So I left, without resisting or arguing or trying or pleading or promising or struggling just one last time. I just took my coat and went to the door, and then I waited for the elevator to take me back down, numb to what I was leaving behind.

I promised myself that I would finish my dissertation that summer. Finish it . . . instead of being with Nancy. I did not. Summer gave way to autumn, autumn to winter, and my numbness lingered, transforming itself into what seemed an unbreakable siege of isolation and immobility. Things fell apart. I stopped seeing people. My notes and books on Duchamp lay in unassemblable confusion. I still saw Mel, but less. I still talked out my ideas with him, but less. Avoiding Nancy, I avoided The Bunch. My teaching marked time. There were no more women, and there were no men. My promising-young-man luster was fading fast.

Meanwhile, I was listening to the muttering of my own mind, listening to the imagined me talking, begging, whispering, shouting, pleading with the imagined Nancy, while outside the winter blew and the radiator pipes on Perry Street banged like a prison riot.

The talk of my preconscious maundered on like a radio that couldn't be turned off, heard night and day through some paper-thin wall.

Nancy, listen to me. I have listened to you long enough. Try, try now to understand. I . . . I . . . I . . . I love . . I need . . . I remember . . . I hope . . . I wish . . .

Nancy, I won't listen any more. I am sick of your side of the story. I am sick of your self-justification. Don't give me your reasons. I hate your reasons. Lies, self-delusions. Canned music. Psychological Muzak. Spare me.

I know your real reasons. They are perfectly obvious. You rejected me . . . you rejected me because . . .

Because I didn't satisfy your schoolgirl fantasy of a man.

Because I am intellectually threatening to you.

Because my dissertation isn't done.

Because I am not rich.

Because I can be of no real use to you in your career.

Because I am not an alliance. I am a luxury.

Because I have the wrong accent.

Because you hate and fear love.

Because you look at me as a gigolo. A cheap fuck. A pastime.

Because I live at the wrong address.

Because I don't live in either a loft or an elevator building.

Because I hate playing tennis.
Because I am also no good at tennis.
Because I couldn't help it.
Because I said the wrong thing. Just once, just once.
Because I tried.
Because you thought I didn't try hard enough.
Because you hate and fear men. The power of the male sex over your feelings terrifies you, drives you to evasion, dishonesty and trivial, repetitive little psychodramas.
Because I didn't come on with a big butch act to please your fantasies.
Because I was too gentle.
Because I was too strong.
Because there is no right way. The right way simply does not exist between men and women. If it existed once, it doesn't any more.
Because I forgot something.
Because I remembered.

So I would sit at my desk, hearing the mute inner tirade babble on and on. *Love, love, love. Stinking, wretched, boring love. I want you I hate you I want you I miss you I banish you I need you I will be triumphant without you. I. You. I. You. I. You.*

Blah, blah, blah.

Once I saw her on the street — the intersection of West Broadway and Spring Street — walking right toward me, though she did not yet seem to see. I ducked into a doorway, and she passed.

Everything honked.

Another time, I was at some party on Wooster Street when my hostess — sadistic creature — stepped into the tinkling assembled company and called out — loud "Jason! Nancy Hopkins is on the stairs. She just buzzed. She's coming up. What should I *do?*"

Then she cocked her head in a cruel smirk.

I stared back speechless, a stick of celery in one hand and a glass of white wine in the other. My eyes narrowed in a sudden spurt of hatred and fear. Mere paralysis prevented me from rising to her bait. First I crunched off a bite of the celery stalk. Next I swallowed. Then I set down the glass — glancing at the surface of the liquid to see if there might be a tremble there. There was not. I was in control.

She was climbing the stairs. In a minute she would be taking off her coat. I stared at the table. I stuffed refusing fists into my pockets. My distress seethed.

Then she appeared. I remember the moment exactly.

She stepped into the foyer slipping off a fur coat — a very beautiful fur coat, very expensive, very undowntown. She draped it over her arm and was busy smiling and saying hello to people. I think she must have caught a glimpse of me, there on that glum couch, but she did not show it just then.

She disappeared into a bedroom, and came out without the coat a few moments later, and walked into the main room.

She saturated sight. Even now my eyes fill, remembering her there.

I picked up my wine glass again and she stopped to talk to a group of people. While she talked, and listened, her eyes wandered, and soon enough they wandered my way. The moment we connected she gave me a bright smile and a small high sign with three tumbling fingers. I responded with a grave nod. I finished the celery, and waited while she talked herself free.

Suddenly she was in my corner of the room.

"Jason. Hi there."

In the blink of an eye, all my labored thinking about it — about us, about her — vanished. She sat down. My fists unclenched. I drank the wine. We chatted and laughed as if neither one of us had ever heard of our calamity.

Six weeks later, in the dead of December, she called me on the phone.

"Jason! It's Nancy."

My life seemed to drain away.

I chirped my answer' "Hi there, stranger. To what do I owe the honor?"

I owed it to a desire for a favor.

"Jason, I'm calling absolutely everyone I know, because we've run into just a little bit of a snag with my gallery assistant, a wonderful person who's had a little bit of a *contretemps*. You see, he had a lover, as a matter of fact his lover was none other than Dennis Stevens, and Dennis Stevens has gotten just a little bit miffed about something that is too long and boring to go into here, and thrown him out. On his rear. Without any ceremony at all. And Cullen is an absolute darling, he doesn't deserve any of this, and I'm just seeing what we can do about arranging some kind of apartment for him, some place for sublet or something. Fanciness doesn't matter, not for the moment, just some place where he can lay his golden little head. I mean . . . we can't have him wandering the streets, can we? With all his pitiful possessions?"

She ended with her sharp, hard phony laugh. In the telephonic background, I heard muffled male laughter. And as happy chance would have it, an apartment was something I actually had at my disposal. It was an apartment identical to my own. Three weeks before, my upstairs neighbor Rhoda had gotten married at last, and had moved out leaving me in possession of her key.

"Jason," Rhoda had cried, wiping away a happy farewell tear, "Goodbye."

"I *knew* it." Nancy was triumphant. "I knew that sooner or later we would have some luck." ("Yes," she was saying, covering the phone, "Yes, he knows about something.") "Jason, you are *such* a sweetheart, you are an absolute *life* saver. How about if I send him over tonight?"

Not so fast, my recent dear. "Tonight . . . uh, tonight happens to be not so hot."

"Well, sometime tomorrow then. See, Cullen is feeling really quite a lot of pressure to connect with something fast. Dear

Dennis is really *very* pissed, he is being not nice at all. It really is awful. I mean, Dennis pulling his whole psychotic number, ranting and raving, and wailing and moaning, and it is ter*rif*ically unfair, if you knew the story, you'd know. Anyway, Cullen has been sleeping on my couch for the last few nights, and that is all very cozy and everything, but how much longer can *that* go on?" I seemed to hear the absent Cullen listening.

"I get your point." I chewed my nether lip a moment, and during that moment felt the very first of what would be many shivers of jealousy over Mr Cullen Crine. But still, it was not quite enough to make me hop to tonight. "OK," I concluded, "send him over tomorrow night. I get back from my last class around seven, and if he comes by then, I can show him the whole place."

"Well, Cullen will come knocking there at seven o'clock on the nose. You'll recognize him. He's blond — blond and *cute*." (More laughter from the back of the room.) "And Jason? Thanks. Really, thanks. You really are wonderful. So incredibly sweet. You know that, don't you? You know — sometimes I wonder if you really do understand that?"

"Who, me? Oh no, my Nancy, you have me wrong, I know, I know, I *know* they just do not come any sweeter than me." I hung up in inarticulate excitement, not having a clue how very soon I was to be restored to her.

chapter 3

The next night, I polished off the sophomore survey's lightning week on mannerism with a grand generalizing flourish, then trudged home in the cold, street-lit blackness of the midwinter early nightfall. My first stop was the gustatory center of my graduate student life, the Mon Paris delicatessen on Seventh Avenue. There I stood at the rear of that unclean, fruity, aromatic shop, bone-tired, amid the Pepperidge Farm and Entenmann racks, blinking in my post-lecture stupor into the white enamel deli-case. From turkey breast and chopped liver and Virginia ham, I assembled my unsharable evening meal, a repast for the exhausted. The next stop was the liquor store, its green windows corroded with frost. There I numbly plunked down my money for yet another outsized jug of Inglenook Navelle Chablis and lugged it the last three blocks home, the big bottle in its plastic carrying bag bumping against my thigh. On both sides of the sidewalk were blackened ridges of snow. It had been a hard winter.

I was slumping in one of my director's chairs, mechanically munching on my second turkey sandwich, mechanically looking for liquid rest in my third glass of wine, when on the exact instant of seven, my buzzer was hit with one peremptory jab.

Him. Nancy's whatsisface.

Wolfing the last of the sandwich and downing a final gulp of Navelle Chablis, I wiped my hands on the dishtowel that was my napkin, and buzzed the intruder in. Then I stepped out into the hall and for the very first time heard the clipped, quick, mounting footsteps of Cullen Crine.

A freezing sight came rounding into view. The fierce dazzling youth who stepped onto my fourth floor landing was a very far cry from the cultural bureaucrat who these days is seen smiling on Page Six and who gets his name in Suzy Knickerbocker. That man is now a medium-to-quite good-looking American male, pushing middle age, somebody who is exactly what he looks like: the chief curator of the Pierrepont Museum, an elegant trafficker in middle to upper cultural power. The person I met on the stairs twenty years ago was an enraged blond boy, with a body as chiseled and trim as flint, and a face in which what might have been an almost banal perfection of feature gave instead the impression of an almost frightening intensity.

Time has changed all that. In the years since I met Cullen Crine, deep and often secret rivers of vodka have softened that golden body and left the chiseled face spongy with an amiable slackness. Many years of the art world's finger-food have blurred those taut, almost professionally boyish lines. What once was a physique like a gift from God now must be worked on at the gym. And the work is never quite enough.

But then — *then*. The person climbing those stairs was so beautiful it scared me. My dubious heterosexuality trembled. I gaped. He was fresh from the winter cold; he was blowing on his hands as he climbed. He wasn't wearing gloves, and he was wrapped in a tight, trim herringbone tweed topcoat which could not possibly have been warm enough — the frigid night was violently still, violently bleak — but which fit his body so you could sense every trim line moving as he climbed. He turned onto the landing, took one step near me, then looked up. His eyes were twilight grey. I knew I wanted him.

He was used to being wanted.

"Hi there," I said. "You must be Cullen." I had deepened my voice a shade and handed him what I hoped would feel like a good solid manly shake.

His fingers were freezing. With an irritable little jerk of his head, my visitor tossed back his forelock of sandy blond hair. He did not say hello, but merely, "It is so *fucking* cold outside that I thought I'd turn black and die before I found you." The comment was not softened by any smile.

"Come on in," I said. "It's warm inside."

"This *climb*," he groaned, coming through the door.

"It *is* a little much," I agreed.

"A *little!*"

"Did you have any trouble finding it?"

"I got lost," he snapped. "I'm never in this part of town." This was Cullen's first lie. In point of fact, a major part of his sex life was conducted within a five-block radius of the spot where we stood.

"I'm sorry," I said, idiotically. "Would you like something to drink?"

"Uh-huh," Cullen purred. Then, with a lazy theatricality, certain I'd be watching every move, he let the herringbone tweed coat slip from his shoulders.

It was true. I watched his every move.

"What have you got," he said, looking back at me.

"I've got some wine," I said, "and I think I have some vodka."

"Vodka," he commanded.

Luckily, I did have a bottle of the cheapest stuff, wedged and forgotten in the permafrost that buried my ice cube trays. As I tugged and chipped the cold thing loose, I called to him, "A little? Or do you want a lot?"

"Oh," he answered. "I only want a little tiny bit." This was his second lie, and transparent. I poured him a decent glassful of the freezing crystal syrup.

Cullen had dropped into one of my director's chairs, where he draped his swimmer's body in an arrogant slouch. I handed him the glass, and I noticed that he greeted the sting of the clear icy liquid against his lips with a secret sensuality. His twilit eyes softened with pleasure as the freezing vodka smarted in his mouth. Then he picked up my watchful eyes with a bored glance.

"Shit," he said, succinctly.

We chatted a bit about apartment hunting and the aches and pains of sleeping five nights on a couch. Of course, it had been Nancy's couch where he'd been sleeping. The thought churned inside me in a jealous mix. I pictured my sometime girlfriend wrapped in the terrycloth robe I knew so well, carrying morning coffee into her living-room and glancing at the touseled hair of the gorgeous sleeper under his mound of blankets. I imagined her blinking a little repressive blink against this vaguely sexual sight. I imagined Cullen's naked golden arm dangling over the side of the couch, his fingers grazing the floor.

We made conversation, and while the talk meandered, I looked and looked. He was a beauty all right: he was Tadzio and Antinuous and Rastignac rolled into one. His looks compelled me, as if they incarnated a mystery — some simple, but unfathomable something about yearning and having. I shifted in my chair nervously, chatting.

I still knew nothing about him, of course. Gossip hadn't yet demystified what I saw — the physical perfection, the chilly sensuality, the wide streak of anger and contempt. It was obvious that heaps of people must desire the creature, and I correctly guessed that he had the seducer's knowledge of how to deepen that attraction and make it compulsive. It was a kind of seductive fury that flickered in the grey eyes. You could see it in the way he tossed the forelock back.

Why does somebody so pretty look so *mean*? I wondered. So obviously somebody prepared to shower slivers of despair into anybody's heart?

I soon began to learn. The gossip of the next few weeks

quickly confirmed my sense that the boy was a heartbreaker. I found out, for example, what had led the devastated Dennis Stevens finally to throw him into the street after weeks of talkative anguish with all his friends, talkative anguish with his therapist, talkative anguish with the whole support system of the New York solitary. I found out how long it had taken Dennis to work up the tragic, self-pitying, desperate courage he needed to expel his invader. It was six months after he had precipitously suggested Cullen to move in with him and six months and eleven days after their first deluded encounter. Dennis Stevens was a man to whom adulthood meant, after much bashful tumult, becoming a psychoanalytically equilibrated depressive — one who had learned to be careful about the treacherous way his inordinate sudden hopes for love were so very often demolished by his masochistic yearnings. Dennis had worked it all out; worked it through, as we say. He had become a successful, circumspect, meticulous, prematurely middle-aged homosexual who had learned how to watch himself. But he had not learned to watch himself well enough to deal with Cullen Crine.

They had met at a party. Yet another party. Dennis was at first a little patronizing and amused by the kid, thinking Cullen just another beauty among the many beauties then as always all over New York. He did not notice the exquisite tact with which a seduction was being initiated, the cool way a second meeting was being arranged. Cullen asked, seemingly sexlessly, if it would be possible for him to come to the gallery some day and look at a little known set of rare surrealist pictures Dennis very rarely showed. Well, why not? Dennis asked himself. Dennis thought it was mildly interesting that somebody so good-looking also should know so much. Why not, he thought. Oh, oh, why *not*.

Famous final thoughts.

Exactly three all-too-interesting days later, Dennis Stevens was no longer an equilibrated sometime depressive in premature middle age, but ga-ga, convinced he had at last discovered his whole spiritual and sexual being made flesh, his soulmate and at the same time, the perfect minx, the most sumptuous of male catamites. And yet so *good*. So *true*. So *interesting*. And so *hot*. Cullen Crine was no longer just a pretty kid interested in pictures. He had made his move — and it had been a smooth supple dive into Dennis' unconscious.

In point of fact, Dennis Stevens had got himself addicted to an extremely dangerous drug known as Cullen Crine. For weeks they went everywhere together. For weeks Dennis was uninterested in any experience that did not feature Cullen. And it had taken exactly eleven days for Cullen to move into Dennis's loft — which was a very comfortable loft indeed.

It was only after Dennis was securely hooked, that the golden angel began subtly to withdraw everything he once had seemed so freely to offer. He invariably withdrew it so both men would feel the sting of mutual contempt involved: You want *me*? Well, for that, I despise *you*. Cullen withdrew — manipulatively, cruelly, opportunistically, always holding out a variety of hope that was worse than despair, and *certain*, every second, that *he* was being put upon, that *he* was the offended one. He was angry about it, in fact. Meanwhile, Dennis was a gibbering Cullen-addict deprived of his daily hit, tantalized and demeaned and increasingly hysterical. Everything that once had seemed so exciting to a depressive like Dennis was now suicidally anguished. Dennis found himself clutching his coffee cup at business lunches and bursting into tears. He staggered to his therapist; he staggered back to his live-in misery at home. In the telephonic small hours, he talked and talked and talked about it, listening over and over again to the plain advice of all his friends, how he must act in his own defense, how he must set himself free, how he must give Cullen Crine the unequivocal heave-ho and reclaim what was left of his life.

Dennis later would call it a sign of health that it took him only two months of grief to act.

Cullen Crine was beauty as refusal.

Sitting across from me, he sipped his vodka over a bored glance, then getting down to business, asked, "So is this apartment that is supposed to save my life, a whole lot like this one?"

"It's just exactly like this one," I said. "It is the very same apartment, the same floor plan, except that it is one floor higher." Cullen took in this information with a God-help-us roll of his eyes.

"Look," I said, really irritated now, "this is up to you. I think the place upstairs is available, and Nancy told me you were desperately in need of *some* sort of place. Well, here is *some* sort of place."

Obsequious little prick, I was thinking. *Kissing ass with everybody but me.*

"I mean," I continued, "take it or leave it. When I talked to her about it, Nancy, at least, seemed to think it would be fine." Not that Nancy ever actually had condescended to even set foot inside my house. Our little affair had been a her-place affair . . . up on the thirty-first floor.

"Don't be mad," Cullen said, lowering his eyes a little, "I'm sure the place has all sorts of absolutely wonderful things about it. I mean, its *perfect* for cruising the pier."

There it was. The Subject. I went defensive. *Get this straight right here and now*, I thought. I hardened my voice, and I leveled my eyes, and my answer did not flinch. "That," I said, "I wouldn't know."

Lying.

I knew about the pier all right. Cullen was referring to an abandoned hulk on the Hudson River, near the Perry Street waterfront. It once had been the warehouse and dock of the Lehigh Valley Railroad; now it was a ruin, its four shambling stories sagging into the slimey water. Once a great center of shouting dockmen and teamsters and dispatchers, now it was cavernous with spaces and uncountable rooms that teemed with anonymous homosexual sex, an abandoned hidden honeycomb on the nasty side of eros, with collapsing ceilings and holes in its floors and huge obscene graffiti everywhere, a place of waiting breathless, nameless bodies in the dark. I knew about the pier all right. It was there I had seen for the first time, glowing on the wall, the anonymous slogan spray-painted by one of art's lost children:

THE SILENCE OF MARCEL DUCHAMP IS
OVER-RATED.

I wanted to get away from The Subject.

"Anyway, the last tenant of the place upstairs was a girl named Rhoda and she moved out a week ago because she finally got married. But back when she lived here, she left a key with me — you know, for emergencies? Well, I still have that key."

Tadzio led the way.

It often happens to me. As we climbed that flight and a half of stairs, a sort of unwritten novel flashed through my mind, an untraceable strobe of episodes. It was American Balzac, all about Cullen Crine. There were images of the middle western kid with his Schwin, beneath the maple trees; then licking through his veins the secret eros that compulsively seemed to promise an irresistible, shameful combination of freedom and ambition and style. Then came the need — indistinguishible from perversity — to escape that paradise of bridge clubs, pheasant hunting, lawn-chairs and ice-fishing; the need to be somewhere else; the need to create a new self amid the splendors and miseries and the subtle beauties of the great urban corruption; the need to transform himself from a provincial boy into a creature of artifice, into Cullen Crine, trafficker in the secret and indecipherable, an angry *arbiter elegantiarum*.

The empty apartment we stepped into was a sad scene. When Rhoda turned her back on the place for the last time, she had left the bathroom light burning. It miraculously still burned. The sound of a leaking faucet came through the door. I snapped on the kitchen lights — two dusty, paint-spattered bare bulbs screwed into a slum sconce — and we got the full view. There was only one touch of color. Pinned to the wall at the far end of the apartment was a huge, pathetic, crepe-paper poppy. The thing must have been three feet wide, and it drooped there, its twisted pistils made of black crepe, in the midst of a huge dusty blossom of red, the whole thing abandoned, a bit of antic outsized feminine pathos left behind in the cheerless place. A bag of trash had broken open. Some liquor cartons were left from moving day. A rubble of some bricks and boards had fallen and was strewn on the kitchen floor. The smell in the room was that of old dirt spattered with Ma Griffe, the whole combination further accented with the faint but pungent stink of simple wretchedness. They seemed like three rooms with bath where somebody had died. The bathroom trickle ran on and on and on.

The trickle was not new to me. Before she left, I used to hear every ripple and splash of Rhoda's pathetic bubble baths above me, just as in the months to come I would be hearing Cullen splashing in that same lewd echo chamber. In fact, I could hear everything, though the sounds in my ceiling were always blurred in a mutter of indistinction. Rhoda had not been happy on Perry Street. She was in the all-too-frequent habit of crying in her bath, and the endlessly renewed sound of her wracking contralto sobs used to make me grit my teeth and writhe. She also paced. I used to hear her pacing above me while the ventilating shafts wailed. And she was a phone freak. I used to pick up on the indecipherable mutter of her endless calls. And of course she had friends. If her visitor was a woman, the sound most often was marked by the jabbing, high-pitched music of half-suppressed hysteria. But the visitors sometimes were men. There even was sometimes masculine laughter in the mornings — I heard it quite often on Rhoda's lucky Sundays — a new, lower sound.

Rhoda was, God help us, an actress. She too wanted to become famous in the big city. One hardly knew where to begin deploring her ambition. Her head was rotten with hopeless wishing. An *actress?* It was intolerable — her teary cheerful bravery before certain failure being the least tolerable aspect of all. I never for a second believed in her future, of course, and of course it was part of her pathos that neither did she. *She needs a man*, I used to assure myself as I sat downstairs and looked up from my desk again, hearing the mouselike scratchings of her misery.

Then would come her timid, unbearable knock on my door.

"Jason, I am *so* sorry to bother you. Is this just a *ter*rible imposition?"

"No, Rhoda, hi. Come on in. How have you been?"

"Oh things are wonderful, Jason, but I have just one little *tiny* request." And then she would ask the favor — could she leave her key, could I fix a light, tighten a screw, always a pretext for some time in my company. Always with the same wearying flattery of my masculine skills.

Rhoda would come in, and I would give her a drink, and we would talk — Rhoda perhaps waiting for what was not going to happen in the pauses — and she would give me all the latest to happen on her endless auditions; her pitiable hopes for a callback; her waitressing jobs; her office temping. I would hear about her classes in singing, classes in dancing, classes in everything. And then I would hear about her work in films. She really did work in films. She was a member of SEG — the extras' union — and now and then she got early morning calls to show up for some walk-by on a big production. She loved to gossip about "the Industry," as she called it, and repeatedly invited me to come and hang around and watch her in these little triumphs. "Oh Jason, you have *got* to drop by the location tomorrow and see Lee Remick. She is just amazing, so beautiful, so well-pre*served*."

Marriage did at last save Rhoda, when one of the Sunday morning voices grew constant. He was there Wednesdays, Thursdays, and Fridays as well — I met him in the hall — a lawyer from Legal Aid. I thought he was great. A little dull —

but great. Rhoda's savior. I gave him a brotherly welcome: shaking hands; having coffee; laughing. When Rhoda told me she was going to marry him in November, we celebrated, like fellow convicts celebrating her miraculous reprieve.

As Cullen sauntered into the apartment, I mentioned — with a hint of apology in my voice — that I guessed the place was pretty dirty.

He shrugged that off. "Oh, I can take care of that."

But he never did take care of it. Cullen moved into Perry Street three days later and not one damp little item of the feminine dirt Rhoda had left behind had been cleared away. It never was. Cullen simply moved in and began to lay down his own masculine crud over what Rhoda had abandoned. The poppy was never even taken down. It still was pinned to the wall a year later, after everything was over between us all, and Cullen had moved out and upward, resuming his social climb.

He was a strange boy. In the outside world, Cullen was notably fastidious; he was, in fact, impeccable. But that was in the outside world. He used the apartment above me as a kind of lair, the secret place where he lived the secret life, a hideout from the great world of culture and power — that is, the world Cullen wished to conquer. Nobody ever visited him there. Nobody except tricks, I mean. The floors never were mopped. The dishes never were washed. The musk that came to permeate the three rooms was that reek familiar from men's dormitories the world around — a spicy mildew of unwashed jockey shorts, of sperm and sweat, of spilled liquor and the sickly cinnamon of aftershave — in Cullen's case, all of it liberally laced with amyl nitrate.

Cullen slowly strolled through the little rooms, making theater out of his inspection of their cramped squalor. When he reached the far windows down by Rhoda's poppy, he darted a quick contemptuous glance from the rear window into the courtyard — that dank pit with its city-winter dirt. Then he drawled — lazy, provocative — "by the way, Nancy said you should call her. I almost forgot. To have lunch, or something."

Keep cool.

"Oh, did she?" I answered in a clipped fake little voice. "Well, all right, I'll give her a call."

Cullen ignored my answer. He strolled back toward me, looking around, his hands languid in the pockets of his Italian trousers. He tossed his contemptuous blond forelock back; he leaned a proprietary shoulder against the little arch that led into the room where the poppy hung.

"It'll have to do," he said.

chapter 4

I called Nancy the first thing the next morning, and we made a date.

The freedom that came to me two days later at that lunch in Little Italy felt like an act of psychological grace. Instead of ebbing frightened and nervous and talking pointlessly, instead of confusing the issues and addressing false emotions, instead of making a fool of myself, I was granted a completely un-Jason-like forthrightness and confidence. I listened to myself perform with a subtle wonder.

"Listen Nancy," I said, lowering my voice. "I don't care how this sounds, I'm going to say it anyway. I miss you and I know you miss me. And I don't see why that should go on. I can tell you something else. Life without you is atrocious. Since we've been apart, I've hated every single minute."

I spoke without self-pity, in a sudden intensity that I think surprised Nancy and I know surprised me. Nancy had been stirring a cup of tea. She looked up, breaking into a kind of smiling half-laughter. But laughter didn't stop me and her smile subsided into an attentive stare, her large brown eyes watchful, interiorized.

"I think we should get back together. I mean more exactly I think we should make love together again. It is a matter of desire. My desire and your desire too. I know it. I can see it and

I can feel it. It is there, and it must be served. It is important. It can't be ignored. I am not talking about love, I am talking about what we need now, right now. Don't tell me there is anybody else because I know there *isn't* anybody else . . ." I knew nothing of the kind; I merely guessed. Nancy kept staring with her watchful brown eyes, the teaspoon in her hand, "and I know you desire me just as I desire you. I think we should act on it, now, today, this very night. It is perfectly plain."

Nancy set the teaspoon down. She tilted her head. She cocked an eyebrow. Then we both laughed, and we made an appointment for her place at seven o'clock.

I was prompt of course. I walked from the IRT through the expensive neighborhood, the storefronts and newsstands I last had seen eight months before flicker back into familiarity, just fast enough to keep my excitement high. *Again. We are together again!* The phrase kept running in my mind, and when I reached the lobby of that pretentious apartment building — monied, faceless, a rich-girl's hideaway — my feelings began to converge. . . .

It was a strange apartment for a girl like Nancy. I remember a party Nancy and I had gone to in Connecticut — and Nancy being met on the lawn by some very important young snob (he ignored me, but so did they all back then). "Oh Nancy, I just *love* your apartment, it is *sooooo* tacky. *How* did you find it? It must have taken months. Either that or about forty-five *minutes*." My blood ran cold. I never have accepted the permission to insult that is endemic to the American art world's system of snobbery. Nancy responded only with her sharp hard laugh. Still, it *was* a strange place, and the time it had taken Nancy to find it was indeed close to forty-five minutes. She had rented the apartment in the course of a single morning, an hour and a half after a momentous decision made over morning coffee, and after a seething wakeful night beside the large long sleeping body of the man she had married at the age of twenty-three. Man — he was then just a boy; the Kier Hopkins of that time would look to me now like any arrogant rich boy, one of my students even. But Nancy and he were near the end. A horrible night had succeeded upon a horrible evening, and it was succeeded by a dawn with stinging eyes, a morning in which the first sign that the moment of resolution had come at last was that she telephoned nobody once Kier was out of the house. She did not call anyone, she did not look for consolation from anyone. She finished her coffee and then put on her dark glasses and walked out for what might almost have been a morning stroll, except she walked with mounting amazement, astonishment that one step could follow so simply, so naturally, from the one before it. She had bought the *New York Times* and stood on the corner of York Avenue and 68th Street ransacking with unexpected avidity the want ads. Her eye fell on one large listing. LUXURY APARTMENTS — HI RISE. She hailed a cab. The moment the cab door was slammed she gave the driver the address from the paper, and rode, saying to herself, *this is real, this may even be real.* There was an office. A salesman. And he took her to the thirty-first floor. There were — counting the closet off the kitchen called the maid's room — five tacky new "luxury" rooms. Nancy walked around them twice, her dark glasses held in her hand, while the manager watched in silence — he *sensed* he should be silent, though he kept a mechanical grin — and after she had made her second tour of the place, in which she had not been looking at all, but thinking, conjugating, *this is real, this is a real place, this may be real . . .* she had turned to the salesman and said simply, "Fine, I'll take it." With that she slipped her dark glasses over her face again and stepped out onto the terrace of the place, looking over the steamy miniaturized Manhattan morning below her and knowing that the moment had come at last; from this moment on she was married no longer, from this moment on her girlhood was over, that she was leaving Kier and the bleak business of adulthood had come.

I came through the revolving door, greeted once again — *why did it never change?* — by the almost indefinable scent, a smell mixing in the crystal turnstile. I'd noticed it the first time I'd ever come to this building, one year before. I had stopped trying to identify it. It was troubling, elusive. Then I knew. It was the smell of *money*. I do not mean money metaphorically, or symbolically, anything of that kind. I mean the literal olfactory smell of greenbacks. Cash. It was as though some enterprising perfume maker had distilled the essence of a wallet's insides with the essence of the U.S.Mint, and sprayed the mixture around Nancy's front door. That musty odor had greeted me on every visit. It was greeting me again.

The aromatic revolving door whooshed me in, and perched behind his oak desk was the familiar humorless doorman I had last seen eight months before. Calling up, he gave not the slightest sign of remembering my name.

The sleek white elevator doors closed behind me and we started our ear-popping rise to floor thirty-one. *Money.* Surely that Proustian impression downstairs has *some* psychological dimension; of course it had to be that money was part of Nancy's allure, since it was part of my exclusion as well. *(Floors 7, then 8, then 9 flashed past on the board.)* I thought about Kier. Kier the athletic. Kier the rich. Kier the husband. Kier and the world of men. There were husbands and lovers — that and homosexuals. That's the division, is it not? *(Floors 17 . . . 18 . . . 19.)* I was no husband. Lover was my role. I was walking back into a system of *exclusion*. That was the deal. I saw it in a prescient blink. And in another blink I thought of Cullen Crine. I thought of his arrival in the city. I thought of mine. *(Floors 22 . . . 23 . . .)* Cullen, the Rastignac of Perry Street. He who saw the world as a world of style. *(Floor 31. The soft bell chimed.)*

At the door, Nancy greeted me with a social kiss which I confirmed in the foyer with something more serious. She poured me some wine, and as if for the sake of ritual, we sat in exactly the same seats we'd taken the night I had come and heard her give me her little goodbye speech. She sat in the proprietary couch, I settled into the polite exclusion of the chair

for guests on the other side of the coffee table. I leaned forward a
little. It made my body feel more firm and real and true to itself.
Then I said, "I've missed you, Nancy. I really have."

She stared at me a moment, just as she had at the restaurant.
I think it is possible even that she felt a bit moved at the thought
that she had been missed. Then I stood up and moved to the
couch. She told me that actually she had missed me too, and I
said I guessed that must be why we were here. I lifted my glass
and said, "Let's drink to no more missing each other."

Then — something in me broke and at the same time,
cohered. I made my move . . .

"Please," I said to Nancy.

"Hi there, turtleneck," Nancy said, hooking her finger into
the garment of the same name, tugging me toward her.

I felt the way a surfer might, riding down into the hollow of a
wave, sinking only to rise. There is no reason to dwell on
details. At that stage of my life, my erotic fantasies, the bisexual
movie inside the mind, seemed to take the form of a
disburdening . . . or is it first an invasion? . . . I was excited by
the real person, but only when she was attended by imagined
beings. The fantasy was crowded and the process of excitement
consisted of working out a way to banish all the imaginary
beings so I could be left alone with her. Most of these imaginary
beings were men; males, all my bachelors, breaking out of what
Duchamp might have called their malic molds, a whole huge
grunting mind's eye allegorical wallful of them, a half-
homoerotic vision of my own sex, all of them wanting . . . *her*.
Men scared, men enraged, men wistful, men greedy, men
fainting with love — groaning and restless, heavy with their
horny impossible burdens, and above all else, *alone*, untouched,
without hope. The great sweating herd of them thronged in my
mind while Nancy and I groped and embraced. As we crawled
on the couch, the masculine chimeras within my mind began to
be torn away. *(Except that Nancy and I were getting into a position too
complex for the couch. She had pulled at my sweater, she had pulled it up
and was caressing my skin.)* In my mind, the bachelors swarmed,

elbowing and shoving one another as they lusted after . . . her. Wishful voyeurs denied, fat and lustful, the whole hot gazing malic gallery wanting . . . *her*. And as their imagined bodies swarmed I moved in on Nancy's. All my excitement mounted, they were being torn away. The weakest, the least compelling ones already had been banished. *(I was working away, firm and fast, at Nancy's blouse, and after a bit of the classic graceless fumbling the bra problem was solved, and it with its classic release just fell away.)* The bachelors' desires were my desires. Their abjection was also mine. Their strength and their secret violence was *my* energy too. I ached alongside them. They were *my* possibilities, their heaving, passionate, imprisoned, unconsummated experience was mine. I had to get rid of the bastards, I had to banish them, the whole bleating impossible herd, bestial, lustful, unforgiving, wishful, never to be real. . . . *I stood up and undid my pants, stepped out of them, knelt to undo Nancy's skirt and while she wriggled out of it, she was looking up at me from the couch.* I laughed a little because my hard-on was poking through my underwear in a pretty awkward way until she reached up and worked it loose.

I got out of the underwear. My turtleneck was the last thing to go. "Don't you think," Nancy said to me, "that it's about time to adjourn to the other room?"

I had left most of the malic herd behind by the time the two of us stood up and started to play together standing. I left even more of the creeps behind when we walked naked together into the bedroom — I managed to leave them all out there, somewhere on the other side of the bedroom door. In my own good psychic time, I eventually would be left alone with the real.

I used to sense that if that urgent, angry, lonely crowd within only were to inhabit me in some different way, my entire life would be lived in a different way, and I might be free.

In the bedroom I had left them all behind except for one. Nancy and I embraced again, and I was wallowing in the softness of her thighs, sliding down her body for my first taste of her secret flesh. *(Free. Free. I was almost free, almost at one with myself, almost rid of all the fantastical figures of my inhibition: my excitement: inhibition and excitement at the same time.)* Suddenly I had access to the kind of happiness that makes for laughter in bed, giggling before the next move. We tumbled down together, manoeuvering into position for *soixante-neuf*, my arms around her middle. I swam in her; I rolled and tumbled and played in the ocean of the woman's presence all around me. . . . *(Only one bachelor remained, a solitary figure left behind, a new kind of tormentor, at once a rival and an object of desire . . . himself wanting her. He bore in on me. He frightened me, he was impossibly alive, mocking, insulting, warning. . . . Mel. It was Mel. He of the slanting hips and dark eyes, near me, part of me, usurping me, being me, a figure of phallic enchantment, dancing in my mind to the rhythm of some unheard song.)*

It is possible to be insulted by one's own fantasy. I was insulted. My erection began to die. I lay alongside Nancy and kissed her again, my eyes open in the bedroom light. Damn Mel. I was seeing Mel as I had seen him the first time in SoHo, back before SoHo even had a name, at the party, pressing a woman against an unpainted brick wall and banging his hips in against her. He had invaded me.

As Nancy and I lay quiet and gently played, reality once again began to take its part. The invading psychic image, and the anger it provoked, began to drift and break. . . . Mel became any man, and any man became somebody, nobody, some husband to be. . . . At last I lifted myself above her on flattened palms and wove in and out above her smiling face, our eyes both open as we watched each other, everything suddenly simple and sweet, the porpoise with two backs, leaping in its slow grace through imagined waves.

We were alone together.

Her legs were still wrapped around me when we opened our eyes again.

"Welcome back," she said.

I sank down beside her and closed my eyes again.

"Happy?" she asked.

Still wordless, I nodded yes. I was thinking, *I am free, I am free again*. We untangled and I stood up, damp with it all. Then I flopped back down, rolled and looked at the ceiling a moment. Then I turned and looked at her for a long time.

Nancy had gone to the kitchen to get some more wine, and I watched all eyes as she came walking back, carrying the drinks. She handed me my glass, then slipped into bed beside me. I went yipping around her like a puppy, holding the glass up high to keep it from spilling, thinking, *I'm free, I'm in love again, the time scared and alone is over. It was all a mistake.*

At the end of recuperation's decent interval we resumed, and the second time everything was untroubled by any untoward intervention of the ghastly malic throng. Things were gentlemanly and classical, and they produced gentlemanly classical results. And so we continued until we were both squeezed dry.

I lay half-dozing on the sheets.

"You know this was supposed to be for dinner," Nancy said, "You want dinner?"

"I am hungry," I conceded, as though mumbling it through my sleep. But I was awake, half-awake, soaking in her presence.

"Well, we could go out," Nancy said, her mind already organizing. "Or, we could stay here."

"Mmmmmmmmmm?" I said.

"What do *you* want to do?"

I told her I wanted to do what she wanted to do.

I loved her again. I was with her again. She was with me again. *I'm free*, I kept telling myself, *I'm free and I'm with her again.*

Outside her bedroom windows the Manhattan lights were beginning to take on their shapes, beginning to form the complex urban crystals of their deep structures in the darkness. The high-rise evening was settling in. *I am with her again, I'm free.* An act of recognition.

Then for the first time I happened to notice a full-length mirror in a freestanding oak frame tilted — toward us. Tilted at just the right angle. I had been too — too distracted to notice it.

"Huh," I said, pointing feebly.

She replied with a wicked, gentle smile.

So it seems that while my mind had been in combat with the bachelor throng, Nancy had been looking at the beast with two backs and seeing. . . .

I poked the tilted mirror with my toe. There we were. In our nakedness I kissed Nancy's side, still keeping one eye on the sight of us. There we were.

We ate our dinner that night standing naked in a darkened kitchen, at the open refrigerator door, licking our fingers and laughing in the light that came from inside. Since this was a "luxury" apartment, Nancy's refrigerator was a grandiose machine, and among its countless compartments and shelves and racks we managed to find a huge hunk of cheddar cheese, some stale Italian bread, and a little fried chicken. Then there was another very cold bottle of Blanc de Blanc. Licking our fingers at the open refrigerator door, we stood there and assembled two primitive sandwiches made all the more sublimely gratifying by their chewy staleness. From the cheddar block, we chipped bits with a knife. We'd brought our glasses from the bedroom, and Nancy poured the wine. Then we took it all to the kitchen counter and pulling up high stools, sat, swallowing hard, to eat.

That was when the telephone rang.

Nancy ran to the bedroom to take the call rather than using the wall phone two feet away near the kitchen sink. I sat on my stool, chewing my sandwich in stolid satisfied imperturbability. I sipped the wine and I found the whole thing extremely good. My mind drifted in the post erotic haze. *I am in love again*, I told myself.

Nancy's call went on rather an irritatingly long time. By the time she came back into the kitchen she had covered herself in a terrycloth robe, and she had a slightly preoccupied look. I suddenly felt a little silly standing there, wine glass in hand, without a stitch.

We hastily finished our repast and I went into the living-room to gather up the heap of once ecstatic, now merely messy clothes on the floor. Everything was taken back to the bedroom.

As sleep was coming, I murmured, for the first time, a question.

"Nancy?"

"Uh-huh?"

"You know . . . I never really understood what got in the way with us. You know. Not really."

Silence.

"So . . . did you? I mean, really understand it?"

Her silence made me vaguely uncomfortable. "I don't know. . . ." Her voice was very sleepy. "I don't remember."

"I know. I know, Nancy. It's strange. Of course, I've thought and thought about it. . . ."

"Jason, I thought we'd decided not to talk about this."

Now it was my turn for silence. At last I said, very softly, "That's right, Nancy. That's right. That's the deal. I remember now."

But Nancy was already asleep.

chapter 5

"Oh *Lord*, it's so *late!*" Nancy's morning whisper broke through my sleep, and her trim, hard girl-scout body was clambering over me, popping to the surface of wakefulness like a firm, clean, new cork. It always had been the same: Nancy woke every morning as if the day were a pistol shot. I, on the other hand, peeked out at the morning while I wallowed in a warm pool of sleep as wide as my guilt. It was a moral drama, this waking business: and it was a sexually specific one at that. The feeling always was that Nancy was in her waking feminine *goodness*, feminine eagerness, feminine right thinking, fresh with the day. I, on the other hand, was sensual sloth decadent, incorrigible, and *male*. She was up, limber and out, while from my mouth came, like bubbles from the oozing bottom of a pond, unintelligible sounds.

Then I closed my eyes again and sank back into the hypnagogic haze. Nancy already had begun to do her virtuous morning exercises, touching her toes in front of the same tilted mirror that had been her louche secret voyeur's companion the night before. When I opened my eyes again, I saw with a vaguely thickening, pointless eros, my girlfriend — girlfriend once again — doing her stretch-up exercises.

"Late for what?" I mumbled.

"Cullen Crine," she said, "He's coming for breakfast."

"Breakfast? I thought he was moving into my building today."

"Oh, don't worry, Cullen will do *that* too. Cullen doesn't have anything to move except clothes."

"What's he coming for?" I asked, hoisting myself onto one elbow and squinting at the sight of her.

"What?" Nancy was heading for the bathroom and her shower.

"I said, why is Cullen coming to breakfast?"

"Oh," she said in the bathroom door, turning her head back to look at me, and in an exquisite gesture one hand lifted to her shoulder, like Diana reaching for her quiver, some ravishing goddess of manlessness, "Oh, he's coming on business," she said, and vanished into the bathroom door.

I fell back into a sleep cluttered with images somewhere between fantasy and dream, vaguely hearing the shattering water of Nancy's shower through the thin bathroom door, and the sound of my own breathing, open-mouthed. Business. My rival. My homosexual rival was about to arrive. . . . I could see his body present, flickering somewhere in my morning morass. . . .

A sharp buzzing woke me and Nancy was back in the bathroom door in a terry robe and a towel twisted in her hair, calling to me, "Jason, could you answer the door?" But then, when she saw me sprawling there, she dropped that idea. "Oh forget it, I'll get it myself. Jason, you are such a *slug*, it's morning you know. . . ." and she vanished out the door, closing it behind her and leaving me entirely alone.

I sat up and grasped my ankles, wishing I'd been fast enough to have actually answered that doorbell, wearing a bathrobe myself, exhibitionistically fresh and just a touch mangy still from the warmth of Ms Hopkins' bed. *Give the malicious little wiseacre a ghastly unexpected peek into the heterosexual abyss of how things stand. I may be ac/dc,* (I scratched my armpit), *but I'm a lot straighter than him.* This thought made me flop back onto my pillow and dozed a moment more. When I woke for good, I was alone, and the sound of laughter, his and hers, was filtering through from the living-room.

God, they seem to have a good time together, I thought, as I pulled myself up and my feet touched the floor. Now his voice was going on at some length, with a rather eager sound. He had something to tell her, he sounded like he knew it would leave her vastly amused. I strained to catch one of the words, but I caught only the music of his narrating voice, punctuated here and there with Nancy's sharp laughter and the sound of dishes being put down on her glass dining-room table. I saw myself in the tilted mirror, unshaved and in my morning ruin. It was time for a bath, time to close the bathroom door to silence the sounds beyond.

In contrast to the trim asceticism of Nancy's style in general, her bathroom was a large, glittering, excessive, expensive, mirrored temple of feminine consumerism. There were chrome racks laden with unguents and oils; there were rattan shelves packed with towels and towelettes. For the bath, frictions and gelées that smelled of all the fruits; there were soaps in Crabtree & Evelyn wrappers, powders of every imaginable description, scents and perfumes to suggest every wildflower from heather and lavender on the heaths to all *les aromates de Provence*, sachets scenting the air, beads in bottles and an array of perfumes that suggested an entire pharmacy of crystal bottles from Givenchy to My Sin to Joy.

But what *I* needed was a razor; just a razor, nothing less. Naturally, there was none to be found. I looked in the medicine chest. I looked in racks and drawers.

I could hear Cullen and Nancy talking, through the walls.

What is it he tells her in that tone of voice? I reached for the bathtub spigots. What is it in that tone that threatens me? Fag, I thought ignobly. Something in his tone seems to mock all my earnest intellectualism. Cullen didn't have to fill out any index cards or write dissertations to know what makes the world go round. I turned on the shower. Art? He understands art without trying. He is so sure he understands it implicitly, in the depth of his sense of style. I stepped into the invigorating steaming blast. In his sense of corruption. His nastiness. Not for little Cullen the dreary seriousness, the graceless, intellectual pushing and hauling of a ... of a Jason P. Something in that gossiping voice, something in that bright hard nasty laughter threatened me. Nancy loved it. He thinks he's too fast for me. He's filled with irony, mockery, sure that the boring Jason Phillips of this world could never catch the beat of his lethal cruel stylish lightness. The water flowed over me. Nancy and Cullen love it together. They are in complicity, in cahoots, they agree about something. Maybe me.

From the bathtub dish, I picked up a bar of jet-black soap and noticed — or seemed to notice — pasted against it several hairs that were not Nancy's. They looked *blond*. Is this possible? Is it *possible* that behind that elaborate homosexual facade of his, something has been going on here between them? That their mockery actually had gone all the way to ... "Now stop being crazy," I said out loud against the crashing of the shower.

I soaped up with the decadent black item deluxe in my hand, massaging the imaginary hairs against my body, and when I set it back in the dish, I discovered, as if set out by providence, the very thing I needed. A razor — a little disposable item of blue plastic, flimsy and used. *Used by whom?* I picked it up and, before I held it to the spray to clean it, saw that clogged in its slightly rusty blade were — reassuringly — very dark, coarse hairs. Of *course*, this is what Nancy uses to shave her *legs*. I turned the thing in my fingers. It *felt* feminine. Then I held it to the shower and washed all my suspicions away.

I shaved at the bathroom sink — the little rusty disposable scratched madly, but worked more or less. Then I stepped back into the bedroom, and their voices were still locked together out there, chattering away, earnestly now, certainly having gotten down to the business that Nancy had told me brought him here on his moving day. Voices earnest, rather low, I imagined the two of them leaning toward each other, across the breakfast table.

It had been a long time since I'd had the always slightly grungy and disoriented experience of reassembling my scattered pieces in a woman's house the morning after. There are few things I hate more than stepping back into yesterday's underwear, or crumpled clothes thrown in excitement on the floor. But I was getting into them, and then came the smell of distant bacon in the air. I was down on my hands and knees, feeling under the bed for one of my wandering socks when the delicious aroma began to seep in under the door. I found the sock, and my tee-shirt too, which after a disdainful sniff at its pits, I pulled back on. It was a navy blue tee-shirt, its color qualified it as something more than underwear.

I decided to wear the tee-shirt and carry the turtleneck in my hand. I wanted to give some room to my exhibitionism, and it seemed to me plainly desirable to make my appearance in that room in some slight ostentation of undress. *Just give him something to think about*, I thought.

I looked at myself one last time in the mirror. My hair was almost dry. The man I saw in that mirror looked . . . really, quite, quite good. Apart from the fact that the man in that mirror was not the man I supposed he ought to be — I was ready.

I turned with a burst of energy and resolution to the closed bedroom door and rakishly draping the turtleneck over my shoulder (*show him*, I thought), I stepped out, greeted by the wonderful classic odor of coffee, feeling the soaring promise of Manhattan's high white morning light. The smell of that bacon was in the air, and there was all that hopeful toast and jam, and I went striding down that hallway, toward a life I knew would never be mine, just like any happy little husband.

interlude

I punched a pillow with my elbow and perched my chin in the right position for talk, damp but drying beside Nancy in the post-coital coolness. The sexual rhythm had been re-established for weeks. I watched her as she lay, staring upward at the ceiling.

"You know," I said, "I have a question for you about Mel."

"Mmmmmm?"

"It is a question I probably shouldn't ask, but I have decided to work up my nerve and ask it anyway."

She gave me a flicker of her eyes and then turned her head to take me in.

Silence. She didn't seem unwilling. "So — ask."

"OK. I will. My question is . . . well, actually it is kind of hard to ask."

"Mmmmmm." There was a little smile on her lips now.

"OK. I will stop beating around the bush. I am curious . . . curious about you . . . I mean, Mel and you. . . ."

Nancy smiled. "That's all?"

"Yeah . . . yeah, that's all. Isn't it enough? I mean, do you want me to be curious about something more?"

"Whether Mel and I had an affair?"

"Well, yeah. I *am* curious."

She laughed. "Of *course* we had an affair, silly."

"Well, I just didn't know."

"Jason Phillips, you cannot *possibly* imagine that given who Mel Dworkin is, he is going to let *me* be the one who got away?"

"Well, I guess. . . ."

"You mean you never heard gossip about it? It was fairly well known for the brief time it lasted."

"No," I said. "I never heard a thing." This last was not quite precisely true.

"Well, we did."

"Uh-huh." I was waiting for more.

She leaned back on the pillow. "Actually, it *was* interesting, and *very* important for me because it was really my first infidelity to Kier, back while we were still married. That's the story — it goes back that far, I mean — what was it — 1961? 1962?"

"Uh . . . what was it like?"

"Mel? Well, I was so incredibly young and everything, and I was this married little Miss Chapin's girl hanging around with a lot of high, wild people, trying to keep up and not doing too well at it. And there was Mel, and he was just getting to be known and he would come into those bars, drinking as usual, and he came on. I mean, he came on to absolutely every woman he could possibly arrange to come on to, so there was nothing so special in *that*, but even so he did come on and for the first time I sat there and I kind of got the point. I mean the appeal of doing it. I was telling myself and everybody else that I was very happy with Kier, and in a way I *was*—"

"Uh-huh," I said.

"But with Mel when he decided to turn on his charm with me, I really got the point. I mean, it was partly my whole Bennington thing, you know, be with a genius, be with a great man and be free in the name of art and all that crap, but it was also that Mel really could have a lot of. . . well, appeal. I mean, he was very intense, and very virile, and there was a kind of recklessness and fire about him, and I was so sick of hearing patronizing remarks from people about what a little goodie-two-shoes I was, and there he was, Mel Dworkin himself, and it was true, he was a very *very* far cry from Kier."

"So did it go on a long time?"

"Yeah, it went on a whole couple of months."

She lay remembering. "Uh-huh," I said.

"I was one of many, I suppose, and that suited me just fine, because I was having mucho trouble with it, *morally*. God knows I did not want a crisis in my marriage. Not at that point."

"Uh-huh."

"But it went on for a couple of months. It was nice. We used to get together in his studio on Bond Street. I mean, he had had that place since he was . . . like . . . completely penniless — you have probably only seen it in photographs — and we used to make love on this incredibly grungy mattress on the floor and I used to think — well now, we have come to this. Wow!"

She gave her sharp hard laugh.

"What was he like," I asked, pushing the point.

"You mean in bed?"

"Yeah. That's what I mean. In bed."

"Now Jason. You shouldn't ask things like that . . ."

"Well . . ."

"I mean, everybody going around telling people about each other?"

"It is the great narration," I said. "Story hour."

"Well . . ." Nancy pretended to be disgusted. We were silent a bit. "Mel wasn't bad. Not for a man who drank as much as he did. He had a *wonderful* body . . . so thin and wiry and . . . nice."

"So you remember."

"I remember . . . a lot. I used to love watching him move. He just couldn't sit still, or lay still, he was always up and moving . . . and he had a kind of fascinating inwardness, a kind of — I don't know — a kind of driveshaft or something going on inside him all the time, and it kind of fascinated me. I used to love to watch him naked. He had a very different kind of body from Kier, much more . . . sinewy."

"Uh-huh." I paused. "He still does."

"Right. And the other thing is that he was so fascinating to *talk* to. And Mel talked all the time, he practically talked while he was doing it with me, I mean — whoever said that painters are some sort of non-verbal people had better correct their prejudices by spending one night of fun with Mr D. He said a lot of very fascinating things. Mel taught me, that was very much part of the appeal. I had been hanging out with a lot of the wrong people. First there were the people Kier and I knew, and all *they* wanted to talk about was babies and Bloomingdales and the Village Independent Democrats. On the other hand, there were all my scenic friends at Max's, talking about amphetemines and promiscuity and parties. Suddenly, along came Mel. And he was so smart. And so interesting. And so interested in *me*. Nobody before had ever seemed so interested in me quite that way before. And he taught me about art. And he taught me about sex. That too. It was very nice."

"What happened?"

"You mean, why didn't it last?"

"I guess."

"Oh, it was never that serious. And then Tanya came along."

"Who was Tanya?"

"The next girlfriend. My successor . . . in Mr Dworkin's . . . affections."

"What happened to her?"

"Who, Tanya? Oh gone. Gonegonegone."

"Did you want it to be more serious?"

Nancy was silent.

"Did you want to marry him?"

"NO!" The syllable came like a gust.

"Why not? Be the wife of the famous artist?"

"Oh, it would have been a nightmare. Mel can't be married. He's emotionally incapable of marriage."

"Why? Really, why?"

"Why? Well, he's too self-absorbed for one thing. He's not

interested, really, in sharing a life. He lives too much inside himself. Too much in his own imagination. Everything that is really important has got to be there, inside him. And not shared. He'd never be able to let the woman . . . assume her role. He'd want even that for himself. He wants it all for himself."

"It's a little sad."

"Maybe. Maybe not. Maybe it's where all the creative energy comes from. Besides, he's very neurotic. He'd put any woman through hell. He doesn't know if he's weak or strong, incompetent or omnipotent. He's incredibly susceptible to women's power over his feelings, and so he has to go around proving how little he needs them. It's hopeless. No, it's in his own imagination that Mel has got to live."

PART 2

chapter 6

Whatever its advantages, whether sexual, social, or intellectual, becoming a member of the Dworkin entourage did not
lead to unadulterated happiness. Mel was not, it turned out,
the simple, plain-talking down-home American boy-of-genius
his charm sometimes made him seem to be. I soon learned that
his relations were filled with subterfuges. He was surrounded
by others, yet he protected the essential privacy from which his
work proceeded through a manipulative balancing of the
people around him against each other. They were manoeuvers
accomplished both because, and despite, his great charm. He
was a *faux-naif*, like many seducers. He knew very well that all
kinds of people were absolutely delighted, especially at first, by
the charm and the reflected glory of his interest in them. He
knew his hello, his goodbye, had powers that others did not
have. He used them. Used them especially with people like
myself, people who came into the entourage at just the tender
level of psychological vulnerability that made his interest feel
like the finest thing that ever had happened to them, the event
that had made a lifetime of long wishing seem suddenly real. I'd
supposed I'd seduced *him*. Wrong. In fact, like many of the
famous, *he* was the flatterer.

Time and again, I poured out my half-incoherent ideas to
him. Thanks to his seeming fascination, I experienced a kind of

intellectual rapture I rarely have known since. I would sit
beside Mel, spinning out variants and tests of the insights that I
was developing for *The Bachelors' Bride*. Mel's interest awakened
a kind of eloquence in me. He would listen to the latest flight of
fancy, sinking deep into his chair, close in concentration. I
could feel the steadiness of his brown, listening gaze. "Oh
yeah?" he'd say. "That's fascinating. Whoever would have
thought of that? That's interesting, Jason. That's *good*."

Even today, I have the impression that I never thought or
talked so well as I did in those cocktail hours of the sixties,
instructing my genius. I would sometimes think, *I wish I were
taping this. I hope I can remember it when I get home.* In truth, when I
got home, the eloquence invariably seemed to have fled: I had
been given my intelligence, through, by and *for*, Mel alone.

I think he deluded me. I love him and his memory anyway,
but I think he deluded me. I think I deluded myself. I have
never known to what degree Mel Dworkin a) *really* agreed with
my ideas of that time, or b) *really* found them even interesting or
fresh, or c) *really* even cared about them, right or wrong. In the
end, I came to feel he despised me, but that was no doubt only
another illusion. In any case, I flew high for a while, thinking
myself the brand new Ruskin to his new Turner.

I soon found I was by no means alone in supposing myself to
have almost magical importance to the man. I also found that
nobody was permitted to stay in that intoxicated, self-deluded
impression for too long. Just around the time one became really
hooked on Mel's approval, he would produce a rival, some new
person who would be showered with his glow, all for
manifesting exactly the opposite traits. This was likely to come
as a shock. It did to me. In my case, the anti-me was the
insolent and inarticulate Jeffrey Hastings. None other.

I intensely disliked Jeffrey Hastings from the very first
moment I ever laid eyes on him — which was the very first day I
arrived at Mercer Street. I have no doubt that on that same day
Jeffrey felt exactly the same toward me. His rudeness made that
plain. There he was, in his inevitable blue jeans and blue work

shirt and heavy engineer boots, playing at being the power behind the throne, the mindless but masterful major domo. He was, of course, a painter, but despite his current reputation, which I reluctantly admit is a deserved reputation, nobody then except Mel took Jeffrey seriously in that capacity at all. Like many of the men in The Bunch, he once had served as Mel's studio assistant, and then had insinuated himself as a kind of permanent fixture in the place, a kind of shadow Mel. He did the errands, the pushing and hauling, the higher trivia. Everybody knew he had "his own work," but only Mel paid attention to it. I regard it as a matter of dense irony that that work is today known and admired.

Anyway, Jeffrey hated my guts from the moment he saw me, and I am now convinced I was introduced to The Bunch exactly for that purpose, as a new foil against Jeffrey. That afternoon I took up where I'd left off the night before, spinning out my views on Dworkin and Duchamp, the future of modernism, the visual experience in neo-dada terms. The Bunch was my audience, with Mel at its head.

It made Jeffrey writhe. I was in the midst of some disquisition on *Chrystie Strut* and *The Bride Stripped Bare by Her Bachelors* when his patience snapped, and he heaved himself out his chair and rudely stomped out of the room. Since Jeffrey always wore the heaviest engineer boots he could buy, that stomp was a noisy stomp. I paused at mid-flight, staring at Jeffrey's offended back as he walked into Mel's workroom, a sanctum he alone among The Bunch had the cachet to enter without permission. Mel too stared after the blue-shirted back. But not, I think, in surprise. A faint smile played about his lips. Then he said, "Go ahead, Jason, you were saying? It was fascinating."

Thus began the rivalry between Jeffrey Hastings and me, orchestrated by Mel, most subtly, to make each of us feel like a threat to the self-esteem we thought we got from the master. Whenever either Jeffrey's or my stock was down on Mercer Street, we always blamed the other one. If I was the anti-Jeffrey, Jeffrey was the anti-me. But there was nothing natural or inevitable in that role. It was Mel, Mel's sense of us, that linked us together in animosity, while *he* arbitrated our standing and played the innocent, every time. Jeffrey and I might be chewing up our guts inside because one was up or down, Mel could go on claiming that *he* was open to everything, just a guy with a lot of friends, who loved them all. It was a completely successful manipulation. Until the very end, I don't think either one of us ever really caught on to what degree it was contrived. Well, perhaps Jeffrey saw it, in the odd, blinded insight, the partly visionary, mostly paranoiac state he sank to before his end. Not me.

Almost everybody in The Bunch was used in some such way. In retrospect, I'd say it was the manipulation that showed you really mattered to Mel, that you'd really reached him, deep down. Those who didn't really matter were simply given the saccharine of his charm and allowed to go away. But to be caught up in the melodrama was to become caught up as an avatar of some aspect of Mel's sense of himself.

Take Seymour Kaplan. Now that he's famous, Seymour doesn't talk much about his days as Mel's protegé. They were valuable days. But costly. Even to somebody as unarguably and unshakably loyal as Seymour, somebody as essentially sane, and who had even then the peerless Iva at his side to deepen the sanity. Seymour Kaplan is one of the great slow starters in art. It took him a very long time for him to define his task as a painter. This is partly because Seymour did not cheat on a single step. The result was that in the latish sixties Seymour Kaplan was working very hard at absolutely unfashionable work that the whole merry scene regarded as doomed to failure. Except for Mel.

Mel was deeply impressed. Impressed as an artist. Impressed as a man, morally. I have no doubt that his respect was also affected by some self doubt. Where Seymour was unfashionable, Mel was the definition of fashion. Where Seymour held on tight in wretched teaching jobs, invited nowhere, Mel was made of money and knew all the wrong right people. Of course it must have bothered him. Yet in those bad years Seymour derived great strength that a great artist like Mel seemed to care as he cared.

Fine. Once this quite genuine, though rather dependent relation was created, Mel proceeded to torture it. I noticed that around Seymour he was likely to talk a lot about the worldly goodies, the gravy of fame, that ordinarily he discussed not at all. The parties, the meetings with other famous people, the signs of deference that flowed in from all sides. Or he would talk about how *easy* he had found the management of his own career. How quickly success had come. How perfectly it fit when he took it out of its box. How very right it felt to him to wear it. Always for Seymour. He never would have addressed such stuff to me. And Seymour would sit there, broke and isolated, being asked to agree.

Then there was the fiasco of some little mixed-media genius, one Les Tureen. He arrived in The Bunch one fine day as a kind of affront to Seymour. He was really a kind of joke, a con-man pure and simple, and though he was filled with fashionable Duchampian twaddle, time mercifully has spared us taking Tureen's work seriously à la Duchamp because he was then, as I suppose he remains, exactly as dumb as the box of rocks he used as his first major exhibition, and upon which his entire reputation rested. No matter. Les Tureen did manage to have a sickening little thirty-second vogue during the sixties, during which time Mel astonished us all by starting to invite him. And to lay it on with a trowel. Flattering his gnomic and vapid little posturings. Welcoming the ridiculous Tureen to the company of those artists who had Made It. It was embarrassing.

I contend it was all done for, as it was invariably done in front of, Seymour. Mel was not for one second fooled by the empty Tureen. That briefly resonant but hollow void was brought in to set before Seymour, a really serious artist, at that point without a gallery, unrepresented, and selling precisely nothing.

It was a perverse and cruel act, all the more so since Tureen — who happily was soon sent on his way, as soon as his fashion drained away — represented in their lowest form aspects of fashionable obscurantism that Mel might, in moments of self-doubt, have suspected in himself.

But we were all of us aspects of Mel's interior drama, and we were all of us played with. If I was to be intellect, Jeffrey had to be mindless intuition. If Seymour was incorruptible, then Tureen would be produced as scene-maker. Mel would tease us into our roles. Many, many times Mel would invite me to make patronizing remarks about Jeffrey, which he promptly would follow by a defense. Jeffrey, he would explain, might not be able to manipulate empty words, but he at least understood what painting really was about. Unlike all these critics with their *words* — if only I could catch the tone of contempt on that word, "words" — he had a truly modern intelligence, an unstructured intelligence, an anti-linear visual mind that people like me — he was not exactly outright rude, but the patronizing tone was there — couldn't understand.

So I'd become defensive. "Oh, come off it, Mel, don't give me that. What are you talking about? Anti-linear? Anti-structured? This is the cant of our time, and you know it. *Anti-linear.* Jeffrey goes around claiming he has no ideas. He is too pure for ideas. In fact he is filled with ideas, except they are all bar room pothead crap like the anti-linear. Don't tell me you are buying into *that.*"

"I am not buying into anything. But there *is* such a thing as a genuine visual intelligence. A genuinely visual talent. Jeffrey may not be good at slinging words, but he has it. You don't. You're an intellectual. Now, you've got to admit the difference. . . ."

"Well, of course, but. . . .," and I would burn with anger and shame. Jeffrey would be triumphant that day. I would walk around gnawing my spiritual fingernails because I'd been condemned as linear, an intellectual, a — horrors — verbal type. For precisely the reason I'd supposed myself welcome, I was now condemned.

In Dworkin's *Notebooks* (1974, edited, with an introduction by Jason Phillips) there is a deceptively simple passage about which much has been said over the years:

> Put two objects side by side and watch what happens.
> The watching is thinking and seeing both.
> Watch slowly.
> Then quickly — put it all beside something unseen, new.
> Watch again.
> The watching is the work waiting to happen.
> The surveyor watches.
> So does the spy.

A great deal of critical ink has been spilled not least by me over these gnomic words, written at the height of Mel's most incandescent neo-dada period. I am here to say that those lines have biographical relevance as well. Slightly edited:

> Put two different people side by side.
> Manipulate them. See what happens.

Mel did it constantly. The process of manipulation seemed to give him both energy and a sense of security. If Mel felt uncertain about some aspect of himself, if he felt doubtful of himself intellectually, artistically, socially, sexually, any way — he was in the habit of adding to The Bunch somebody who reflected that anxiety in some way. Then he would play that person against their opposite number. And when the panic began, he'd feel strengthened, reassured. It was as though the two contending people somehow invalidated each other, and left him autonomous, free. Then there is the cryptic remark about surveyors and spies. The critics have said much about the images as metaphors for pictorial space and the like. But the surveyor is also the man who makes himself visible, defines the terrain, and says what belongs to whom. This was Mel the star, assigning people their roles. The spy, on the other hand, is the secret manipulator, prizing his invisibility. This was Mel the voyeur and covert sadist. Both were roles he held and used incessantly.

It was also standard procedure with women, on a sexual level. During that night of pillow talk, when Nancy conceded that she'd had an affair with Mel, she mentioned Tanya without much dwelling on her, who she said, had ruined everything. I have since learned in considerable detail what *really* went on in that exchange.

For one thing, Mel was no light little infidelity that had passed through Nancy's life and vanished into the mists of pleasant memory. Their affair had been a wrenching and major event in her life. Mel had been intensely attracted to Nancy, and he had laid on his full, very potent, powers of seduction. He told her he loved her. That she was bringing sanity into his chaotic life. He became involved in her breakup with Kier. He became involved in the first faltering steps toward the founding of the gallery. He flattered her, talking about the wonders of her good sense and lucidity. Loving her straightforwardness. Her nerve. Her organizational power. Her social skill. On and on. It was exactly what Nancy had needed to establish her autonomy against the strength of all that female conditioning. She began to believe that maybe Daddy had been right; maybe she could do anything. Even open the Hopkins Gallery. Maybe she could dare and succeed. I think it's plain the Hopkins never would have come into existence without Mel's encouragement. It was not that he'd ever promised to let her represent him. Never. At that early stage such a thing would have been absurd. But at the right time with the right words, Mel was there, as lover, and as friend.

Then, as soon as Nancy was well out on the limb, the effervescent Tanya appeared on the scene and blew everything to bits. Nancy soon discovered that she was in an open relationship with Mel. Surely she wasn't so narrow as to imagine he could be tied to one woman? Besides, Tanya was so wonderful. Everybody loved Tanya. She had such a rich, rewarding, exciting personality. Couldn't Nancy *see* that? See it? Tanya was in fact the anti-Nancy, simple spit in the eye of all the qualities Mel had been telling Nancy he loved so much. If Tanya had been forced to choose between balancing a checkbook and hanging, poor Tanya would have had to opt for the rope. Where Nancy was order and sanity, Tanya spread chaos with every step. Where Nancy was systematically tasteful and very womanly, Tanya played the *cucaracha* and gave the impression of carrying a vibrator in her purse at all times, just in case. So Mel went on and on about his freedom, his new zest for life with Tanya, how much Tanya understood true pleasure, how good she was at real living, what a lush and inexhaustible source of new sensations, new truths Tanya was.

Nancy took it with Nancy-like self-possession, but in fact it was a fist in the guts. The fledgling gallery was moving into its first real life-or-death crisis, and suddenly everything she'd felt Mel helped her believe in came crashing down. She passed a number of very painful and frightening weeks, wondering if either her self-esteem or the gallery would survive.

It was then, and only then — once the bond that Mel himself created had been broken and demeaned, once he had taken away everything he once had seemed to offer, that Mel suddenly turned around, sweetness and light, and announced he was leaving Leo Castelli and coming to her.

It was a thunderclap. Reduced to powerlessness, Nancy was suddenly "saved."

And the manipulation was complete.

This erotic web also spread to men, since without being precisely homosexual, Mel's impulses of seduction, rather like his impulses as an artist, were quite polymorphous. Nobody could rest immune. His sexual involvements were certainly deeply with women, but even so, there was a homoerotic edge in the way Mel enticed men into his circle of power, and in his fascination with their dependence on him. I've mentioned how, at the age of 23, being invited into The Bunch made me feel like a genuine person, a real live grown-up man, for the first time. Mel subtly made himself seem indispensible to that new sensation. And in some way every man in The Bunch was enticed into some similar dependence. But I am convinced that we all are projections of his own anxieties, avatars of himself. That night in bed with me, Nancy said Mel lived too much in his imagination to marry. Well, the men around him were also too much aspects of himself for friendship. You'd think that might be grounds for a good — in a way, the best — friendship, that profound recognition of the self in the other. But in almost every case, certainly in my case, and Seymour's, and God knows with Jeffrey, the recognition became a ritual of seduction and humiliation. And it could become a nightmare.

Take Jeffrey. Jeffrey's macho posturing, that studied sullen inarticulateness, appealed to Mel. He saw its absurdity of course, but still he saw its . . . use. Besides, he liked to play. One form of playing was to needle me with Jeffreyism — I who was so much the opposite, with my babbling intellectualism and doubtful sexuality. Then there would be the usual crap about verbal types and visual types. But another form of play restored the brief authority of Tanya in her starring role. When Mel later told me that at various times he had shared women with Jeffrey, I was shocked. I am now virtually certain that Tanya was one of those women. Since Jeffrey tended to feel that Mel was in possession of some magical quality Jeffrey lacked, the hint that Tanya had told Mel what a humpy, sexy fellow she thought Jeffrey seemed came as deliciously welcome news. Next, Tanya, who had a flaky streak a mile wide, was likewise delighted to pick up Mel's hints about what fun it would be for her to hop into the sack with his great buddy Jeffrey, what a fascinating glow that would give everything. Whether this adventure ever was enacted as a literal threesome may be a piquant detail, but not very important. In any case, I do not have the Polaroids. What matters is that Jeffrey would find himself with Tanya and flying high on a new sense of intimacy with . . . . Mel. Not Tanya. Mel. And he would be feeling a euphoria which for a while nicely masked Jeffrey's dependency and his no doubt veiled and secret homoerotic yearnings.

That euphoria did not last long.

Mel next would proceed to hint ever more strongly to the errant Tanya that fun was fun, but he really did think it was time for this empty, purposeless sleeping around to stop. Tanya, in no hurry to lose the star in her bed for Jeffrey, promptly informed Jeffrey that the party was at an end. And Jeffrey would now confront his own brand of consternation and self-contempt. If he fought for Tanya, Jeffrey would be rewarded by certain rejection by Tanya and probable rejection by Mel. Without fighting, he would merely be humiliated. He had to choose between rejection and rejection, and the all the more deeply humiliating recognition that his addiction to Mel, the essential drug of his ego, was, though it had dragged him to the bottom, unbreakable.

And so it remained until at last Jeffrey did, in his desperation, try to break the spell. And thereby brought down a holocaust.

It has just occurred to me that the single person in this story who really was never enticed into the magic theater of Mel's system of dependencies, the one person never made to feel moved and manipulated by the power of that imagination, was Cullen Crine. As Nancy's gallery director, he must have dealt with Mel on an almost daily basis. But Cullen never really got enticed into The Bunch. He always stood a bit apart, never really under the spell. I suppose when it came to manipulation, it took one to know one, and Cullen had manipulations of his own, elsewhere, to effect. Besides, the sex was all wrong. Mel had no real interest in Cullen's kind of homosexuality — that narcissistic, icily obvious, and if-you-don't-like-it-drop-dead manner meant nothing to him. On the other hand, my kind of bisexuality represented the ambiguity that precisely suited Mel's *modus operandi*. As a result, Cullen Crine strolled through the whole burning fiery length of the Dworkin furnace entirely unsinged. Somehow or other, he simply never got under Mel's skin.

It was *my* skin Cullen Crine got under.

And how!

chapter 7

Nancy darling, listen to me. Let your own sweet Cullen Crine clue you in. Lose this man. You know that you are going to get rid of him sooner or later. Do it now. Put him out of his misery.

I sat alone in my little work alcove on Perry Street, listening to the imagined voice of Cullen Crine yammering on and on, a new nasty note for my private inner music. My upstairs neighbor had slipped into my psyche, and there in my psyche he sat with my girlfriend, locked in malicious discourse. On some ghastly couch of the imagination, Nancy sat calmly nodding assent to every vicious word. *Lose him, my darling. Lose him.*

I slumped at the desk, distracted from Duchamp, lost in eavesdropping on my own mental processes.

Nancy darling, do try to to remember: You are powerful. You are rich. You are beautiful. You are everything these new feminists say you ought to be. You have it all. Except for the right man. Why Jason Phillips? Answer only that. What has he got? Darling, you know me. You know I understand zilch about the emotions, so-called, of straight men. I don't want to understand. But you can do better than this. From the whole range of masculine talent in New York, you come up with Jason Phillips? Minor intellectual? Permanent slum dweller? Four star bore? Puh-lease!

I shifted in my seat. I dug my fist into my chin. I kept listening.

He's a bore. Surely you see how dull the man is? Never in my whole young life have I met anybody even comparably tedious. Listen, I live above him. I know. Do you want to know what I hear filtering through my floor? What signs of life and vitality? Pathetic as they might be? I will tell you. None. None at all. Zip. That hole he lives in is as the tomb. What rises from its precincts is deathly silence. That silence is not because I have thick floors. Face it. JASON PHILLIPS IS A BORE. See it. And act. I beg you. I implore you.

Enough!

With a sigh that originated in the black center of my mind, I pushed away from the desk, stood up, and shuffled wearily to the kitchen, looking for some sweet silence within, reinforced by coffee. Bitter, unconsoling companion of my dissertation work-day. The blue gas flame burst on under the pot. This masochism! This sick self-hatred! If only I could forgive myself for . . . I stood watching the coffee reheat. The whisper returned.

Nancy darling, a word to the wise. Next time try a real man. You deserve la vraie chose. *Select. Don't settle.*

The coffee cup hung loose in my hand, while I listened to Nancy's hard, sharp laugh. *Let me explain something. Out in loser-land, Jason, your boyfriend, occupies a uniquely dreary place. With his hideous little teaching job and his hideous dissertation and his hideous everything. I know, I know, everybody keeps saying, at least he's smart. They yawn while they say it, but they do say he's smart. Honey, they all say that when they reach the bottom of the barrel. For men, smart is the equivalent of women with lovely smiles. Well, they say, it is true he has no charm, no class, no wit, no money and no dick but AT LEAST he's got brains. Sweetheart, that way lie madness and misery. Then last but not least, let's face the clinching truth. Jason Phillips happens to be the world's most obvious closet case.* (The imagined Nancy crossed her legs and leaned forward: *"You really think so?"*)

Do I? Darling, puh-lease! Don't let me com-mence!

I was falling into something I might call anti-love with Cullen Crine. I was discovering a perverse *promesse de bonheur* in everything that seemed hard and hateful and unapproachable about him. I was *drawn* to his coldness. It was not just in my mind that I heard him. I heard him all around me, up above my head; in the ceiling, in the walls, on the landing outside my door. In the morning I was wakened by the crisp clatter of his Bass Weejuns in the stairwell. At sunset, I looked up from my books, hopeful at the sound of his footsteps, mounting. Then, when darkness had come, I used to hear him going out, once again, into the New York night. Going out, going out, and then deep in the small hours, making his debauched, frightening return.

Because Cullen led two lives. They were lives notable in the geometry of their unlikeness, lives linked as opposites, bound in a paradoxical interplay of the abstract and the concrete. One of them was the life that Cullen led in the art world, the world of his ambitions. The life he had at Nancy's side. That life was all talk. It was entirely a matter of what you said and who you were. Everything in it, from what you wore, to how you sat, to whatever you liked, from cuisine to cathedrals, counted for something, was a sign of something. It was Cullen's job to read the signs.

On the other hand, there was Cullen's nightside existence. It was harsh, mute, classless, wordless, done in the dark. In Cullen's art world, all that mattered was who you were. In his nightside world, you were a body, and that was all. What I heard through my ceiling was Cullen making the pit stops between them both. That apartment was where he existed in neither. Alone. Sometimes, working at my desk — my dreary desk, as the imagined Cullen would have called it — I would hear him running his bath and padding barefoot across the room above me. My heart would start. I was infatuated. I would wait, listening, until I heard him ease his body — his naked body, his golden body — into the tub. He settled into the steaming heat, and I would try to get back to Duchamp. But there was only the splash and trickle of his play. I'd push back from the Smith Corona and glance up at my dry ceiling, while my mind raged. *You degenerate! You disgusting little narcissist!* I sat still, flailing between unenacted jealousy and unenacted desire. *I know you. You're the kind who poses naked in front of mirrors. You're the kind who perfumes your tub. I bet you jerk off in your fairy bubble bath. I bet you kiss your own armpits. You tongue your own mouth in your sick smudgy medicine cabinet mirror. I hate you. I hate you.*

He would come home from work filled with energy, just when I was hitting my slump of the day. In the first evening darkness, I would hear his busy footsteps above me, at least until they were drowned out by his inevitable Ronettes or Rolling Stones or Maria Callas soaring through *Vissi d'arte* for the nth time. *Vulgar little opera queen!*

Silence returned only when his evening toilette was complete, and Cullen was on the stairs again. Not that he ever paused at my door. Ever. He would be on his way to some dinner party: his average night's invariable phase one, as well as his final daily duty to the life of visibility. I myself might, or might not, be going out. That depended almost entirely on Ms Hopkins and her busy schedule. But whatever I did, Cullen would be home again by midnight at the latest, mounting the stairs a little more slowly now, and stepping into his apartment almost with stealth.

The time had come to begin his entry into life number two. Cullen's second toilette of the evening was prepared in silence. The Italian tweeds would be shed. The Paco Rabanne tie would be tossed onto the bed. The Saint Laurent shirt slipped to the floor. I could imagine it all. Replacing all these, in a slow ritual, garment by garment, was the black tee shirt, the crusty Levis, the boots, the bomber jacket. I *heard* the clothes of Cullen's visibility dropping above me. I *heard* him step into his jeans, heard him struggle with his boots.

And then those boots would resound on the stairs. Cullen was on his way to the nether regions of his cruising anonymity: the back rooms, the bars, the pier. Two or three hours later came his stumbling return, in ruins. I think it was a fairly rough world that Cullen frequented. I pictured some fierce devouring consuming frenzy. Violent. Awful. Sometimes I heard his body slump against the staircase wall. Sometimes there seemed to be two pairs of boots in the hall. Sometimes, half-asleep, I half-heard groans of both pleasure and pain.

It was a life heard through walls. Cullen made no particular secret of that life: the secrecy was entirely mine. His tantalizing, shameless, blond existence coming and going, moving around, living above my head, became the focus of all my swarming secret yearnings. And sometimes the swarm was so intense it was at the extreme edge of what I could do to keep it secret. More than once I followed Cullen through the covert dark as he made his way out to one of his after midnight prowls among the river slums. I would trail a block or so behind him as he made his dangerous way west, aching for him to turn and uncover me, aching that he might. Then I would check myself and walk home, pleased that sanity had returned. Until one night I was caught. Or at least I think I was.

The event came after dinner uptown with Nancy, and an evening during which neither of us had had a very good time. Nancy had been distracted, and I was only half there myself. I had come uptown sullenly, hoping we'd make love before the restaurant. Instead we'd quarrelled. So instead of life being like the fine first days together, we trailed out to Martell's. I still remember the place: Martell's. The meal was desolate, and when the tip had been paid and the coffee cups left behind, I stood on the sidewalk with Nancy and, giving me a weary you-will-forgive-me smile, she announced she was tired. Swell. A Checker cab swept her away, and I made my way to the subway, through the murk of my lingering mood.

I was halfway down Perry Street, almost home, when I saw Cullen stepping off our front stoop, in full regalia, boots and jeans and bomber jacket, dressed for his darkness. For some reason the sight of him instantly transformed my depressed mood into excitement. Excitement and fear. I know that I was once again going to follow.

I drew one long breath, closed my eyes and thought, *All right,*

but why not follow him all the way this time. He is only going off to some
damn bar. So follow him all the way this time and when he gets where he is
going, stroll right in after him, and give the irresistible little monster your
best smile.

A block and a half ahead of me, Cullen stood under a street light, his hands on his hips. I ducked back into the dark, suddenly terrified that he might turn and see me. *Oh, come on now*, I thought, huddling in a dark doorway, *what if he does?*

In those neurotic days, whenever I found myself edging into a homosexual adventure, my thoughts would slip into my college French, as if by thinking in a language I only half knew, I might be only half present for the awful sexual lapse. Only half compromised. So I would trail along behind my act of madness in another language.

In that shadowy doorway where I was hiding, the sickly whisper of my pidgen French started up again in my mind. *Tu peut le suivre, Jason. Tu peux trouver ses lieux secrets. Suis-le. Il est tellement beau. Suis-le dans le noir, et après . . . peut être . . . peut être . . . tu peux te reveler. Là, dans le noir. Comme il est merveilleux. Suis-le. Sois sage. Mais suis!*

It still was winter. I can remember seeing the small white gusts of Cullen's frozen breath caught against the night light. He strolled along slowly, calmly, slightly hunched from the cold. His golden head was bare. The small freezing wind stirred it. His hands were dug deep into the front pockets of his jeans. He was quite unaware of me.

Suis! Mais sois sage!

I stepped out of the sandstone doorway where I had been hiding, and started creeping down the dark edge of the buildings, keeping my distance, about a third or a half a block behind Cullen's walking figure. I felt plain, simple sexual excitement, intermingled, so excitingly, and so boringly, with fear. I was afraid, among other things, of losing him. All it would take would be just one turn around a corner and he would be gone. I hurried. *Il est prèsque disparu! Plus vite, plus vite!*

I hurried enough to get him clearly back into my field of

vision. I was quite near him, and frightened by my excitement, when I saw him turn a bit, as if he *might* look back.

Il me voit! Il me voit!

I ducked desperately into the darkened doorway of a cobbler's shop, and closed my eyes and huddled around the rush of my desire. *Damn Nancy! If he sees you, tu prétendras que tu fais une promenade innocente. Tu diras que tu marches pour marcher. Just remember that. You're just out for a little walk.*

Actually, Cullen had stopped and was talking with somebody. Is that possible? A friend? A police car, its roof lights dark, cruised harmlessly through the intersection. Cullen did not even glance at it. He did not glance, either, at me. Still not taking his hands from his pockets, he turned away from his acquaintance and continued west.

The stranger passed by my way, and gave me a glance.

But Cullen almost had reached the corner. *Il va disparaître. Dépêches-toi!*

I did hurry, but at the corner he was gone.

Gone from the face of the earth.

Merde!

A little further down the street there was a bar, exactly as I had foreseen. *Eh bien. La déstination. OK. OK. Now is the time.*

Cullen had stepped in and vanished, and I followed with my slow approach. There was a crowd of men loitering on the sidewalk outside the entry, and as soon as I was no longer alone my poor French fled. *Oh Christ Jason, get off it and grow up. If it's so damn tempting, just walk into this perfectly ordinary gay bar and say, Hi there Cullen, how's tricks, having fun?*

Dare. Just dare, you fool.

I pushed open the bar room door and held it open. The place was warm with its crowd of men, rank like all such places with the smell of mildew, its jukebox wailing in the dark. It was filled with bodies, with joyless merriment, with the reek of wishing. I scanned the crowd a second, and then there was Cullen in profile, just about to turn toward me, a slight smile on his face. He too was vaguely scanning the room, and his gaze was moving toward the door and me. He was certain to spot me in a second's time, and then it seemed to me I did indeed see that cold ravishing face light up with cynical recognition just as I jumped back into the darkness and fled.

chapter 8

As I went hustling home from that bar by the docks, I tried to talk myself into believing Cullen hadn't seen a thing. Close: it was true, he'd come close to seeing everything. But I was certain I'd ducked out of sight just in time. This was insane, I told myself. Never, never again. The men I passed cruising westward could not catch my eye. They were not for me. I had let one pretty, perverse,sneering face stir up some ancient fantasies, but I was not going to let one moment of half-horny curiosity be transformed into a destiny. Not by Cullen Crine I wasn't. So what if Cullen did get under my skin a bit? So what if I found him irritating in an . . . interesting way. Did I have to transform my life just because of that? I trotted across Seventh Avenue, hunched against the dark. That icy, promiscuous, unfeeling, enticing little killer! Was I supposed to tear up my life with Nancy and plunge into a life of God knows what for that? Was I going to toss away my whole life on that saucy, half-educated little snob? On what he had to offer? Like that sewer of a bar, for instance? Thank God he hadn't seen a thing. At least I was pretty sure he hadn't seen a thing. It was as close as . . . that. Think how treacherous he could be with Nancy. With Mel. With everybody. But I guessed I was safe. When I reached the Perry Street door, I glanced back, seething with the thought that perhaps Cullen had followed me home. But no. Thank God. He hadn't seen a thing.

I had managed to work myself into a good solid scare, and in the weeks to come I managed to use that fear quite intentionally to sublimate my obsession with Cullen into something that didn't scare me. He was my neighbor and Nancy's closest associate. I couldn't avoid him, and so instead I sought him out, especially with Nancy. I'd suggest we have dinner together, go to parties together. This had some positive results. I let the fantasy of Cullen freshen the stale edge of things with Nancy. Secret obsession was dangerous; I was clear about that. So I set out to demystify the little beast. Instead of cringing at my desk when he passed in the hallway, I was at the apartment door saying hi. We became almost friends. I was no longer, I told myself, acting like a child. Following people in the dark! Running home from bars, scared!

And then Vicki arrived on the scene. I was deep in work. Picture me seated, slumped at the desk on Perry Street, all my intellectual muscles sore at the end of a long, hard-thinking, hard-typing Sunday. Picture on the slide rack before me, one 35mm image, glowing. It is Duchamp's *The Passage From the Virgin To The Bride (1912)* — a pot of hot, cubist-derived greens, reds, and browns. Picture, on the pages slowly ratcheting up from the Smith Corona, this from *The Bachelors' Bride*:

Esotericism and the erotic: From a very early stage, both these apparently separate themes had played large but mutually distinct roles in Duchamp's juvenilia. Yet, between 1910 and 1912, this apparently clear-cut distinction between the esoteric and the erotic begins to be blurred, and at last erased, as Duchamp enters his struggle with the esthetics of cubism and, we are obliged to note, enters likewise upon the parallel traumata of his young manhood. By the time we reach *The Passage From The Virgin To The Bride (1912)*, the two salient though seemingly distinct elements of Duchamp's art — hermeticism (that is, his *symboliste*-derived fascination with the allure of a secret and only half-readable language);

and eros (that is, his involvement in a cult of desire and a cult of woman, construed as *the* driving motive of art) — have become not merely linked, but indistinguishably fused. From this point forward — indeed, until his death—desire will be the omnipresent figure in Duchamp's art, although it invariably will be figured in some mocking and hermetic fashion. Henceforth, desire will be mystified. Any simple impulse toward union or communion will be baffled by one or another of Duchamp's sundry mockeries of ordinary human yearnings, whether sexual or otherwise. From this point forward, wishing and incomprehension will be a single entity, confounded, and — as it were — wed.

I heaved a sigh, and without re-reading, stood up and strolled to the kitchen, checking the refrigerator for whatever consolation might, by some lucky oversight, still be left inside. Nothing. Instead, I made some coffee, and while waiting for the water to boil, the next phrase came to mind. It was this: "This marks a very considerable change." A very correct sentence. I carried the freshly steaming cup back to the desk, and began again:

This marks a very considerable change. Prior to 1910, the eros so pervasively running through Duchamp's work, while hardly simple, is at least unmysterious. In his nudes, we sense the plain ache of a young man's yearnings for woman's flesh. There appears nothing at all odd about his motives. But by the time we reach *Portrait, (Dulcinea) (1911)*, or *Sad Young Man on a Train (1912)*, the erotic obsessions of the young painter will be more and more evidently troubled. Any manifestation of eros now seems laden with sexual menace. The sad young man is literally shaken by his desires' power. Soon, eros will be more and more linked to the mindless comic potency of the machine, its erotic pistons imbecilically churning. Energy is figured as invariably grotesque, thrilling perhaps, but finally a laughable, grinding contraption — conjoined to the incomprehensible plumbing of some ghastly drainage system. In truth, all eros has come to be seen as a deracinating, family-shattering force, tearing up the young man's earlier life of sunlight and lawns and teacups, that sister-consoled bourgeois idyll of which the boy Marcel was so extremely fond and the mild pleasures which we glimpse in what might be called his youthful nostalgia for that dying impressionism so evident in his juvenilia.

Now I was cooking. The idea was in place and crossing the page like notes climbing a scale.

At the same moment that cubism conquered advanced painting, Duchamp's affective life changed—the specific triggering event being his sister Suzanne's hated, intolerable marriage in 1910. His own experience of desire became more troubled, and Duchamp began to mystify once fairly plain erotic concerns in the language of a private and vaguely *symboliste* "esotericism."

I have put the word "esotericism" in quotation marks. I cannot find that Duchamp's grasp of, or interest in, any established hermetic science — numerology and alchemy are the most often proposed — ever was anything but cursory, slight, and merely bemused. No: the "esotericism" of Marcel Duchamp borrows permission from the symbolists to generate an entirely autonomous system of idiosyncratic signs, personal images, and private myths. Though the entire enterprise may be proposed under the sign of desire, it is nonetheless a system whose impulse to subvert meaning is engaged less in any already existing hermetic vocabulary than it is in a critique of language itself. By language I mean something much more radical than mere mockery of the newly discovered vocabulary of cubism in painting. I mean a critique of *all* language, visual and verbal: a critique — indeed, an immobilization in irony — of the mere idea of human communication and human interchange, nothing less, a private — indeed, all but artistically self-referring — devastation of the very instruments of knowing and being known.

The link between all this and eros is simple. As a man, Duchamp experienced the Other, in that Other's most provocative and dangerous form, as Woman. At the center of his self-generated hermetic system is a self-generated, ironic, hermetic cult of Woman. With *The Passage From The Virgin To The Bride* — a canvas which marks Duchamp's farewell to cubism and to the classically practiced art of oil painting itself — this private cult of Woman finds its first normative expression. Here Duchamp engages with the all-provocative, all-desiring, all-desired figure of Woman and baffles her, reduces her, endistances her, transforms her into. . . .

Into . . . Into . . . I leaned back in my desk chair, stuck for the moment. I closed my eyes to think. At that moment, a musical little knock-knock at my apartment door coyly interrupted.

Damn! All the elements of my concentration came clattering down like a juggler's dropped pins.

Double, double damn!

I wasn't trying to hide my annoyance when I yanked open the apartment door, and so I probably flashed a jolt of sexual surprise at the sight before me on the landing. There slouched a blond stranger, female, her head tilted in bewilderment, lazily goggling me through lavender-tinted aviator glasses that perched cockeyed on her round young face. She was chewing gum. She chewed with her pretty mouth open, making lots of sexy noise. She chomped the spearmint in slack voluptuousness.

"Shit," she said, addressing nobody in particular, blandly turning her back on me. "*You're* not who I *want*." She took a few steps back onto the landing, sinking her weight on one hip, and peering around for the truly desired.

I stood still, trying to master a small, almost erotic fit of impatience, listening to her chew. Her long hair hung over her olive drab canvas jacket in a tangled, unclean veil of blond strands spreading almost to her waist. The face that had just turned away was wonderfully creamy and smooth; there

obviously was more of that creaminess beneath the canvas —
but that femininity swam submerged under masculine yards of
army surplus: an olive drab field-jacket caked stiff with dirt,
and basic training fatigues rolled over the clunking laced boots
of an infantry grunt. Still lost, still chewing, my visitor glanced
back at me, struck dumb with what might be called bored
amazement. She continued to chew. It was as though some
slatternly Eve, stumbling through this dump they had the
nerve to call a garden, had come across the impossible: not
Lucifer himself, just some irrelevant, perfectly pointless Other
Man.

"Vicki, will you please stop molesting my poor neighbor?" It
was Cullen, calling down from the landing above. "Vicki, look
up. *Up*! I am up *here*!"

"Wha?" The disoriented girl could only moan her answer,
first looking around her and only a few dazed seconds later up
at the beauty leaning on crossed forearms over the railing.
Cullen was immaculate in his latest fifty-dollar haircut, his
Italian pants, bunch-pleated in the front, always a half-step
ahead of chic, and a sleeveless sweater pulled over a Saint
Laurent shirt.

"Oh there," she said.

"Just one little flight more, Vicki. It's not hard. Don't be
lazy. And watch yourself with my neighbor, because he's my
boss's boyfriend."

"Oh." This had made her give me a size-up glance.

"Jason, the apparition in front of you is named Vicki Mercer
and she is my oldest friend in the entire world."

Vicki goggled me through her cockeyed, dandruff spattered
lavender lenses.

"Gee," I said. "Hi Vicki."

"Hi" she answered, without cordiality. She did not extend
her hand.

"Jason, why don't you come up and have a drink with us?
Protect me from her. She's rapacious, you know."

Vicki glanced at me charmlessly. "He's such a liar."

"Well, I'd love to Cullen, except just now I was sort of working. . . ."

"Oh *fuck* your work, Jason. In God's name, it's Sunday afternoon. You work too much anyway. It's making you a bore and driving me crazy, with that damn typewriter of yours for-fucking-*ever* tap-tap-tapping away." "I'm sorry," I said. "Not to mention your *incessant* pacing. Come on. Have a drink. At least pretend to be civilized."

Scratching through khaki the undoubtedly luscious inside of her thigh, Vicki stood squinting upward, while I pulled the apartment door shut behind me. I had abandoned Duchamp. Why now? I wondered vaguely while Vicki climbed. Why an invitation now? She clomped in her boots, her hands deep inside her frayed field jacket sleeves, like the little hands of the playground's poor girl lost in some immense hand-me-down.

When she reached the top of the stairs, Vicki let herself be given a bear hug by her oldest and best friend. Then she sidled through his door.

"So *this* is your new place," she whined, walking into the apartment. "Pretty *dégoutant*." With a kind of shrug, she let her battle jacket slump to the floor. Then she sank, loose and luscious, into the room's one comfortable chair. "God," she said, "what a hole this is."

I myself had not seen the place since I'd shown it to Cullen weeks before and apologized because it was dirty. By now, "dirty" had become far too crude, too simple a word. The place was dirty — plenty dirty — all right. The sink was a reeking heap of dishes resting in what appeared to be cold brown slime. But the floor was not merely dirty. Obscene would be more precise. It was a whorehouse floor, littered with the dreck of Cullen's nightside life. Near Vicki's coat lay Cullen's heavy black cruising boots and a few feet away sprawled Cullen's bomber jacket. Against the molding an empty bottle of Smirnoff vodka had rolled into balls of dust. On the linoleum, eight or ten white plastic ampules of amyl nitrate were scattered, smashed inside their white plastic nets, tiny broken beasts. I spotted a tangled and knotted athletic support on the floor near Cullen's foot, which for some reason Cullen stopped to pick up, fastidiously pinched between forefinger and thumb and delicately pitched through his open bedroom door. Cullen himself, on the other hand, stood before us in boyish freshness, and I suspected that in some closet beyond, his whole straight wardrobe was hanging in perfect order.

"You want a drink?" Cullen asked us both.

"I've got something better than that," Vicki cooed, her eyes wicked behind her glasses. She reached into the capacious side pockets of her fatigues, and extracted two joints already rolled, holding them to us as if offering some irresistible game of patty-cake. Then she tossed back her hair in a movement exactly — but exactly — like Cullen's habitual toss of his fifty-dollar forelock. Nonetheless, Cullen and I only drank.

"Vicki and I," Cullen explained, pouring me a vodka over ice, "have been friends ever since we were five back in Ohio, and playing dirty games with each other in the bushes. Right, sweetheart?"

"Riiight," Vicki said. She lit one of her reefers and sank back into the soft chair as if into a warm pool of sex. With her jacket on the floor, Vicki wore as a top only an oversized faded scarlet tee shirt, beneath which her body moved, bra-less.

"So you two grew up together?"

"Uh-huh."

"That's fascinating," I went on, "you do really look a great deal alike. It's actually rather amazing. I mean, the resemblance seems almost genetic." I paused. "Has anybody ever said that before?"

"Uh-huh," Vicki answered, toking.

"You're *sure* you are not really brother and sister? Maybe a secret strange mix-up in the baby baskets way back there in Ohio?"

Vicki coughed her pot-cough, then tilted her head and produced a sparkling coquettish smile. "No mix-up. But wouldn't it be *great* if Cullen and I really *were* brother and sister?"

"God yes," Cullen said. "Incest!"

Over the rim of his vodka glass, Cullen held Vicki's eyes locked in a twilit gaze of deep affection. Meanwhile, I sat there trying to balance their resemblance in my mind, and noticing, as if in some kind of light reflected from my attraction to Cullen, that I found his soul sister likewise very alluring as she slouched there in her army fatigues, exuding her enticing sullenness. And then the thought occurred to me, quite suddenly, that this twin-sister look-alike from his mid-western boyhood — a past Cullen usually most ostentatiously renounced — was the only person of either sex anywhere that Cullen loved, or would, or could, ever love. Vicki goggled back at him through those lavender glasses, which were specially polarized to make all the world look as though you were seeing it high. They tilted at an ever more precarious and radical angle at the end of Vicki's very pretty nose.

"Riiight," Vicki concluded after a longish druggy pause in the chemical elsewhere. "Well, Cullen, the difference between us is that you are a fantasist and I am a realist. I face facts."

"It is such a shame. If we could commit incest, think what an *evil* time we could have together."

"Right," said Vicki, chomping her gum.

They sat across from one another like two of the Midwich cuckoos, blond and pretty in their old argumentative affiliation, two androgynous cream-puffs, one dirty, one clean, both filled with lots of fluffy but cynical sweet cream.

"So where are you staying since you got back."

"Sally's house," Vicki said.

"Ya wanna stay here instead?"

"Are you kidding? I'm not that hard up."

"So how was Europe?"

"Europe was simply great. I love Europe. I hate being back here and I can't wait to go back there, which is what I intend to do the minute I manage to get ahold of some money. Cullen," she switched into a little girl voice, "I need some *muh*-neee. Can you get me some? I mean, like, can you get me a job or something?"

Cullen rolled his eyes. "God, doing what? Driving people crazy?"

"Cute," said Vicki.

But on reflection, Cullen seemed to take the question seriously. "Well, come to think about it, it might be possible to dig up something . . ." He considered the question. I wonder if the idea he eventually produced, the one that would so deeply affect us all, flickered through that calculating brain of his then or later.

"Of course," Vicki added, "I don't really *want* a job. What I really want to do is get enough money to get back to Europe. I know a lot of interesting people there now. I've got a boyfriend there, and I have to go back and figure out whether to get rid of him."

"So what do you want to do? I mean for the job."

"Oh Cullen, don't ask dumb questions like what I want to do for the job. OK, I'll tell you: I want a fascinating easy job where I can have lots and lots of fun all day long and I make heaps and heaps of money so I can walk away from the job as soon as possible and fly back to Paris and dump or decide on Jean-Pierre gracefully, that is with a bank account. *Capeesh?*"

"I get it. Something simple. A matter of a phone call. Vicki, I have a suggestion. Why don't you sell your body?"

"Cullen, you are so inexpressibly witty. Did you learn that kind of elegant wit kissing ass in art galleries, or what? Why don't you sell yours?"

"I can't find any takers."

At this point, Vicki removed her gum, held it out toward Cullen and asked if there were someplace she could get rid of it. "I would *hate* to mess your place."

Cullen pointed to the unspeakable garbage pail beside the sink.

"So, sweetheart," Vicki said, strolling back, "tell me about this new job of yours. Are you finally a big shot in the art world? Who is this Nancy Hopkins you've sold out to? Not that I think for a second you ever wanted to do anything except sell out, of course. But who is she? Not that it matters. Film is the only art that matters now. Painting, sculpture, all that. The nineteenth century. *Fi-neet-o.*"

"Thank you, Cassandra, for those prophetic words. And here I am telling you about my job, and wondering where to get you one. But whatever you want, we're finished. The answer to your question is that Nancy is a newish dealer, operating downtown. Very good, very smart. Properly capitalized. A lady."

Vicki rolled her eyes. Her body moved, maddeningly, under her tee shirt. "And as I said on the stairs, Jason here is her boyfriend."

Vicki tilted her head toward me.

"So watch your mouth," Cullen added.

"What's so im*por*tant about her?" Vicki asked, thinking, toking, disregarding me.

In one smooth transition, Cullen effortlessly became businesslike and lucid. I glimpsed why he was good at his job. "I would say the Hopkins is an important gallery because, first of all, it is very active — by which I mean, that we do real business instead of pretend business. See, a lot of galleries in New York do pretend business. In other words, tax business. We really sell real art. The other thing is that Nancy is ready for the next phase of taste and is building her connection to it, and at the same time she's grounded and bankrolled in the big money-makers of today. Something else: people believe in Nancy. They believe in her because she has class and because she has first-rate connections here, and in California, and in Texas, and in Europe. The clients are a nice mix of private and institutional. We have good artists, we are building on the best newcomers, and we represent one or two major ones. Meanwhile, Nancy has a *fabulous* gallery director. Namely, me."

Vicki still was thinking. "So who is this major artist, so-called?"

"Mel Dworkin," Cullen produced the name as if playing an ace.

"Ah well, in that case. Hot-ze-*tah!*" Vicki stared at its celebrity a moment. "You used to say that Mel Dworkin was nothing but a has-been."

Cullen, found out, flushed with annoyance. "I said nothing of the fucking kind, Vicki. Believe me, you and your French film boyfriend will be has-beens when the Dworkin reputation is just beginning. Mel Dworkin is not a has-been, he is a classic in his own time."

Silence. Vicki toked her joint. "Don't be snotty about Jean-Pierre. I might even love him. You never can tell."

"I'm sorry Vicki, but you say irritating things sometimes."

"It's finished anyway, this art thing. It is just a whole upper bourgeois scam that won't matter in a radicalized world. It is bourgeois beauty. And bourgeois beauty is dead. You know it. You love dressing in Saint Laurent shirts, so you go around saying it is really in some kind of vanguard, but it isn't. It's finished. The only art that is going to matter at all in the seventies will be film. And it won't be American film either. So forget that."

"So it's going to be you and your French boyfriend and Sally and. . . ."

"*And* Godard, *and* Bertolucci, *and* all kinds of people. . . ."

"And all kinds of people you have met in Europe. . . ."

"Meeting. I'm meeting them."

"And we know Bertolucci would rather die than be seen in a Saint Laurent anything."

"So tell me about him then. Mel Dworkin."

Whereupon I settled back and listened to Cullen launch into a description of Mel.

Two nights ago, I had dinner with Cullen and the subject of Vicki came up, as it always does. That impression I had so

suddenly, all those years ago — that Vicki was the only person
in the world that Cullen could love — has proved surprisingly
durable. In the years since Mel died, Vicki has been a regular in
that branch of international middle-Bohemia where the boy-
and girlfriends of the famous drift, taking with them their
gorgeous bodies and their petulance and their many, many,
many problems. Vicki has drifted from New York to Paris to
Rome and back to New York again; she has drifted from lover
to lover; from radicalism to radicalism. She has passed from the
rough narcissistic theater of feminist rage to the terrorist
chit-chat of the seventies into the greedy eighties, all the while
sliding through high, halcyon summers among the glamorous,
settling into less lovely winters of elaborate traveling, elaborate
drinking, elaborate drugs and boredom. . . . weeks and months
of bored, worried *waiting*. I think there was a marriage — I
mean, a real marriage — somewhere along the way, but it was
not the right kind of *real* marriage for Vicki, probably was as
blanc as they come. Strictly for the passport office. There was a
time when Vicki's feminism shaded into radical Lesbianism.
And then radical Lesbianism gave way to Lesbian chic, a very
different thing, so Vicki flourished on *those* yachts for a while.
Then, it was back to heterosexuality, for a much-publicized
round in Hollywood, and for a moment it looked as though
things finally were coming together for Vicki. But no. Not
quite. She went back to Cullen in New York, where Cullen was
as usual making his way from success to success, inexorably.
Then back to Europe, and (between moments of homosexual
refreshment) men. A few too many men. Vicki has drifted
toward middle age with the simple good health of a
solidly-made, middle western girl. The Ohio Swede in her
managed to keep her looks in place year after year after year.
Her bedroom Italian and French long since had become fluent,
and she was and is always in contact with the *real* man in her
life, Cullen Crine. Always under his watchful eyes. Always
helped by him. Always linked to him. And still capable of that
allure that did not quite work, still making rumors move like

flickers of pointless light as she strolls at a long evening's end into the Piazza del Popolo.

"Vicki and I," Cullen said the other night at the Odeon, "have decided to spend our old age together. I have got it all laid out. Once the inevitable comes and we both look like hell, we will move in together and face the horror of it side by side." Of course, the inevitable already is making itself felt. At forty-four Cullen's sometime beauty in all its exquisiteness has sunk into mere amiable masculine handsomeness gone just a tad fleshy from the liquor. "It's a perfect arrangement. After all, I love Vicki and Vicki loves me, and that's what counts in any marriage, right? I have laid it all out. First of all, if we must be not gorgeous, at least we'll be not gorgeous in Italy. So it's going to be winters in Rome — with maybe a little Parisian salt and pepper every once in a while — then late spring and summer in Sestri Levanti. Fall will be either travel or else Venice. Vicki doesn't have a *dime* of course, but we'll live on my money, the little I have tucked away here and there. Plus perhaps a little dealing from the living room in the old masters or the post-modern. After all, I have wasted my youth on this racket to *some* purpose, and I do have *some* sort of reputation. I think Vicki and I will make an ideal couple. She is the only person on earth I possibly could live with. She is such a *fab*ulous whore, I figure she and I will be able to comb the beach of Sestri Levanti with maximum effect. If you get my drift."

"Sounds wonderful, Cullen."

"Now then, what do you want to eat here?"

It is an odd but devoted and unbreakable union. Oceans may separate them, but Vicki and Cullen's relationship gives the appearance of being indissoluble, oddly loving and life-long. Not to mention, most importantly, pre-emptive. It is by now perfectly obvious that theirs is a romance that can be challenged, really challenged, by nobody. Cullen still spends every long vacation he can with Vicki in Italy or France, and whenever she is in America Vicki is promptly installed, long term, in the high style of Cullen Crine's much publicized loft, which is, as I guess is fairly well known, Mel's old Mercer Street loft, the shrine that Cullen bought from the estate in the early seventies. I wonder what Vicki thinks when she arrives at the place and settles in, not with Mel but Cullen. I guess it is all in some kind of family. She still is as dependent on Cullen as she was that day she arrived in Perry Street wearing battle fatigues. She has been painted by David Hockney and photographed by David Bailey, and she knows everybody. And she still doesn't have a dime.

"So when I finally get through with this art-world crap," Cullen continued, "Vicki and I are going to grow decrepit together on the Italian coast." Cullen glanced at our hovering, very handsome waiter, who had very obviously recognized who Cullen was. "I'll have the chicken breasts, please," he said.

So it was going to be Cullen and Vicki together in Sestri Levanti, Cullen and Vicki in the *passagiata* on Capri. Together in the end as they had been in Ohio, in the beginning. That is the only way that either one of them could contemplate the otherwise unutterable inevitabilities of time.

Our newly self-conscious waiter pulled the cork and poured a taste of wine into Cullen's glass. Holding the bottle half high and ignoring me, he stepped back and sank into contraposto, waiting for the career-maker's reply. It is true. Cullen is now really a very powerful man. Hard to believe. My impression was very distinctly that the waiter would not have minded if Cullen liked more than the wine. I could see the moment of refusal pass, ever so subtly, through Cullen's features. He has gotten to be very good at what people want. Very good at No. Cullen accepted the bottle with one cold nod and a toss of the forelock, and while the hovering beauty poured, Cullen froze him into the absolute distance, with the absolute indifference of his twilit eyes.

chapter 9

Though it had seemed the new age would last forever, we now had reached the winter of 1969. Affair number two with Nancy Hopkins had survived almost another entire year. The night before the decade ended, I took the subway uptown for a quiet time with Nancy. She and I were going to be sane; we were going to say goodbye to the old decade, welcome in the new, with dinner alone. But when she opened the front door, my girlfriend groaned as I kissed her hello.

"Well *that* is an unforgettable greeting," I said, and while I unloaded all my winter trappings, she sank onto the couch beneath the Morris Louis and sat, her eyes averted from the spectacle of my shed stocking cap and boots, depressed, preoccupied, in a heap.

I took it in for a moment. "Happy New Year. I am very sorry to have interrupted. I should have remembered that suicidal people do have a thing about being alone."

"Oh Jason, don't make things difficult."

"*I* am making things difficult? Oh, I get it. I should have known a simple kiss would trigger despair. Callous of me. Sorry."

Nancy leaned forward and covered her eyes.

"Hey now, hold it," I said. "What *is* this. Come on, Nancy. What is the matter?" She did not respond. "What should I do?

Do you want me to sit down? Do you want to talk?" Nancy shook her head as if declining the offer of an aspirin. "What *is* it?"

"What's what?"

"Oh come on, honey. Tell me."

She looked up at me. Her dark brown eyes seemed to meditate indecisively, one hand pressed for support into the soft cushions of the couch. It was as if she were considering some crucial question. About me.

"All right, Jason. You're right. Something has happened, and I am going to tell you about it. Ordinarily, I would keep this to myself. But this time I can't." Her voice sank a shade deeper. "And maybe . . . I don't have to. Anymore."

Well now. That was at least a start.

"Is it all right if I sit down?"

Nancy straightened herself up on the couch and I pulled over a chair. "Jason, this little story isn't . . . isn't a little story. I think it may be kind of a big one. And a serious one. And I have no idea at all where the damages could end. I need . . . I need your discretion. Your *absolute* discretion. This has to be between us. Really. But I mean *really*."

"All right," I said, leaning back in the chair. "I agree to that. You have my discretion. Really."

Nancy closed her eyes for a moment, gathering her thoughts, and then she began. "Four days ago, while I was out to lunch, a man came ambling into the gallery. Don't worry about his name. He's just a man. He introduced himself to Cullen and he said he had brought in some prints which he was hoping to sell. He added that these were prints by Mel Dworkin. Signed lithographs. Quite recent. Cullen said fine, fine, let's have a look. So, out they came. Well, the prints were very good prints indeed. In fact they happen to be some of the best prints Mel has ever made. But Cullen was also just a teensy bit startled, because they come from a series which has not yet been put on the market."

"I am not sure what you mean."

"I mean that a member of the general public had come sauntering into the gallery trying to sell us back a print that we have never released in the first place. Never even shown. Informally or any other way. It was impossible to explain how this guy had ever come into possession of it."

"Hm." I took it in.

"Cullen stayed very cool. Cullen is so sharp, Jason. So competent. He really is wonderful. I don't know what I would do without him."

Splendid. My shadow rival was indispensable. I smiled my wan smile.

"He told the guy that these were indeed very nice prints, and yes the gallery might very well be interested, but that the decision was not his, that I was out of the gallery for the moment. Might we hold the prints for a day or two, just to decide? And a *bit* to Cullen's surprise, the seller said sure, he'd leave the prints overnight, why not?"

"So you think maybe the seller doesn't know anything about what might be wrong?"

"So far as I can understand this thing," Nancy answered, "the seller is completely on the up and up. *He* is not our guilty party. Well, the second I got back from lunch, Cullen took me into the back office and showed me the prints and the bottom of my stomach just dropped into the basement. I mean — Jason, you have no *idea*. Those prints are absolutely top secret. They are the best work Mel has done in a long time, and their impact is everything for Mel's reputation at this stage of his career. We have not shown them to anyone. Not to friends, not to you; nobody. They are under lock and key. Period. That is the policy. So right away, I knew that something was desperately wrong."

"Obviously."

"Anyway, the first thing I did was telephone Mel in Springs and tell him the whole story. And Mel absolutely could not believe what he was being told. I asked him if there were any way, any way at all, that there might have been some leak . . .

some gift, some set of proofs left behind at Gemini. Anything. Absolutely not. He was certain that the whole edition was still locked in their drawers in New York, and nobody has access except Mel and me and, of course, Jeffrey."

"Uh-huh."

"So, I hung up feeling odd. The next day, the seller duly returned to the gallery, all bright and innocent, all set to get rich selling me his beautiful *beautiful* Dworkin prints. And so I met him in my office, and we talked, and I said yes indeed they were very interesting prints, very beautiful, blah, blah, blah . . . And yes, we might very possibly be interested in them, but by the way did he happen to know the — uh — the *provenance* of these beautiful prints? And without a blink our man says, sure he knows the provenance. He had bought the prints from a very nice young painter way, *way* downtown, somebody he'd been sent to by a friend in the art world, somebody who used to work as an assistant to Dworkin himself, who had been given the prints by Dworkin personally, as a gift. Now the guy was doing some work on his loft, and loft work being terribly expensive, he was selling them, and he was selling them for a thousand dollars apiece.

"Well, I said, that certainly sounded very interesting and heaven knows he had been given a very handsome bargain at a thousand dollars apiece. Then, as if I were going through the ritual of a dream, I asked if he recalled the name of this nice young assistant and he said, sure he recalled it. The name was Jeffrey Hastings."

It was my turn to cover my eyes. Then I looked up.

"You're telling me those prints were stolen by Jeffrey?"

"That, my dear, is exactly what I'm telling you."

"I can hardly believe it."

"Well, sweetheart, *believe* it. Dear Darling Jeffrey, sweet Jeffrey of the soft brown eyes, Jeffrey with Mel's complete confidence, Jeffrey the buddy of buddies, with the key to absolutely every closet and drawer on Mercer Street."

"It really is kind of horrible."

"Horrible is only the beginning. Before I called Mel back I called, just on a hunch, a couple of resale places around town and made a discreet inquiry or two. It took about four calls to find out that there are stolen Mel Dworkin prints out all over town. Every one with the same nonsensical story behind it, the studio assistant forced to sell his little gift. It's incredible! So obvious. So transparent. So easily traced. . . . *Really*!"

"But Jeffrey? He always seemed so admiring. Almost abject."

"Well? Do you need to look any further for a motive? Happy New Year."

"Does Mel know about this?"

"Of course. I called him back right away."

"What did he say?"

"Well, he's naturally terribly upset. But I think he's upset about the wrong thing. He keeps talking about protecting *Jeffrey*. We shouldn't jump to conclusions. Who knows if it might not be some crazy mistake. Blah, blah, blah. Well, that was before he called Jeffrey and very gently raised the issue of this odd unimportant business of some guy trying to sell some prints."

"And?"

"And the conversation then turned step by step, insane. First, Jeffrey got all huffy and confused. Of course he claimed he had never in all his life heard of the guy with the prints and he couldn't understand why Mel was even calling about him. Mel said that as he talked, Jeffrey's voice was choking up, getting a little crazy."

"I *bet* it was getting a little crazy." He who was so proud.

"Well anyway, Mel persisted. He told Jeffrey the seller had really been very definite about where he got the prints. At which point Jeffrey turned nasty, snapping out something about how maybe he had sold a print or two, and what of it. Mel gives away lots of prints."

"Which *is* true. . . ." I interjected.

"Yes, it is true. But Mel pushed a little harder, saying well, maybe so, but he hadn't given any of the new series away. At this point Jeffrey started really going bonkers. He started snapping into the phone — you know, with that awful little giggle he has? — well, so what? So what if maybe Jeffrey had once or twice helped himself to some drawing or print left laying around. What difference could that possibly make to Mel? It was no skin off Mel's ass. So what, if once in a while Jeffrey took a little compensation for the shit Mel dished out."

I simply stared.

"That was just the beginning. Mel stayed very calm, very together, and he said, now Jeffrey, of course, you can have any print you want. You just have to ask. But this situation doesn't seem to be a matter of just a couple of prints. Because it seems that there were all *kinds* of prints out, all of them unaccounted for, in all kinds of outlets, all around the country. . . .

"At which point Jeffrey Hastings proceeded into a full blown psychotic episode. He began to *scream* into the telephone all about how he didn't care anymore, all right, go ahead, accuse him! Forget friendship and service and slavery, simple slavery. It was just like Mel to turn against his friend, against his slave, ruin him, destroy his whole life . . . over property. Then he started to cry. Can you imagine? Blubbering about how Mel had ruined Jeffrey's life, humiliated Jeffrey for years, blocked his career, crushed out his talent, ruined his manhood. . . ."

I laughed. "Manhood," I muttered. "Jeffrey and manhood."

Nancy closed her eyes. I watched her sink into herself. Her arms were clenched across her chest.

At that point the telephone rang, and Nancy stood up to take the call in her bedroom. I went to the window and stared out in the early fallen winter evening from our grand Manhattan height. I was absorbed in the story, and yet I also at that moment felt disoriented, dangerously close to some kind of frightening victory. The colored lights crawled below, but I felt I understood Jeffrey's crisis better than anybody else ever could. I felt party to it, implicated in it, almost as though I somehow or other had planned it myself. I was linked to his humiliation in a way that excited me, and though I was in a deep, dubious, shameful way pleased with the ruin of my rival, I felt also drawn to it as well, as if the moral forces that had brought him to such a desperate condition might very well destroy me too, that as his rival I too might drown in the same quicksand where he was now drowning. It frightened me, and yet something in me sang in the deep, frightened, rising joy of seeing his defeat, he who was always so hostile, always so quick to despise, always so filled with masculine menace, now, now at last, self-destroyed, deep in self-loathing and humiliation, going down. *Good*! My terrified heart sang it. *Good. Bring him down. Bring Jeffrey Hastings down. I love the sight of it.*

When Nancy came back into the room my forehead was pressed against the freezing window pane and my eyes were closed.

"That was Cullen," she said, "and he's on the way up here. Everything is in motion. Mel is driving in from Springs now, and Cullen has just been at the loft, checking around. It's worse than we thought. He looked through the drawing drawers and it seems all kinds of stuff is . . . poof! With us no more. Unbelievable."

"It really is sad," I offered hypocritically. "I've just been thinking about Jeffrey and what he must have gone through to sink to this point."

Nancy instantly closed ranks. "Oh no, you *don't*. Spare me the poor suffering Jeffrey Hastings crap. I've been listening to that all afternoon from Mel. Jason, you don't seem to grasp the scope of this. You don't get what's been done, financially. This is not just a personal betrayal. It's not just some sniveling neurotic getting his jollies in a pathetic act of symbolic revenge. This is a system of *thefts*. It is a *racket*."

"Well, it looks like he tried to be caught. There must be *some* neurosis in it. . . ."

It really was too perverse. For the first time in my life, I was defending Jeffrey Hastings.

"Of *course* there's neurosis in it. There was neurosis in Auschwitz. *That's* no excuse. I refuse to find Jeffrey pathetic. I find him sickening. The betrayal of trust. *Trust!* The very word is a joke. When I think I actually suspected Mel of holding back prints. . . . Mel! When all along it was that strutting, lying. . . ."

Then Nancy did something rather strange. She sighed, as if sighing away her anger, and pulled me to the couch. She sank down onto my lap. She wanted to sit on my lap.

"Oh Jason, all this makes me feel so . . . awful. Life shouldn't be this way." Her fingers went into my hair. She wanted to trail them there, and slowly play.

"It's just so nasty . . . such a horrible look into life. . . . That crazy little person. Then this bad dream breaks, tonight of all nights — stupid, disgusting New Year's Eve. 1969. The stupid end to the stupid sixties. I hate it." She hugged me tighter. "I hate New Year's Eve, I think the whole holiday should be shot dead in its tracks. Put out of its misery. I really do."

She was silent a moment, while she clung to me.

"So hold me," she said.

I held her.

"Nancy," I said at last, "let's not sit here crushing each other," and I stood up to lead her by the hand into the bedroom, where we lay on the bed, side by side, and lowered our voices.

Even though the winter evening was early, night had fallen over the cold city.

"*Are* you going to call the police into this?"

"I don't know," Nancy answered. She kept touching my cheek with her fingertips. She kept looking at me. "I wanted to call in the art squad of the FBI. Just so we could track it all down. But Mel won't let me. He says it's immoral. He says all he wants to do is talk to Jeffrey. . . ."

"So Mel would not call in the establishment?"

Nancy laid her wrist across her forhead and released a little snort of laughter. "The *establishment!*"

We were silent a while.

"This thing has got to stay private, Jason. I am relying on your absolute discretion. Really. Please. Promise me."

"Nancy, I've promised you once. If you like, I can promise again."

She turned and looked at me, very tenderly, and then she hugged me, her eyes wide open. "I guess I don't trust you, Jason. I don't know why. Maybe because you are a man. I think that's it. I feel like I hate men right now. I do." I swallowed rather hard. "And I don't really care what you think when I say it. I hate every last one of you." She laid her hand on my forehead and looked at me very deeply, as if trying to get to the bottom of the fear I was attempting to hide. Fear — fear kept tight with the tingle of excitement. "To me, this whole story stinks, just stinks from top to bottom with the male ego. With male competition and destructiveness. These feminists are right about so many things. I really think half of you are just lost. I do. At this stage of history you're ruined, a whole sex hopelessly . . . turned against itself. I don't know."

She flopped back onto the bed, thinking through a long stare at the ceiling. "When I think of that little twit, with his macho, and his basic weakness, I could vomit. I *hate* hearing Mel defend him. I *hate* Mel's insistence upon seeing him. His . . . sentimentalism about this."

"What sentimentalism?" I asked.

"Oh, Mel is busy pretending to be *good* about this. I think it is dangerous. Literally, physically dangerous. I wouldn't put any violence past Jeffrey now. Let a threatened male ego loose, and death and violence are . . . anywhere. An inch away."

"Nobody has done anything violent," I murmured in as unhysterical, unthreatened a tenor as I could muster.

"Jeffrey was *insane* on the phone."

"Women get crazy on the phone, too."

"Not like that. But Jason, don't let's talk about this anymore. I've talked all day. Hold me some more." She was nuzzling her face against my chest, like a little girl recovering, unconsoled, from a long tumultuous cry. I held her. I held her for quite a long while. Nancy had been talking about fury, but fury was not what I felt running through her body. I felt instead the slow flow of grief. I lay there drawing an unfamiliar stillness from my excitement and her grief and the smell of her woman's nearness to me, until the lobby intercom burst upon us with its hard rasping squeal.

"That will be C.C.," Nancy said, sitting up in her businesslike way, disentangling herself. She stood beside the bed, composing herself in the reflection of the sometimes pornographic tilted oak-frame mirror that was now so chaste, and then she walked into the living room to answer the door, smoothing back her wonderful chestnut hair.

chapter 10

And so, that final night of the sixties, our gloomy little New Year's Eve party consisted of uncorking one sad bottle of champagne and toting up a list of stolen goods. Cullen arrived with a preliminary inventory from Mercer Street, and we contemplated the damages, debating the disaster until eleven, when we heard from Mel, who'd driven to the city and gone straight to Mercer Street to prepare for a midnight confrontation with his Nemesis.

Nancy opposed the meeting, but she was supportive on the phone, warning him, while Cullen and I listened, slouched over our joyless bubbly, to be careful and promising to be at the loft the next morning at ten, with Cullen and me, to make a more systematic inventory of the losses. "But Mel? *Do* be careful. Remember Jeffrey is frightened now, and he *is* crazy. So don't stay up all night trying to talk sense to him. He is beyond sense. Get some sleep . . . What? . . . Oh, right. Happy New Year. Ha. Ha. Very funny."

Cullen and I left early together, wading solemnly into the reprobate night, breaking our silence in the cab only occasionally to denounce, once again, and in a strangely forced and half-hearted way, the man we despised. When we climbed the stairs of Perry Street together, we did so like friends.

The next morning we walked to Mercer Street and arrived

at the very moment Nancy was pulling up in a Checker, kitty-corner. We climbed the stairs to Mel's place, solemn as a funeral delegation bringing condolences to the house of the dead. When Nancy's gentle tentative knock did not rouse Mel, she let us in with her own key.

"Mel?"

No answer. She closed the door and then, half-assertive, half-afraid, tried again: "Mel?"

In the sleeping claustral air, stale with Mel's long winter absence, the smell of marijuana hovered like an aroma of exhaustion. The many high narrow windows of Mel's living space seemed pulled into mourning by long white shades drawn to the sills. The big coffee table in the center of the room looked like the scene of some sullen debauch. Among some emptied champagne bottles and two smudged glasses, the roaches of several joints lay like papery dead bugs poisoned in the marble ashtray.

Nancy slipped off her coat and assumed the brisk manner of a registered nurse taking charge of a sickroom. "Jason, will you go wake up Mel and let him know we're here?" She picked up three empty bottles and carried them to the trash.

Mel slept in a small bedroom tucked away near his studio. I knocked gently, and then, on tiptoes, let myself in.

"Mel?"

He lay sprawled under a cobalt blue quilt which he clutched in a sleeper's embrace. His feet stuck out, bare. One arm had reached out, naked, and his silencing hand was clamped asleep over an alarm clock.

Looking out, I could make out the whole outline of Mel's body. My eyes lingered on the arm that extended from the quilt on the bare shoulder. Mel had set his glasses neatly beside a half-emptied champagne bottle and one overturned tumbler.

"*Mel!*,' I made it loud.

"What!" Mel flailed out of sleep, twisting onto his back, snatching the covers and squinting up at me in startlement.

"Sorry," I said. "Sorry to wake you. Just wanted to let you

know we're all here." And before he could speak or make a move, I made my escape.

Half an hour later, Mel emerged into the kitchen, wearing an undersized boy's bathrobe of hideous green — something that must have belonged to him when he was in high school. The smell of fresh coffee was now in the air, and Mel shuffled past us at the table to the stove, where he poured himself a mug, reaching without apology for a bottle of bourbon on the shelf above. He uncorked it with a nonchalant squeak, and spiked his first day's sip of anything. He proceeded, judiciously, to take that sip. Then he walked back to us and sat down.

"So?" Nancy said. "What happened?"

"With Jeffrey?" Mel was slow to begin. He lifted his mug again. "Well, Jeff came over," he said. "And we talked. We talked a lot. Jeff sat over there, and I sat across from him". Mel stared into space as if to imagine the scene, "and he was speeding. He was very nervous. He kept saying that . . . uh, saying that people were lying to me. That it was all a mistake. He said he might have taken a couple of prints, but it was basically a mistake. And all the while," Mel lifted his hands as if to frame the sight, "he kept battering out these jazzy private rhythms with his fingers. On the edge of the coffee table. Like the main thing was that he kept the beat." Mel laughed. He was the only one among us who found it funny. "Like he was trying to keep up with this bongo in his brain." Mel laughed again. "So . . . I sat there and I was thinking, he's lying, true, but he's also crazy. Why did I never *see* he was crazy? He's just crackers." He laughed once more. "And then I thought something even more interesting, even though it made me want to have a whole lot more champagne. And this is, well, he's not just crazy. The important thing is that this person sitting here smoking dope at my coffee table hates me." He paused a moment, looking down. "I mean he *hates* me. Just . . . blind, total hate. And the funny thing is that he is my best friend." Mel squinted down into the liquorish heat rising from the black surface of his coffee. "My best friend. Paradoxical." Then he looked directly at me with a sad, pale smile. "Explain that. Explain that."

I responded with a small pale smile of my own. "I can't, Mel."

Like hell.

Mel leaned back in his chair. "Well, has anybody else got any suggestions? My best friend hates me."

"I have plenty of suggestions," Nancy said sharply, "and there's nothing paradoxical about them. First of all, he is not your best friend. He is a cheap hanger-on."

Mel's face hardened at the harsh words.

"Secondly, the source of this behavior is envy mixed with greed and those two are not a paradoxical mixture, they are the oldest story in the world. This is a matter of money. Plain simple money."

"He could have gotten money," Mel said, harsh now himself. "I would have given him the prints. I could have given him new work. I could have gotten him grants. I'd fucking well have given him the money outright — just given it to him. But no. He used to make big speeches about how he was going to make it on his own. His work was something else. He just wanted to be here. With me. With us." By now the jaw was clenched. "The son-of-a-bitch."

"This is what I like to see," Nancy said, standing up to pour herself another mugful of coffee. "A little anger."

I sat silent, looking at Mel in his absurd green bathrobe, his black hair tousled, staring into the shining surface of his coffee mug and sniffing the bourboned steam. The situation did not really seem to me so very cryptic. I am not certain I articulated it to myself then, but it is quite obvious to me now: for all my seething intellectual contempt, I had much more in common with Jeffrey Hastings, I understood his disaster far more intimately, than I ever would have dared confess. It was really absurdly simple. Mel was quite simply everything — the only thing — that Jeffrey thought he wanted. *Really* wanted, I mean. Mel was Jeffrey's image in the pool of Narcissus, irresistible with the promise of everything Jeffrey did not have. Of *course* he was hated. Of *course* he was needed. Jeffrey thought Mel held the whole secret. To be whole. To be strong. To be one's self. To matter, to be admired, to be loved. It was really very hard to beat. At first it must have been magical for Jeffrey, finding himself at the center of a life that seemed to offer everything he . . . needed. But true to the classic Ovidian logic, as Jeffrey became more and more absorbed in the icon of Mel's fullness, the absorption created, not surprisingly, emptiness. It just drained away more reality from that never quite real thing called Jeffrey. But as the bitterness of failure closed over Jeffrey like black water, as the Mel-magic turned thief, Jeffrey likewise turned thief. What could not be given, would be taken. Taken in the bitterness of his heart. I understood it all quite well: I was in fact a kind of scholar of the process, and I saved myself from drowning in it only by thought. Thought and caution. The thought and the caution of which poor sappy Jeffrey was so obviously incapable. Later that very morning, while Cullen and Nancy counted the missing prints, Mel confided in me, "You know, when I was a kid, the big dream was that I wanted to be Picasso. That was, like, *really* in my head. I wanted to be just like Picasso. I had pictures of him, I had books, I'd hitchhike five hundred miles from Palo Alto just to see a print. That for me was what being an artist . . . *meant*. You know? I wanted to be him." Sure, I said. Sure, and I thought: now out there the kids want to be you. Except for me. Except for me. I don't want to be you. *I* just want to understand.

I glanced over at Cullen. The twilit eyes watched Mel with new interest. Then the beauty tossed back the fifty-dollar forelock.

"Anyway," Mel finished, "he's coming back over later. I told him we'd all be here today, and he insisted that he was coming by, too. This afternoon. So, I said. All right. OK."

I proved to be little help taking the inventory of the missing prints, and I was soon relegated to the main room to keep Mel company. He had no heart for the task, vanishing into his bedroom to emerge an hour later dressed and shaved and looking fresher. Then the two of us sat together in the joyless winter light flooding the room (once we'd raised the shades) and talked like peers. Mel's mood was slow, gentle. He asked about my life. About the job at N.Y.U. About my future.

About me and Nancy.

"I mean," he said, "what kind of future do you see with her?"

It stopped me at first, and then I answered: "None." It just slipped out, the truth. "I don't see any future with Nancy at all. We have a relationship without a future."

"That's interesting," Mel said quietly. "What do you mean?"

I listened to the sound of Nancy in the workroom beyond, sliding shut one drawer and pulling out another, I heard the muffled sound of her speaking to Cullen. I didn't think they could hear us, but I lowered my voice anyway. "Because," I said, my tone was now low, but level, "to a Nancy Hopkins the future means husbands, and to Nancy Hopkins, Jason Phillips is not husband material." I spoke with absolute lucidity. It was a subject which I ordinarily kept hoarded in my neurotic secrecy. But I felt quite clear. "That does not mean I am undesirable as a lover. As a lover I have much to offer. The main attribute of lovers is that their place is the present. The future lies before them, of course, as it does for anyone, but strictly speaking they do not possess a true future. They have the present because only the present defines them. That is what makes them lovers."

"I don't quite understand that," Mel said. "Explain it a little more."

"It's simple," I said. "A marriage is an alliance. It is conceived as an act of anticipation, of futurity. Marriage is a *vow*. It is about what *will be*. From Nancy's point of view I have nothing to offer an alliance, no futurity, nothing to avow. Let's face it. Nancy Hopkins is simply not going to marry a graduate student who is maybe going to be a junior professor of art history at N.Y.U. We both know that. We all know that. It's crazy."

"It doesn't really sound all that crazy to me," Mel said softly. "The world isn't that hierarchical."

"The hell it isn't," I said, perhaps a bit too sharply. "The truth is that as a lover I am perfect, and as a husband I am ineligible. The future that I see with Nancy is an ending. Don't know where. Don't know when. But an ending, nevertheless. Inevitably."

"Inevitably?"

"Barring major transformations."

"You're a pessimist."

"I don't think so. The oddity of it, you know, the paradox, is that in all other aspects of my life right now — like, professionally — I am nothing *but* future. Nothing but."

We also spoke of Duchamp that morning. "You know, when I first knew him," Mel said, "I really did feel like the kid who'd won the prize. I would wake up in the morning, and I would lay there in bed, thinking, 'well, these are the days, Mel my man. It's not just that I sold a picture this week, and it is not just that there is going to be the European exhibition next month. The *real* thing is that now, this afternoon, I am going to have *lunch* with Marcel Duchamp.' I mean, that was *the* prize. Marcel was big on lunch, at least he was with me. And the thought of it would just fill my morning, pure happiness coming up. I really was going to be having lunch with Marcel Duchamp. Your thesis subject. Back in those days, I used to see Andy Warhol, and Andy would say, 'Gee Mel, do you think that maybe Picasso has heard of us?'" Mel imitated, quite exactly, Warhol's little boy stammer. "'Do you think anybody has ever told Picasso about *us*?' And I never said anything to Andy, but I always thought, Picasso? That isn't what matters. Of course, I understand what he meant." And at this point Mel told me about his youthful hero worship of the old man of Mougins. "But see, I had been cured of Picasso. By Duchamp. I said to myself, Picasso isn't what matters. For me the whole joy was that Marcel Duchamp actually wanted to know me. That I actually got phone calls from Marcel Duchamp. To me, that was like getting a call from . . . from *Giotto*, or somebody. Duchamp came to Bond Street. He looked at the pictures and said he liked them. He had even accepted a painting of mine as a gift, just took it. Said, 'Thanks, Mel.' It was on his wall. Man, you just have no idea. On Marcel Duchamp's *wall*. I was a happy man. So far as I was concerned, it was all worth it and more. I was loved.

"Anyway, so Marcel used to go to lunch every single day to the exact same Italian restaurant on Sixteenth Street, this completely unknown place where he'd been going since God knows, since the Armory Show, or something. And I mean, *nobody* went to this restaurant. We were very often the only people in the place. Very, very cheap. I mean, this was a place with nothing, no tablecloths even. Just pure Napoli: formica tabletops and paper napkins in chrome dispensers, and those little hot dry red things you shake out of a shaker? I've almost forgotten where it is. Anyway, Marcel loved the place, even though he had the exact same meal every single day. It was also the cheapest thing you possibly could order. One simple plate of plain spaghetti with butter and garlic sauce, and one plain glass of red jug wine. Beside it, a bowl of grated Parmesan. That's it. Very, very austere. Really, Marcel the monk at work. But then, across the table, there was me. I definitely was *not* Mel the monk. I ordered all kinds of stuff. Meat balls? Sausages? Bread? A salad? Plus a whole little bottle of wine? Well, Marcel would watch me, with this faint little smile, sort of taking in my gluttony? At first I was embarrassed. I thought I should be the same way as he was, and then I thought, the hell with it. He's Marcel Duchamp, but *I* am hungry. So I'd order what I wanted. And then I noticed something about old Marcel. He used to sort of like to ask little prying questions about me and my love life and stuff? Me and women. He'd sit there while he was being elegant and I was on my third glass of

wine. 'All right, Mel, tell me, are you encumbered these
days?' That was his way of saying it. Encumbered. 'Are you
encumbered these days?' and there I was, this wise guy from
California with a plateful of peppers, and I'd say 'encumbered?
You mean am I fucking?' ''

We laughed.

"But it really was interesting to me, that contrast I used to
feel around him. I would leave that lunch with this peculiar
sense of being kind of . . . animalistic? Appetitious, you know.
He didn't want anything, and I wanted everything. Just all
kinds of tastes. Wine. Women. Meat balls. I felt animalistic,
but I felt I liked it that way. And that he did too. And there he
was, so ascetic and monkish, so devoted, I thought, to art. It
really was a little like Villiers de L'Isle Adam, you know, in
Axel's Castle. Living? We have servants to do that for us! That
was what I was doing. I was doing the living for Marcel
Duchamp. Like, I was doing the eating, with my sausages and
my fifth glass of wine. He was so thin and delicate and ascetic
with that modest little plate of the plainest possible spaghetti,
that single glass of wine for his French stomach's sake,
wondering if I was 'encumbered,' and sort of elegantly hinting
around that he wouldn't mind some more hot info on exactly
how and when and where I was encumbering her, just exactly
what kind of encumbering we did. And I had this strange,
really kind of *flattering* sense, sort of flattering and insulting
both, I guess, that I was the living servant. I was doing the
living for Marcel. Everybody joked, how I was his adopted son.
If so, it was because I did the living for him. Then once I had
another thought, once, over my gluttonous meat balls. Which
was, *maybe I am doing the painting for him, too*. 'Make art? We have
Mel Dworkin to do that for us!' ''

Mel paused. "It was pretty flattering, and pretty insulting,
both. But that didn't matter — I liked it. I think the reason the
insult didn't bother me was that I'd decided already that the
only reason I could work at all was because Duchamp already
had called the whole thing off. Called off my Picasso dream, I

guess you'd say. See, I'd started out this kid who wanted to paint masterpieces. I wanted to be a great artist. I wanted to be Picasso. And I found out I couldn't. You know? I couldn't even be a really good artist. I tried it, tried hard, and it was impossible. Like what I'd been told being a good painter was, just made me turn out . . . crap. I couldn't do it. I had to give up being a good painter. It was the only way I could become . . . whatever it is I am."

"A good painter?"

"Well." He frowned. He didn't like the cute turn. "Anyway, that was what Marcel did for me. Like, Marcel was my failure. I mean he showed me where the failure was, inside of it all. He made sense out of my failure. I wasn't . . . alone with my failure. You know how he used to say, 'there is no solution, because there is no problem'? To me, that sounded like freedom. It was like Marcel became my failure, and that way I could go ahead and make art. Mine, I mean. It's paradoxical, I guess — if I may use your favorite word, Professor Phillips — but it happened that way for a lot of us back then. Duchamp was my failure so I could be his success. Anyway, that's the fantasy. Still, I wonder sometimes whether maybe the fantasy was something he felt too. You know, sitting there, hinting about me encumbering girls, with his plate of plain spaghetti, watching me eat."

The rough inventory was finished around two o'clock. When Nancy emerged she sank into the couch beside me, her expression one of rage subdued. "All right," she said wearily, "we can be pretty sure that there are at least — *at least* — fifty prints missing, or that we can't account for. We've really only begun, but the main point is that there is a hell of a lot gone. Fifty is a conservative guess."

Neither Mel nor I spoke. He seemed numb.

That was when the buzzer announced Jeffrey's arrival. Mel was up in an instant, suddenly alive with a kind of grim excitement. He was like a man who'd spent the day waiting for his beloved.

He opened the loft door on an extremely high Jeffrey Hastings. I have no idea what pharmaceutical cocktail he had used to fortify himself, but the man who stepped into that room was in a chemical elsewhere. I remember he kept nodding his head in a slow self-pacifying druggy rhythm, as if bowing to the toxic Buddha within.

"Well, well," he said, nodding. "I see the whole . . . whole *gang* is here. Everybody has gathered. I see. I see."

Nod, nod.

"Hello Jeffrey," Nancy said.

"Miss Big. Hi there. Hi there."

"Jeffrey," Cullen said.

Jeffrey silently continued nodding. He ignored me altogether.

"So," Mel said. "You want a drink or something?"

Jeffrey considered this offer . . . too long. He seemed to be scooting down some chemical slide in his mind. "No. I'm just fine."

"OK," Mel said. "Whatever you want." (Nancy had looked down at her thumb rubbing against her nails.) "Uh . . . so . . ." Mel continued, "Let's us just go back into the workroom and talk for a little while, OK?"

Jeffrey shrugged a concessive shrug.

"If that's what you want. You don't want The Bunch here listening in?"

"Oh no no no," Mel said. "This is just between you and me, Jeff. Just between you and me."

Jeffrey continued to nod. But more slowly.

The instant the two of them left the room, Cullen favored us with a god-help-us roll of his eyes.

After the door to the workspace closed, their voices filtered through inaudible, merely a kind of muffled vocal music, unsyllabled. Once, through the closed door, we heard Mel shout, "I'm not *saying* that, Jeff! Make *sense*! *Listen*!" That was followed by a long, muffled time again.

Then they emerged.

"Go ahead, man," Jeffrey was saying, coming out first. "Go ahead and accuse me any way you want. I don't care. I just don't care."

"Jeffrey, I told you already. Can't you *listen?* I said I am not interested in accusations."

"Not interested in accusations? Not interested in *accusations?* I don't know what the fuck I am listening to, if not accusations."

"Jeffrey, listen to me. I tried to tell you, and I will try to tell you again. It's just a statement of fact. They tell me something like fifty prints are gone."

"It's a lie."

"Don't say that, Jeff. I know what is in my drawers. We have the inventories."

"Like hell you do. You don't know *half* of what goes on in your own studio. *I* know. You live someplace else, man, so don't tell me things like . . ."

"Jeffrey, let's stop talking about how many prints are missing. I am more interested in my friendship with you than I am in a bunch of prints. But don't stand there and tell me the prints aren't gone. Because they are. They are *gone.*"

Jeffrey's nod had grown agitated. "Missing? Missing? OK, so they are missing. OK. I'll settle for that. You want that? OK. Fuck it all. So I took some prints. So? I took them. I did. I took them." Jeffrey turned to us sitting ten feet away. "You all like hearing that?" He repeated it. "Miss Big, you satisfied? You like that? I *took* the suckers." He turned to Cullen and me. "You like it? It pleases you? You faggots getting an earful?

"I don't care what you think," he went on. "And I don't care what *you* think, Mel. Because, fuck you. Really. I am glad this finally has happened, glad it's all hanging out. Now we can see each other for real, which is nice and refreshing. Listen up, you all, listen up. This isn't going to be too pretty. Your hero, the genius here, is going to *squirm.*"

Jeffrey had begun to pace. "I like to have all this coming out. It is a first step for me. A first step toward . . . toward *freedom.*"

Mel stood with his fists driven into his front pockets and his arms pinched inward, as if he were shivering with cold. "Because, man, for years, *years*, I have been your *slave*. You call it friendship. Your great wonderful friendship for me. No way. I call it slavery." He moved in very close to Mel: he seemed about to put his hand on Mel's shoulder. Their eyes locked. "Because you don't *understand*. For years, you have been like a drug for me. A bad drug. *My* drug. My meanest high. That's what you are. You aren't a friend. That friendship shit is just one of all the hundreds of lies you tell yourself. You are a drug. You're smack. That's what you are. You are a *thing*. The sick thing I can't get out of me, the sick thing I can't live without. *Friends!* Piss on friendship. You don't understand friendship. You don't understand *any*thing. You live *alone*, man. You live alone." At this point, Jeffrey reached out and dug his fingers into Mel's shoulder like a claw. "So I'm glad this is out. I'm going to break you. I am going to detox on my Dworkin habit. I am going to be free of you. You have been in my life. You have been in my mind and my blood and my being and every god-damned breath I draw for all this time has been you, you, *you* — that's all I am. I am just *you*, tortured. But now I am going to be free."

At this point I realized that Jeffrey's face was wet with crying. He was not about to release Mel's shoulder. "I hate you," he said. "I hate your fucking guts. I wish you would die. You know, I used to lay at home in bed, and I'd think, well, the only way out of this is death. I will never be set free, not until one of us has died. Either he's got to die, or I've got to die. But with the two of us alive, I knew, *knew*, I'd never, *never* be free. Not going like I was going. I mean, I *couldn't* detox on you. I just couldn't do it man, I couldn't get free. Do you understand what I'm saying?" Jeffrey peered at Mel. "No, of course you don't."

"Jeffrey," Mel groaned, "How many times have I told you I don't *care* about these prints."

"Man," Jeffrey went on, "you don't get it. I don't *care* what *you* care about. *I* care about the prints. I took the suckers because I *wanted* them. That, and another reason. Because I hate you, man. I really hate you." Then the hand was released. "So I took them. I stole them right out from under you. So . . . go call your cops. Call them. One of us has to die and it might as well be me. You are going to call the cops. I know you will. I know you. It's like bringing in your dealer and the whole faggot brigade here and the whole palace guard. That's what everybody calls them behind your back, you know. The palace guard. Cold blooded pricks . . . Anyway. You are going to go to the law. I know you better than you know yourself. Pain makes me know you. Pain. You fucker. You're going to call the cops."

"No Jeff. No. You are so high you don't know what you are saying. Nobody is going to call the cops about anything."

"Oh yeah? Is that why the palace guard is out here in force? Just so we keep it all in the family? The way you lie to yourself! You lie to everybody. You are going to the police. I know you."

"I won't Jeff. I swear. I won't." Suddenly, Mel was abject.

"Well, I don't give a shit what you do, Dworkin. I don't. Call the police or don't call them. I don't care. All I know is that you are not a person, and you are not a friend. Nothing like that. You are a drug, the dirty white powder that has destroyed my life. I used to have a life, you know. And you destroyed it. You made it into something not worth living. But I am going to be free now. One of us had to die before I would be free, and I'm glad, I'm really glad you know it all now, how much I hate you, how much I hate and despise you and how now finally, finally, I am going to be free.

"You want your prints? OK. I have got your god-damned prints. They are here." Jeffrey walked back toward the door where he had left a mailing roll leaning against the wall. "Fifty prints gone? Here they are. *One* of us has to get free. *One* of us has got to die. You want your fucking *art*? Take it. Take it, you god-damned cocksucker."

Then with one mad sweep of his enraged drug-pinned eyes around the room, Jeffrey laid the roll on the table and swept up his coat and was out the door, sauntering out in slow, demented dignity.

None of us spoke. Mel picked up the roll and unscrewed its metal end. He extracted what was inside.

In 1961, at the height of his youth and powers, Mel Dworkin did a series of eighteen silkscreen drawings which are now among the most often reproduced of his work. They are also among his masterpieces, and the most valuable works on paper in his *oeuvre*. The title of the series is *David's Quick Dreams*.

It was one of the most beautiful of these works — Variation Number Seven of *David's Quick Dreams* — which Mel now extracted from the roll. It flopped open before us on the table. This was not one of the stolen prints. This print was inscribed: "To My Good Buddy Jeffrey, who's going to do a better one some day. With my admiration." Then, maybe a touch oddly, it was signed: "Love, Mel." Something else was written on it. Scrawled in lurid magic marker in the center was the word:

SHIT!

And above that word, as if to make it into a mouth, Jeffrey had drawn in an enormous, curling, black moustache.

Mel stared at it a moment longer, then with a numb movement of his hand sent the print sliding to the floor. But there was something else in the tube. Nobody spoke,. His face as solemn as that of a hierophant at a rite, Mel lifted the roll and onto the table and floor poured what remained of the companion print of that gift, Variation Number Eight of *David's Quick Dreams*, which Jeffrey had torn into a thousand bits and which now fluttered in a stream of lacerated color onto the perfectly varnished hardwood floor of Mel's success, confetti for a brand-new decade.

interlude

Not long after that meeting with Jeffrey Hastings, I dreamed a dream that stands as an obscure watershed in my writing of *The Bachelors' Bride*. In my dream, I played chess with Marcel Duchamp.

I had worked at home during a long and extremely concentrated day of thinking and note-taking. I had been struggling with the conundrums and mysteries-within-mysteries of Duchamp's relation to language — and not merely his visual language, but all language, and above all the relation in his work between what is written and what is seen. It was a day like wrestling with the Hydra. The old man's dodges and subversions and perverse baffles and word-plays multiplied from within. To solve one problem was to make another one. A moment of understanding produced — unending bafflement. Flashes of illumination only deepened the murk. Hour after hour of intellectual pushing and hauling merely accumulated heaps of dead information, blocking my way.

At last I stripped off my clothes and crawled to bed, though (undefeated) I carried my pen and yellow pad with me, always hoping for some last-minute glimmering. I planted the pad on my weary knees, but . . .

Nothing. My mind was squeezed dry. The pen began to slide down the pad, trailing a wavering incoherent line with its blue point . . . I gave up. I dropped the pad and pen to the floor, snapped off the light, and surrendered myself to sleep.

The dream formed quite quickly. Out of sleep's first incoherent mutterings in the murky hypnagogic glow, the chess-board formed, and the pieces were all there before my closed eyes, in full array. I understood that I was already deep into my gambit. Yet I felt a little . . . unsure.

I looked up. Across the board sat Marcel Duchamp, smiling at me, but old, old. He spoke — not in English, but in French, and in a French moreover that at that stage of my life was far, far too fast and idiomatic for me possibly to have followed awake. But my unconscious seemed effortlessly to understand every mellifluous syllable. Was that some preconscious superior knowledge liberated, or merely the dreamer's delusion? I do not know. In any case, it seemed to be real French I was hearing. Effortlessly understanding, I felt some anxious, hurtful burden lifted from me, almost magically repealed. It was his smile that freed me! His smile was so easy and simple. It wasn't the dry sneer I knew from photographs and that I remembered from that real night I'd met him and he'd said, *"I am not sure that is the best thing to do with my work. Understand it."* The smile of mockery that had taught me that Duchamp was in the tradition of the *philosophes*, the very same little curl of bemused contempt that's on Voltaire's statue — that national monument of French intellectual life — at the foot of the rue de Seine. How I had feared that sneer. I had anticipated defeat from its power.

But no more. Not now. Duchamp was being so . . . so clear. So warm. I ignored our chessboard and I listened, rapt, while he talked. What was he saying? He was quite simply explaining himself. And in copious detail. Duchamp was opening his mind to me as I suppose he had never done for anyone in real life. Every theoretical and esthetic problem I'd wrestled with was being explained. With such simplicity! Such forthrightness! And all for me! Me! I, whose name the real man barely could remember the night I met him!

This was revelation.

I understood it all. *How kind he is,* I thought. *Who'd have dreamed the old man would be so kind. So open. This candor, this concern, this wish to explain and instruct.*

It was almost like a father's love.

Comprehension was mine.

But I had to thank him, respond. I opened my mouth and began to reply in French. Oh, it was a wonderful French I spoke to Duchamp that night. My questions and compliments flowed with eloquent ease. How smoothly the language presented itself to me. This, I thought (in French), this is in itself a kind of reward. This sudden sweet availability of meaning. You undertake a language. You fumble its vocabulary. Your pronunciation is a verbal smear. You wear out the dictionary looking up the obvious. You half-drown in the bitter obscurity of simplicity turned incomprehensible: Cat; Mat; Rat — the language of a child is a conundrum, until quite suddenly, you finally get it! It happens! The language that had resisted you, that had sadistically withheld itself, suddenly is yours. All yours, deliciously, ecstatically yours. Beloved!

So it seemed that night as I spoke to Duchamp. He listened to me, and from moment to moment his ancient face seemed to brighten with comprehension. He was all openness, all sweetness, all lucidity . . .

Ah oui Jason, he said. *Je suis reconnaissant. Je comprends. Mais quand même, attendez. Vous avez oublié notre jeu, notre echequier.*

It was true. I had forgotten our game. I looked down at the board to find it transformed before my eyes. The boring grid of chess problematics had become a glittering cube, a crystal of possibilities — all possibilities — all arrayed in the three dimensions of glass through which the translucent pieces moved, ascending and descending, proposing and resolving, very much, I thought, as the angels might have ascended and descended Jacob's ladder. It was exquisite. As I looked into those crystalized dimensions I seemed to see it all, outside time, and outside perception too — every momentary movement of the game, from the first small move of the crystal pawn, to the death of the queen, to the extirpation of the king.

I looked up. Duchamp was no longer there.

And with a kind of thump in my brain, I woke.

The room was pitch dark. *You've got it!* I thought. *Get it down! Quick! Don't lose it!*

There was not so much as a sliver of deep city night-light silvering my slum wall. *Don't lose it!* Naked, I slipped from the covers and slapped the dusty floor for my paper and pen.

Don't turn on the light, I thought. *Light will lose it. Write in the dark before it slips away.* With the pad, I hopped back into the warmth, ready to scribble down the Revealed.

Ka-thump!

It was really rather loud, that thump. Because it did not come from my brain.

Ka-thump!

It came from upstairs. Above me.

That sex-crazed faggot beast!

Ka-thump!

Does he never stop? Doesn't he sleep? I am dying down here writing this fucking dissertation and that sleazy erotomaniac is driving me to distraction. . . .

Ka-thump!

I heard him tumbling with his trick.

Ka-thump! Ka-thump! Ka-thump!

I could hear their voices, stifled.

The bounce was speeding up. It grew louder, until I heard Cullen's tenor, plainly drunken, jabbing higher and higher, jolting upward — *KA-THUMP!*—before the dying call, his last trailing squeal.

Damn him! Damn! Damn!

I flung the paper and pen back to the floor and sank back into the pillow. As the sexual racket subsided above, it seemed to me I could hear the dry, deathly cackle of that vicious old man's laughter growing louder and more mocking, accentless and triumphant, in my assaulted ears.

PART 3

chapter 11

Some rather momentous news has just come across my desk. When I came in this afternoon, I found in the department office a long-awaited letter from the French Ministry of Culture with their decisive commitment to my appointment as curator in charge of their great show two years hence: *Marcel Duchamp and his Heirs*. Of course, I have been pretty sure for weeks that this would come, but here it is at last: triumph! Ever since I opened that letter I have been basking in a steady strong flow of pride, the surge of quiet happiness felt over a life's work confirmed.

It is going to be an epochal show. I've spent half the afternoon musing once again on all the things I'm going to accomplish in Paris. The challenge is vast. In one of the two great museums of modern art in the world, definition of a phenomenon that spreads like a secret web through the whole of twentieth century art, radiating out from *The Bride Stripped Bare by her Bachelors*, even. . . . And I am the man who will uncover the web.

Me

I've particularly been giving thought to the actual building where the show will be mounted, the great tin construction in Beaubourg, and the more I consider the space, the more dazzling scope my prospects take on. This show is going to be about more, *much* more than merely the life and work of Marcel

Duchamp. I want to lay out a completely coherent view of the whole moment in modernism and spread it all through that mechanical labyrinth of a building. I want to funnel the crowds from Dada to John Cage. I want to roll them down ramps from Raymond Roussel to Merce Cunningham and Twyla Tharp and Robert Wilson. I'll march them on catwalks from Picabia to Rauschenberg and Johns. I'll escalate them all the way to Mel Dworkin and back again. And then, as if at the altar at the center, right in the structural heart of the great tin beast, I will set up the masterpiece, brought from Philadelphia: the *Large Glass* itself, with its spidery cascade of cracks snaring all its silvery icons, insectoid and unreadable. *The Bride Stripped Bare* . . . that window into the end of art, its array of rigid, immovable, hollow, armored bachelors huddled in contemptible stolidity beneath the great grinding gassy Bride.

Come to think of it, the architecture of Beaubourg itself rather resembles the look of Duchamp's *Bride*. The parallel never struck me before, not until this very moment. But it is perfectly obvious. That structure is really very much like Duchamp's naked and ghastly concatenation of plumbing and wheels and tubes. On the one hand, the mad structure of the Bride; on the other Beaubourg, with its tunnels, its funnels and ramps; its perches and catwalks and escalators. A transparent mass of moaning erectile ventilators, denuded sucking blowholes — it is all very like Duchamp's vision, a monstrous stripped-down machine for consuming consciousness, a huge Rube Goldberg contraption (this is a very good point to make in the catalogue: though be careful . . . it might very much offend them), a contraption for chewing up seriousness. In fact, I see it quite clearly now: Beaubourg itself is a kind of a horrible, unconscious — well, half conscious — architectural parody of Duchamp's antic, mechanistic, misogynistic, misanthropic vision. . . .

Misogynistic? Misanthropic?

Sudden words. Hard, unexpected words.

Well, let them stand. It is remarkable how there in these

pages, success is setting free my thoughts, making my conceptions grow. In the grand plaza in front of the building, out among the fire-eaters and jugglers, and the whole fast-food eruption of Parisian vulgarity that the Centre Pompidou created, perhaps a Robert Morris sculpture and the banner: MARCEL DUCHAMP ET SES HÉRITIERS.

Inside, in the three-story atrium, an immense mounted blow-up of the old man's photograph would be just the ticket (I think I'll use the Irving Penn photograph, the one with the pipe), the picture presiding over the whole exhibition like a great grey ghost. Duchamp can seem to muse over the scene like a modernistic Buddha. So amused. So bemused. Smoking his pipe. Arrayed below him, all around him, larger-than-life blow-ups of the héritiers. I see Rauschenberg and Warhol and Johns and Yvonne Rainer and — of course — most visibly, Mel. I already know exactly the picture of Mel Dworkin I'll be using, and I don't care that it is one of the most famous from the class-postcard racks. I mean the strangely plain, strangely romantic photograph of my sometime hero back in the very earliest days at the Bond Street studio, looking tall and young, a boy with his hands slipped into the back pockets of his jeans, gazing at the camera in attentive mistrust, numinous with his dark shyness, waiting for fame. . . .

Well, enough of that for the moment. I must draft my letter of acceptance to the French, and when that is done, I want to make a few more notes on the whole subject. I feel my mind opening up in a quite fresh new way, even after all these years. There is nothing like a fresh new confirming challenge. Then there is the Feldman's dinner party tonight. I have been looking forward to it all week. But think how much greater pleasure I am going to have when sometime, over the first course, I can drop, ever so gently, my momentous news.

11:37 p.m. Deep night.

Night and I am back in the office again. I just closed the door on the echoing hallway outside, and I am here in the studentless solitude.

I am back from the Feldmans. What dear people they are! I had a splendid time. I did ever so discreetly drop my news, and we made it a party. It was a marvelous meal, and how the white wine did flow! *Deux Colombes* it was called, and those two doves did flutter and fly. I left the Feldmans with them flying at my side, and they have fluttered around my spinning brain all the way back here to the office. Rather than face the walk back to SoHo, I came here. So — no home yet. Home can wait. I let myself into the deserted building, slipping by the watchman as I have long since learned how to do. Why? Because . . . because there is something I want to note down here in these pages. Something that has been troubling me. Something I want to . . . confide to this book. But what is it?

It seems to have slipped my mind . . . just a little. I am a little high. It will come. Give me time. I think it was some notion I wanted to jot down about the Beaubourg show. Oh yes. I remember. I remember now.

I HATE MARCEL DUCHAMP.

That's it. The very thing. Exactly what I wanted to recall.

I BLOODY WELL HATE MARCEL DUCHAMP.

I might as well put that down now. Tonight above all. I hate that despicable old man from the bottom of my scholar's heart. I hate him with a loathing that is deep and implacable and absolute. My angry passion is a thousand times more profound than the mild contempt most scholars eventually come to feel for those to whom they have given that unreturnable attention of attention. Posthumous attention. I despise Duchamp beyond any mere contempt for those merely human failings that any scholar will discover in any figure to whom he gives his scholarly allegiance. It is true that no man is a hero to his intellectual valet. But what I feel about Duchamp passes far beyond mere disabuse. I hate that cruel, insidious snob with an unforgiving understanding that is deep in my heart. I hate him with a bafflement which, as his explicator, I do not hesitate to proclaim (here in my secrecy) to be *absolute*. I stare, I gape in consternation at everything the old beast ever concocted.

Monster! Creep!

"The Silence of Marcel Duchamp is Over-rated." Has any truer slogan ever been sprayed by an art school rebel onto a rat-infested city wall? None that I ever have read. Sometimes I think about him. When I think how I have served him. When I think how I — *I* — am putting him back on the map he destroyed. What a *profoundly* uninteresting artist he was. I hate his influence; I *hate* the way he dominated the art of the sixties. Meddling beast! Destroyer! Corrupter of youth! Above everything else, I hate his influence on Mel. *My* Mel. I should let myself say all this at last. Maybe I will. Maybe I'll finally put it into the Beaubourg catalogue. Maybe finally I'll let the vicious old manipulator have it, let him have it just the way he deserves. . . .

Jason, stop. You must stop this now. You are a little high and a little disoriented by the admittedly mixed events of a very exciting day. This is enough. Come tomorrow, ravings like this will only be something you will read through the awful glazes of a morning-after mortification. You know that Duchamp's place in the history of irony, his role in establishing the post-modern vocabulary of the visual arts has been established beyond any serious dispute. After all, you are the one (along with several other colleagues, however little you may think of them) who established it.

Well, the hell with serious dispute. The disputant is drunk, and so let it roll out, the whole mad fatuous truth. I think Marcel Duchamp was a cold-blooded, self-protected, crippled, fetishistic, half-psychotic and more than half-autistic old *mocqueur*. I think he was a jeering little *philosophe* in the lowest and most shallow French tradition of them all. I think he was a mean-spirited, snobbish, self-satisfied little prick. The most over-rated reputation, probably, of the twentieth century. The great sneering false inevitability of our time.

Anti-Artist! My foot!
I HATE MARCEL DUCHAMP!

False logic! False measure! Doctoral candidates come to grief if they fumble the way I treated of these subjects in *The Bachelors' Bride*. Let me confess it here. What *deeply* boring, what depressing little ideas. Duchamp the radical? Duchamp the subverter of retinal art, received opinion? Please! Shall I say what I really think? Ah. Let my real thoughts wait a moment while I brew some deep black instant coffee.

In my opinion, Marcel Duchamp was a somewhat talented and not entirely uninteresting second-rate French middle-to upper-bourgeois, consumed, driven, from a remarkably precocious age by the leading desire of all too many talented second-rate French bourgeois, which was and still is this: *To Be a Genius.*

D'être un génie.

Many and daunting were the obstacles and impasses that lay between Little Marcel and his goal. For one thing, he was a bullied younger sibling in a crowded French family every one of whom was rotten from top to toe with precisely the same aspiration. Yet on the other hand, Little Marcel had much on his side. He was bright. He had a certain talent. He was . . . educable. He had the many fatuous blunders of his older siblings out there clamoring in the big world of genius to learn from. Above all, he found himself savoring the rising sap at a crucial moment in the nine years between 1905 and 1914, the very moment in which modernism emerged as the definitive force in the arts of our time: they were great days in the genius game.

Save for this: a genius is precisely what Marcel Duchamp was not. He was a quick study: he saw enough about Cubism to pull off a couple of quick smart tricks over things like nudes descending staircases. He saw that, and something else — the simple truth. With a lucidity that was unflinching; with an intelligence much to be admired; with a historical consciousness uncannily attuned to the resonance of the hour, Marcel Duchamp inspected himself and his work, and he saw with perfect clarity that he was his generation's definitive example of the intelligent and talented second-rate. A hard truth. A truth that might have made many another one doubt. It might have made many another give up. It might have made many, even, want to die. But not Marcel. Not our ingenious Marcel.

What to do? In the words of the ancient American wisdom: *WHEN YOU'VE GOT A LEMON — MAKE LEMONADE.*

There the *true* Duchampian art was born.

There the true meaning of his visual language leapt into the annals of art. Duchamp feared meaning; mystification was all, he knew that. He saw perfectly well that to traffic in the language of the vulgar herd jeopardized the whole enterprise, demolished his childish fantasy of being set apart in immortality's elite. More precisely, more radically ... Meaning, the human exchange, proposed itself to our Marcel under the auspices of death itself. For if Marcel was to play Orpheus, there remained the danger that his song might be heard; the danger that his hearers — the whole wild ecstatic throng — might enter his ecstasy and turn on his precious Orphic body with their ravening hands and start to tear, tear, tear. . . .

I am getting ahead of myself. I need more coffee, I need time to think.

That's better. Now then. Much has been said — said by me — about the interpretations one might bring to bear on Marcel Duchamp's many androgynous strategies and disguises. Well, here is the simple truth. For good old Marcel, androgyny was safety. Androgyny was distance, distance from the Bride. It is in androgyny that the Bride's dangerous allure is defeated. It becomes the emblem and fetish of a mind that wishes to live beyond the terrifying dangers of need. He need not hate what he is, and the others out there in the world must be rendered harmless. Woman above all must be divested of her power to compel. She must be mocked.

Eros, c'est la vie? Bullshit. Duchamp used the modes of androgyny to defeat desire, never to enter it.

Eros, c'est la vie? Eros is precisely that invitation to life which must be stilled.

Loathsome little man! Impotent coward!

Stilled. Stilled. That is the notion on which hangs the whole logic of his celebrated treatment of movement and time. Stillness. Immobility. Paralysis. They were the old bastard's whole obsession. He loved them. Thus, motion is subdued in the *Nudes Descending the Staircase*. This mounting excitement is mocked in *Sad Young Man on a Train*. Thus we get eros as hypnosis in Anemic Cinema. This is solipsism, solipsism itself, the empty fortress of the beast's whole project from beginning to circular boring ending.

How I despise him. How I hate him. How he frightens me.

It is madness I have been writing here. I know it. Madness. It is all just crazy, a jumble of angry paranoid half truths. Stupid passions, poor secret little things.

When I came to New York, Duchamp was the presiding spirit, the great grey ghost of neo-dada, then performance art and minimalism, the great good godfather of the avant-garde.

Now his professor sits sobering up in an office in the middle of the night, musing on age and death, and feeling alone.

Duchamp and His Heirs.

Who is his heir but me? I who have followed him, plodding, perplexed. I who used to be so earnest about understanding him one day. Mel is gone. The others mark time, they wrap themselves in their wretched money and vanish, die on their feet. I am the heir, the true heir. The scholar. Me.

Well, thanks. Thanks a whole lot. It has been some swell heritage — this increasingly academic, this hopeless insoluble struggle with one old man and his contempt for the dying platitudes of energy and freedom. Oh, my spiritual father out there in SoHo . . . thanks. Father of coldness, father of dissociation, father of contempt for the senses and the appetites, thanks a bunch. Great grey despiser of all the passions and freedoms, *merci*. Thanks for nothing. Nothing exactly.

What could it *possibly* have been, back then, back in the sixties, that drove me with such unquestioning energy to understand this man, this *thing* . . . merely because I did not understand it. The Large Glass. That Rosetta Stone of Paralyzed Desire. Why, why was I so obsessed with penetrating *The Bride Stripped Bare . . .?*

When I was an undergraduate, reading Nietzsche for the first time, I was baffled. Flat out baffled by *Zarathustra.* There was not one comprehensible page. I do not understand this, I kept telling myself, turning from mystery to mystery. But someday, someday I will.

Well someday, more or less, I did.

I HATE MARCEL DUCHAMP.

Yet there are times when the old man feels very close to me. I have by now a kind of unbearable intimacy with the grey ghost of his mind. I could almost imagine, under the sound of the typewriter, his footsteps in the hall. I sense his hateful face, his old, old face near me: as it was back in 1968, in River House. Who was that ridiculously rich collector? I should remember. I have forgotten. I remember only that the apartment was immense and Mel had brought me. The collection dazzled with every fourth step; outside, beyond the high windows was the truly deluxe urban darkness, lights streaming through lights in the black water of the East River below; inside, all the grand rooms, crowded with clusters of high celebrity. For this was a famous-person party — my very first. The moment we arrived Mel was swept away. I was left, of course, quite alone. I didn't care, exactly, being on those sidelines. I remember standing by the windows and taking in the streaming river lights and a tugboat moving below in the water, sipping at my glass. I even leaned my warm forehead against the cool window pane a little, and I thought: *Life! O, life!*

"Hey, junior," Mel broke into my thoughts. "You want to meet the old man?"

"What old man?"

"Marcel."

At first I did not say anything. Then: "He's *here?*"

Mel cocked his head, turned away and beckoned over his shoulder with a hooked finger and sauntered off, leading me through the crowd. I caught up by brushing past some movie star. "I was just telling him about you," Mel said.

"Me? What about me?"

"You. Your dissertation and all. . . ."

"What!"

But it was too late. On a couch about six feet ahead of us, Marcel Duchamp looked up and at the sight of Mel smiled, a smile of renewed delight, an old man's smile of relief. He was dressed in brown slacks and an earth-tone, rather worn tweed jacket and a subtle green tie. Duchamp was grey, God knows he was grey, but I remember being conscious of color, color everywhere around him and realizing in a moment that this was because I was seeing him for the first time outside the photographic black and white.

Beside him was Teeny Duchamp, the woman old Marcel had married at the eager breathless age of sixty-seven.

Resting one hand on the back of the couch, Mel leaned over the old gentleman, speaking quite distinctly, close to Duchamp's ear. The image of them there remains in my mind as an almost Renaissance image of filial attentiveness. Mel at his most graceful leaning over Duchamp, Duchamp listening with his aged hard intelligence, two generations of dissociation leaning together in perfect affiliation. It was at that moment I could see that Mel really did love the old monster. Duchamp listened to him with his thin mouth in repose, his old, old eyelids half lowered, nodding very slightly and a little . . . coldly. Then he looked up and produced, just for me, his wide, engaging, 'American' smile.

"Well, Mr Phillips," Duchamp extended his thin hand toward me, "My good friend Mel Dworkin tells me you are foolish enough to be trying to understand me. Such ambition!"

I stepped forward and took his handshake with what — given his seated position — may have slightly resembled a bow.

"Well sir, that is true. I am trying."

I was thinking. *One of the giants. One of the visionary company!*

"And have you?" he asked.

"Sir? Have I what?"

"Have you understood me?"

"Well, sir, I have to admit that I have not yet quite accomplished that. But I am on the case, I am working very hard."

"Oh, that sounds dreadful," Duchamp was fast. "I've always hated hard work myself. I've done a very great deal in my life just to avoid work, any kind of work. But this understanding me, it may not be so simple, you know."

"It hasn't been as yet, sir. But I am very persistent."

"You *look* persistent. I like that. I'm persistent too. Still, you may experience some delay in this crazy project." Duchamp spun his finger as he spoke. "I am not sure the best thing to do with my work is to *understand* it."

"Yes, yes, I understand what you mean, I suppose. . . ." I said this with some hesitation; I wanted to extract the maximum possible meaning from the banalities of this exchange. "Well, surely understanding is one thing we are free to do with it."

"That," Duchamp said, tilting his head doubtfully, "that is . . . entirely up to you."

I took the fine edge of insult in that.

"If you believe in understanding," Duchamp persisted.

And so I played the young fool. This after all was the man who had said, *There is no solution, because there is no problem.* I was a fool. I decided to persist in my folly, and barged recklessly ahead: "I am going to solve your secrets, sir. I am going to undo them like a puzzle. I will."

"*Oh,*" said Duchamp in mock fear, "so terrifying — so violent, you make me want to hide." Duchamp tugged at the sleeve of his belated bride. "Teeny," he interrupted her, "this young fellow thinks he is going to break my code. He's told me so. . . . Uh . . . Mr . . . ."

He had forgotten my name.

"Jason Phillips," I said very distinctly, hoping he would remember.

"Well, Jason Phillips, when you are done, send me the results of your research. I am fascinated by myself, you know. Besides, I love surprises."

"Mr Duchamp," I said, "you have a deal."

"That's what I like to hear," he said a little dryly, in a tone that made it plain my time was up. I drifted into a short conversation with Teeny, while her husband's attention went elsewhere.

"Will you be spending the fall in New York?" I asked her, and "Oh no, no," she responded, very amiably, "Marcel and I always go to France at this time of year, we leave for Neuilly tomorrow."

Duchamp heard this remark and looked over at me. "Oh yes," he said, "we are leaving for Paris almost without delay."

Then he turned back to Mel, speaking, I guess, about his health. I talked a bit more with Teeny, while trying to eavesdrop and catch a little of what he had to say. "I'm fairly well," I heard him confide to Mel, "but at my age if you have a headache . . . you never know. Death appears."

I never saw him again. Two days after their return to France, after dining with Man and Juliet Ray, Marcel Duchamp went to bed early and died in his sleep at five minutes past one o'clock in the morning of October 2, 1969, in Neuilly, far from Mel, far from America, while his decade waned.

Enough. It is one-thirty in the morning. Enough. I am sober again, I have exhausted the triumph of the day. My future for the next little while is clear. I will be in Paris next year. There the whole myth will rise to a new level. Now there is nothing left for me but the walk home and even now I don't want to leave. Why, I wonder, have I come to love this office so much? I really don't want to go home. Let home wait. Here I am my simple self, stripped clean by my exhaustion, here before this naked clattering machine, where the chatter of its keys is the only sound in the empty halls, here in the small hours, here in learning's empty space, here where I am too tired to feel my triumph anymore, now that it is late, and Mel is dead, and Duchamp is dead, and there is absence all around me, and at last I am no longer thinking about the future.

chapter 12

Once Jeffrey Hastings had been torn with such angry violence out of Mel Dworkin's life, it was Cullen Crine who with exquisite shrewdness guessed that Mel might want to console himself with a woman. That first January of the 1970's was brittle with a cold so deep and unmoving that it easily could look like hopelessness universalized. Mel pulled back from Jeffrey's accusing cry of rage by retreating to the house in Springs, and there, half in a fury of his own — almost unmangeably enraged by mad Jeffrey's demolition of his illusions — and half in penance, Mel did nothing: futzing with make-work during the day, and drinking, often alone, at night. Halfway through January, during one of Mel's sulky and infrequent visits to the city, Cullen produced, as comfort in grief, his soul sister Vicki. That first day I'd met her, Cullen had promised he'd try to find something, a job for Vicki. And so he did. The strategy was a complete success.

Mel seized his chance; he fled from the insult he'd endured straight into a *folie à deux*. His mood reversed: he went around telling people he felt reborn in the life, the eros, the tenderness, the energy he'd rediscovered through Vicki. She was warmth; she was sweet simplicity; she was sex. At first he hustled her off to the house in the Springs, but in full mid-winter that could be pretty dreary, their only recreation being crunching walks along the icy freezing shoreline. So the next step was Saint Maarten's, in a lavish house by the water, where they could romp in real conditions very like those of Mel's fantasy redemption. Unfortunately, one can play on and on *à deux* just so long. As February ended, Mel intuited that this love affair needed to be fed with the nourishment of a social life even though life with The Bunch, and in New York in general, was precisely what he had been running from. So the next step was Europe. In Saint Maarten's, Vicki had babbled about Europe incessantly — though of course her luckless Parisian, Jean-Pierre, had been unceremoniously jilted, over the telephone, mere days after Mel made his move. As it happened there was to be a big Dworkin exhibition in Berlin that March. Ordinarily, Mel would not have attended such a thing, but now he made an exception, and much was made of it. I remember feeling the pressure lift a bit when Nancy flew over for the grand Berlin week. Paris followed. There were parties and there was press and Vicki was of course thrilled.

The birth of this new passion roughly coincided with the beginning of the end between Nancy and me — the first note in what was to be a dying fall. Like stories, love affairs run to the humming of a certain kind of internal clock, and like stories they move according to that rhythm toward a certain inevitable ending. And it is the type of their ending that defines them both. Moreover, the profile of those endings usually is, if not foreseen, at least forseeable, though romantics may for a time obscure the inevitable in the cloud of unknowing they call love. Marriage on the other hand does not foresee its end. Or rather — usually inaccurately — it foresees its end only in death. Nancy was the marrying kind. She and I had entered our decline.

Yet our precise hour had not yet quite struck. There was to be one more spotty summer between us, and with Mel and Vicki's April return to America, all the talk was of a Hamptons summer. The evil spell seemed broken. With Vicki at his side, Mel seemed ready to resume his life, and he seemed to want The Bunch around him once again. He played the real estate broker, pulling Mel-strings to find places for all of us to stay. He found a cottage deep in the woods for Seymour and Iva Kaplan. He located a Victorian farmhouse near the Springs town square for Nancy and me. The idea was that we would share the place with Cullen, who'd have a bedroom he in turn might share with some more or less presentable companion, should one turn up. Nothing worked out that way, of course, but such was the plan. It is true that nobody took the affair with Vicki terribly seriously; everybody expected it to be swallowed up, like its predecessors, in some neurotic intrigue. But no matter. It had brought the old Mel back. Everybody was going to be together again, just like the good times. That summer was, in retrospect, perhaps the first of our efforts to recapture the — recently lost — golden past.

Mel had found our house in late April, and I was the first of the prospective renters actually to lay eyes on the dream-find. He invited me to see it in early May and made rather an odd point of my taking the train out early, a day before the others. "Come on Friday," he insisted; "let Nancy and Cullen follow Saturday night, after the gallery has closed." Then we would all have a party at Mel's house, the first big party of the season. Mel was very excited about it all; he had it all planned. "Come early." He wanted to show me the house, but there also was new work in the studio he wanted to hash over with me. I felt a twinge of the old flattery in that. "Come early, get to know Vicki better." A flicker of the old intimacy in that. Besides, there were some other, unspecified, things he wanted to explore with me, things we'd never have a chance to cover at the party. "So come. We'll have a great time. Just the three of us. Come."

And so I went, fondly, eagerly supposing this was a turn back to the good old days, instead of what it was, a step into something new and dire.

I pulled out of Penn Station early Friday afternoon, jolting from Jamaica almost to the end of the line in a creaking parlor car, a sad young man on shaking suspension, trying without success to read the book that jiggled uncontrollably before his eyes. It was dark when the exhausted train pulled into the East Hampton Station and groaned to a stop, tilting as if sinking into the sand. Alone on the platform, Vicki stood under a cone of light, waiting to drive me to the Springs in nothing less than Mel's Porsche, parked behind her in somber splendor. The soft-breathed twilight was deep. As I stepped down, Vicki approached with a languid little wave.

"Hi Jason." The girl I had met slouching in her outsize army fatigues in Cullen's apartment seemed very changed. The petulant complaining little girl now was playing satisfied adult. "It is wonderful to see you," she said in elegantly modulated tone, and planted a gentle kiss of welcome on my cheek. "Is that," pointing to my one small bag, "all you have? I mean in the way of luggage?" It was.

Vicki slipped into the Porsche as if she owned it, and I must say there was something about the Porsche that did something for Vicki. Dropping into the driver's seat she tossed me one conspiratorial glance of delight, and then igniting the engine of that amazing instrument of luxury and power, her face assumed an air of serene mastery. The pouting child vanished; the woman of privilege emerged. Wrapped in the exalted whine of that engine we drove beneath the just-budding trees out toward the house on the shore of Gardiner's Bay.

Mel was waiting for us inside the house, and he greeted me with an air of nervous formality that set a tone diametrically opposite to the easy infatuated intellectual camaraderie I'd hoped to recapture now that Jeffrey was gone. Mel moved forward to shake my hand as if crossing a curtain line, as if stepping out from a tense time in the wings onto the false smiling stage. He made too elaborate a point of showing me my room; he was too fussy pouring my first drink. We had that drink sitting around the big round feast table in the brick-floored kitchen, the way we always used to, but things were not as they used to be. I sat there perched on the half-apprehensive, half-curious tension of a new guest in a not necessarily friendly house, with the weird feeling all these smiles might cover the worst.

Vicki and Mel were not exactly nervous with each other, but they were oddly formal. Or perhaps their manner should be called merely tense and false. They talked about their time in Europe, the time in Saint Maarten's with the bland orchestrated enthusiasm one might reserve for some unusually dreary and correct aunt.

As to Mel's alluring promise on the telephone, the siren song of a visit to the studio and a look at new work, the subject never even came up. He didn't mention it that evening; he did not mention it again for the rest of his life. I was not ever again to stand in front of some half-completed work of Mel's, letting what was there liberate my intellectual fancy, winging my way through some words-to-image flight that would give me the really intoxicated impression of giving voice to whatever gave coherence to that web of meaning Mel spun out of his sense of inspired dissociation. That was over for good. That sense of being there beside the crucible, that old fantasy of mine — new Ruskin to the new Turner of our time — was being demolished, before my eyes, but without my recognizing it. It would never resume. Not during Mel's lifetime at least.

It is true we did talk a bit about art that evening, though I ended wishing we hadn't. Mel began to talk in ways I never had heard before; as if gently taunting me, Mel became boastful. Once we'd begun cooking, he made a great point of saying how during the Berlin show some German art magazine had published a numbered ranking of the most important living artists in the world.

"I came in number *five!*" Mel crowed as he stood over the pasta water. "Number five in the world!"

I was standing at the sink peeling some potatoes, and I answered as if I were talking to the old Mel — therefore missing the point completely. The potato peeler fell slack in my hand while I groaned and rolled my eyes. "These stupid editors. They really don't seem to understand how silly, how degraded that sort of show-business is."

But Vicki promptly became all interrupting earnestness. "Degraded? Silly? Oh Noooo. *Noooo.* Jason, you have that all wrong. This was an extremely serious publication. It was one of the very best art magazines in Europe. Tom Cotter told us all about it."

I stared. "Who's Tom Cotter?" I asked blankly.

"Don't you know Tom?" Mel asked. "That's just amazing. I would have been sure you'd know him. Well, it doesn't matter, because Tom Cotter is going to be at the dinner party tomorrow night. Maybe — but probably not — with Elaine."

"Elaine?"

"Elaine's his wife. Maybe you've heard of her. Elaine Welch?"

"No. Should I?"

"Naw, Elaine used to be an actress, but she hasn't done a thing in years. Anyway, Tom's very rich — you know, Wall Street, the commodities market, crap like that. But smart. A very intelligent man. A collector."

Ah-ha! The light dawned. So the mysterious and newly popular Tom Cotter was a collector. This added another unexpected dissonance to the evening's new raw tone. In the past, Mel rarely had wasted time flattering his collectors in front of me. His act always had been to feign complete indifference to where the money came from.

"Tom was with us in Germany a lot," he said. "He was there on business, and he speaks perfect German, and he's a wonderful guy. You'll see."

The old vice of jealousy, so familiar from Mercer Street, had begun to squeeze.

"He's the one," Vicki added, "who translated for us that article about Mel being the fifth most important artist in the world."

I stared again. I did not at that moment actually grasp the transaction, but in fact, somebody to replace the banished Jeffrey, a new foil for Jason Phillips had been found, and as Mel stood behind Vicki, undimmed by her smirk of delight, I saw playing on his lips the little smile I had seen for the first time that first afternoon on Mercer Street, when, enraged by all my talk, Jeffrey Hastings had stormed out of the room.

That little smile spread into a great deal of good old boy amiability shortly later when Vicki left the room for a few minutes and we were left, just the two of us, beside the steaming stove.

"Well," I said, having nothing better to say as Mel stood tasting a sauce, "it looks as though you are madly in love."

With the spoon poised an inch from his lips, Mel fixed me with a glance and said, "Love? What are you talking about. Love with Vicki?"

It almost shut me up. I fumbled, "Oh well I . . . I don't really have anything to go on, of course, but after your time in Europe, after the trip to Saint Maarten's. . . ."

"Vicki is wonderful," Mel interrupted, and setting down the spoon, his test concluded. "She's great. She couldn't be better." Then he turned to me directly and for the first time that evening, I felt the warm blanket of Mel's charm spreading out to at last include me. "See Jason, being with Vicki for me has been much, *much* more interesting than just love. Being with Vicki has been more like some phase of self-discovery. I mean, it has been absolutely transforming for me. I think you can see that. It really has brought me out of the slump that came after all the shit with Jeffrey. But Vicki . . . Vicki," he seemed to search for his meaning. "I find that being with Vicki is like being wrapped up inside my own fantasy. And for me that is Vicki's whole role. She is the way I uncover *my* fantasy. She's wonderful. I love her, I mean I *do* love her, in a sense, but I guess. But — " he shot a furtive glance toward the door, and then with a just-between-us-guys glint in his eye, he lowered his voice — "except there are times when Vicki seems to me more like my own fantasy than a person. That is what is so rich and so revealing about Vicki. That quality of . . . of fantasy that she gives me access to. I sometimes have the feeling that I am only encountering myself with her, but in the most passionate, deepest possible way. That Vicki is . . . not a person at all."

Then Mel grew even more confidential, even more confiding. "I mean, it's not like," once again he seemed to be searching for the easiest example at hand — "it's not like you and Nancy for example. I mean, you tell me that you think Nancy would never marry you, that so far as Nancy is concerned you are just a kind of lover for her. But even so, even so, what has happened between you and Nancy is a real encounter between two human beings. And of course I don't mean to say that Vicki isn't a real person, not a real human being — of course she is. But there is something about her that is so . . . pliant. So supple. So changeable. She really is like a fantasy, and that makes me reach a kind of wellspring inside myself. Do you understand? There is some kind of force that is released from being so deeply involved . . . that close . . . to the real . . . real *flesh* of a pure fantasy." Mel drew even closer to me. "She's a kind of minx." He burst into a vast, unnatural smile. "She's alive in a way that is absolutely compelling. It reaches me very deeply."

The pasta pot steamed. I remained silent, but I drained my gin and tonic.

"But love?" Mel continued, "I am not sure the question of love is even relevant to the thing that is happening between Vicki and me. Do you understand what I mean?"

I faltered again. "I . . . I am not . . . sure," and instantly afterward I surpressed a gasp and broke into a false smile of my own as Vicki, also beaming theatrically, came striding back into the kitchen. Had she, *could* she, have heard the end of what Mel was saying? Could she have heard it *all*? I had not heard any footsteps from beyond before she came back into the room. Was she standing in the doorway and listening to every word? And there was her smile, that wide smile she wore as she walked in. If she did hear, what kind of shock, what kind of hurt or rage must it evoke? To be spoken of that way by the man who you imagine loves you.

"Well," she said. "We're almost ready to eat."

When we sat down to the meal, we all went back to the stiffness that had begun the evening, while my mind raced in the effort to catch up to the evening's secret agenda. While it did, I proceeded to babble about almost anything that came to mind, in an effort to break a spell which, if not exactly stilted, was anything but spontaneous either. While I talked, Mel watched me, still glowing from the odd confession he just had made. Vicki meanwhile seemed to hang on every chattering word with almost imbecile interest. It was not until brandy was produced that the true subject of the evening was broached at last. They had waited for the brandy. They figured they'd need it.

"Vicki and I" Mel began, "have lately been giving a lot of thought to ways for opening new possibilities in our lives. In our feelings." Vicki, who until that point happened to have been gently leaning against Mel's shoulder, straightened up as if to give her full schoolgirl attention to the speech.

"Oh?" said I, feeling my anxiety deepen a shade or two. "What kind of possibilities are those?" I took a merciful sip of the brandy. "What do you have in mind?"

"Well," Mel said. "There are various kinds of options. For . . . feeling."

"No doubt. No doubt," said I, taking yet another sip.

"We have discussed the whole thing very carefully," Mel went on, "and we've both come to the conclusion that you" — here Mel paused again and gave me another of those painfully wide smiles — "you are absolutely ideal as a candidate to help us in that regard."

He stopped again. And held that damn smile.

"Oh?" said I. "Always glad to be helpful. How can I help?" It seemed to me that the moment, the room, and everybody in it were for some reason holding uncannily still.

"You can help with your desire," Mel said, still smirking. "Especially — your suppressed desire."

I responded with a long silence and another long sip of brandy. Since it seemed to me perfectly plain that Mel's cryptic remarks could not possibly mean what they . . . *seemed* to be

. . . suggesting, my mind now raced in overheated incoherence, searching for what deeper, truer suggestion they were so mysteriously imparting. I was getting nowhere. So I at last blurted out, loudly, "desire?" The only desire I was feeling then was the desire to run. "*What* desire?"

"Your desire," Vicki said very softly. "For us. Us." She didn't move at all. For some reason nobody was moving at all. Except me, as I lifted, with perhaps a little tremble, the brandy glass.

Then I spoke very slowly. "I think," I informed them, "that maybe I am beginning to get an inkling of what you have in mind."

"There's a lot of pleasure there, all wrapped up in what we have in mind," said Vicki, leaning toward me just a bit.

I couldn't speak.

"You *do* desire us, though. Don't you?" Her voice seemed to me to have sunk to an absurd parody of a seductive purr.

I still couldn't answer her. I was getting very scared.

"Both of us," Mel added with a new gentle emphasis. "You desire both of us. Don't you?"

"Oh Lord," I burbled, "I . . . I don't know about that."

"Yes you do." Mel said. "I've known that from the first day I met you. From the first hour. That you were attracted to me. That you desired me."

Despite the fact that the impulses of terror had been let slip and were racing wild inside me, I knew I had in some way to regain my balance. That was not terribly easy, because the room had begun to spin. I sipped the brandy again, finished it. Then I poured myself another glass.

"I think we should explore that, don't you?"

"I . . . I don't know."

"*I'm* ready for it," Mel said. "*I* think it would be fascinating to explore my homosexuality."

I was terrified, and as the brandy surged, the one thing I could not bring myself to admit, out loud, was how afraid I was.

I was not quite able to make out what, if anything, I had to be afraid *of*.

"And *I* know," Vicki said, warming more, "I know you like *me* too. That day we met at Cullen's house it was easy to see that. It was easy to feel it. The feeling was very strong. Very sweet. Very strong," and at this point she reached out and brushed my cheek with the back of her fingers. It was a move, and I suppose it was my clue to take ahold of that hand and respond with my first move — let's say, perhaps, a kiss. Instead I snapped back in terror, and Vicki snatched her hand back too.

"Oh *wow*," said Vicki, "You are touchy. Why don't you stop being such a good little boy, Jason? Why don't you try to have some *fun* for a change?"

"You're all words, Jason," Mel said. "You're all words and you use them. They're the masks for all your yearning, and they are draining your body of life. Don't you want to give your body some reality, too?"

"Here we are," Vicki said. "Offering it."

"Gee," I said, "hadn't you guys heard? I'm involved with Nancy. We're having a love affair. We're all mixed up together."

"So? Nancy doesn't need to know," Mel said. "We know how to keep something quiet when we want to."

"Besides," Vicki added, "are you so absolutely certain that Nancy would really mind, even if she did know?"

Once again I only stared at her, though by this time I am sure my eyes had a glaze of shock laid on over their terror.

"This is all too fast for me," I said. "I'm sorry. You're just interested in going someplace I'm . . . I'm not ready for."

"I wonder," Vicki said in a slow, gentle taunting voice, "which one of us it is that scares you. Me? Or him."

"Oh," I shook my head and with my hand tried to wave the question away. "I suppose," I went on, "that a braver person would . . . do what you want."

"*Eros, c'est la vie*," Mel said. "I thought we agreed about that.

Don't give yourself a hard time about bravery, even though I think if you were braver it would be kind of a discovery, wouldn't it? *Eros, c'est la vie.* I just think maybe you need a little coaxing."

For a moment I was terrified that Mel might reach out and touch me with his hand. But he did not. The room by now had come entirely unmoored. It was tilting and spinning at will.

"Well," I said at last, "everything you say may be completely true. It is certainly true, it can't be denied, that I have been mightily attracted to both of you. Just as you say. Together you seem to scare me, but separately, yes. Yes. Desire."

"So?" said Vicki.

"Well," I continued. "I also have a little theory about all this. This desire. This situation. My fear."

"I had a feeling that you might have a theory," Mel said. Was that mockery I heard in his voice? I could not quite decide. For one thing, his voice seemed extremely far away.

"It is a theory about threesomes, really," I went on. "The theory is that all threesomes, whether actual, or merely metaphorical, are really twosomes. Twosomes in disguise. There may be some ambivalence, even a whole lot of ambivalence, but it is always ambivalence trying to make up its mind. I think a threesome is a ritual people use to find out what the true twosome is. They really are not what they seem — all openness, all . . . everybody in the pool! We'll all have fun together. Oh, no. They really are a ritual of Odd Man Out."

Vicki tried to say something, but I raised my hand in professorial authority. "Let me finish. It is a game of Odd Man Out. And I have a funny feeling, here, now, that I know, know in advance, before we even give the game a try, which of the three of us the odd man out is intended to be."

Vicki was outraged. "But we don't *intend* . . . ," and then with that hand I stopped her again.

"I know, I know. Intended is perhaps not the right word.

Destined. I think I know in advance who the odd man out is destined to be."

Vicki remained outraged, but I had captured Mel's interest and I knew it. The one time in that week-end that I, however briefly, held his interest the way I had in the old days. "Why," he asked. "What makes you so sure that. . . ."

"That it would be me? That I am the destined odd man out? All right, let's take a look at that. Let's look at our own situation, here in this room." That room now seemed to be spinning slightly less, and the liquor seemed to me to be supplying what I now imagined was analytic eloquence. "What are the possible combinations? There is, to begin with, Vicki and me. Of course there would be some three-way playing to reach that eventual resolution, but let's say Vicki and me. It is very difficult for me to believe that you — whose idea this is, I suppose — you really are prepared to watch me in a literal enacted physical sense steal Vicki away from you. Before your eyes? Play voyeur to my triumph? I doubt it. I doubt it."

"But how do you *know*?"

"I know. I know. Then let's take the even less likely possibility of the odd man out being the woman. You say that you are interested in exploring your homosexuality. Your so-called homosexuality. Now, I am sure that is very liberated and all, but in fact you have left it unexplored — at least with me — for a very long time. Why now? To what purpose? Oh, that is very hard to say. But whatever the exploration, you and me somehow together? With Vicki rejected? In a mad embrace? Oh no. That is not what I foresee."

I drank again.

"I see myself at the center of this game, all right. I am the pivotal figure, all right. But I am certain that the real meaning of this adventure in polymorphous perversity is not generalized narcissistic eros. And it is *certainly* not Jason finding fulfilment in the arms of either one, or both of you, admittedly very desirable people. Whom I love. I do. And whom I would love to go exploring with, if I weren't so *damn* scared. But I know that the real meaning of this evening, its real theme, is Jason as odd man out. Jason as the rejected one. Jason at the primal scene, reduced to the role of watcher. Jason losing. This is a ritual of exclusion, an excommunication. With me as the lucky star."

Now it was Mel who was staring. He was smiling no more. Was it anger I saw on his face? "That is quite a theory, Jason."

"It's always been my strong point," I said. "Theory."

"What fascinates me about it," Mel went on, "is that what you predict that Vicki and I would end up together, and you would be odd man out? Well, it has happened anyway, hasn't it? You've made it happen, with the theory itself, by making that speech. Vicki and I are together, and you've made yourself the odd man out. We've just skipped the sex."

It was a shrewd point. I never claimed Mel was dumb.

"Eros, ce n'est pas la vie. La théorie, c'est la vie."

"I said it was destined. There was no other way."

The happy couple did not reply.

"And now," I said, standing up very unsteadily and lurching toward the kitchen door, "I think it is time for the odd man out to clear his head with a walk on the beach."

They didn't pursue me. The deck off Mel's kitchen was built out on stilts high above the shore, which was reached by a long snaking staircase of wood that descended all the way down to the sand. The spring fog still was thick; the night was starless; the water far below almost unseeable. I gripped the two-by-four handrail and felt my way down, testing every step afraid of the darkness, afraid of my drunken, frightened state. At last my foot tested sand, and I was on the shore.

I walked out to the tideline, by the lapping bay water, and stood there deep-breathing the cold night air, trying to burn away some of all that alcohol. It was surging through my body in waves of humiliation very like nausea, very like physical pain. The blurring lights of the Connecticut shore, all the way across that vast pregnant sheet of treacherous black water danced and smeared when I tried to squint them into stillness. I told myself I was a fool. Fool! Mel, my errant genius, comes home and gives me a whistle — and so I come scampering out to the Springs, dancing with the hope of some new privilege at my master's side. Instead I am manoeuvered into a choice between humiliation and humiliation. Rejection and rejection. Instead I am placed in a situation so dense with jealousy and mockery that all I am left feeling is my own self-abasing fear. Here alone by the cold black water. Fool! I looked up, back toward the house perched so high above me. Mel who has everything invites me into even deeper rejection. His invitation *is* rejection. It is an invitation that takes the form of rejection. Mockery. The kitchen lights, still burning, made the white-painted hand rails of the deck and stairs into an irrational web in the darkness. They were still in the kitchen. Talking, no doubt, about me. About my running away. Laughing it up. Sharing their perverse triumph.

Mel was a shrewd one all right. He always had seen the sick edge to my devotion. The shamed dependency. The secret, denied erotic yearnings. *And* used them all. And now here were all my embarrassed motives teased out and demeaned. I tried to make my soggy mind reach out past my confusion and grasp instead the anger that ought to come with my pain. Ruskin! That joke! Turner! I go for his lure like a fool, and I am rewarded with this mockery, mockery of my motives, mockery of my commitment, my thought, my belief — the whole thing turned into a squalid sex game, with me as the patsy. Is *this* what Mel did with Jeffrey? Is *this* what finally unbalanced that paranoiac? I sank down on a cold angry rock by that cold angry water and pressed the heels of my hands against my walloping temples.

What were the two of them doing up there now? I glanced back and it seemed perhaps the kitchen lights were off. Damn them! I was thinking exactly the envious excluded thoughts they wanted me to think. *Eros, c'est la vie.* Damn them both. And their game, which had only begun. It was not over. My withdrawal meant nothing. It had only begun! *Eros, c'est la vie.*

At this point a fantasy flashed through my mind. I pictured myself, with Nancy, the next night, when she would have arrived with Cullen. I saw us in our bedroom, and saw myself trying to whisper an explanation of all that had happened here tonight. I imagined Nancy listening with a cold stare. I saw a dismissive toss of her head. *So what's the matter with you? Sounds to me like you should have tried it.*

I stood up and stooped at the waterline to splash my face with some of that still very cold bay water of spring. This was madness. I wanted to stop my head spinning, spinning out thoughts like these. I splashed my face again and felt slightly better. You are just words, Jason. You are nothing but words. *Eros, c'est la vie.*

I had to walk. I began making my way down the strand, still driven not only by my intuition that this event tonight was an invitation perversely disguising certain humiliation, but that it was proof that a turning point had come in my friendship with Mel. That what had begun as the confirmation of my adulthood had now turned into something Mel wanted, by rendering it physical, to destroy.

But what if I was wrong? What if I misunderstood everything? What if I were nothing but a frightened young man, stumbling down a shoreline, trying to keep a black universe from spinning and in desperate flight from his own pathetic, secret desires? Words. That's all I was. Words. And I had gone about a hundred yards down the shore when the rescuing convulsion seized me and I sank onto my knees to retch repeatedly, onto the sand.

Half an hour later, feeling better and steadier, washed and cooled by the cold water from the tide, I climbed the long wooden staircase back up the high bank to the house. The door to the darkened kitchen had been left politely ajar. The table had been cleared. The dishwasher hummed. I went to the sink and in the dark rinsed my hands and mouth again, and then went up to the second floor. As I passed Mel's closed bedroom door, I supposed for a moment that I could hear his voice and hers, playful, deep in eros, muttering, laughing, mingled. I paused for a moment. But perhaps I was wrong. There was only silence. Nothing. Just silence.

chapter 13

I snapped into wretched wakefulness just before dawn. Some dark, terrible killing night-riding terror had been bearing down on me in a dream: It was powerful, and it was cruel, and it was getting closer — and I jerked awake to the sound of a woman's cry. Silence in the guestroom.

Was it a cry of pain? Anger? I felt awful. I felt assailed by that awful luminous blackness that lights some insomnia like a strobe. All that brandy in my blood had become liquid sleeplessness, liquid fear.

I ground my head into a pillow as last night came back — the lascivious couple, the rolling surges of sexual mortification. My mind caromed from exhaustion to anxiety, to remorse. It was awful. Once again Mel was dancing his demonic dance in my mind, and I heard once again his voice from last night: "You've always wanted me." I remembered his invitation to play. I remembered his serpentine condescension. But why couldn't I? Why couldn't I play?

I flailed in the bed.

I squeezed my fingers between my knees and the answer pinched my soul. I couldn't play because something in me was defective, dead. Last night was the proof. I didn't understand what love and freedom demanded. I was only words. Mel was right. Dead words. Joyless, disembodied words.

Opening my eyes to minimal slits, I tried to think about the
real word. In the guest-room window, dawn had begun. Night
was almost over. Night. I closed my eyes again.

If only Nancy had come out with me! If only her body were
beside me. As I clutched my pillow, my insomniac tensions
softened. I slept again, gently, as if uncertain whether this was
sleep or not. A little after eight I rolled onto my back and with
liquor-blasted eyes saw the plain ceiling above, lit by the plain
light of a new day.

A day which was supposed to be splendid. Today I was
supposed to look at the house Mel had found for us. Tonight
was the first party of the summer, here at Mel's. Fun. Think of
it as fun.

I creaked to the bathroom, tiptoeing amid the shattered glass
of last night's spiritual havoc. In the bathroom, I carefully
avoided any glimpse of myself in the mirror. The shower burst
over my aching limbs.

When I descended Mel wasn't in the kitchen, but Vicki was,
and she was being simple and sweet. The night that had
demolished me seemed to have transformed her from being a
mocking blond sorceress into a pretty midwestern girl in a
bathrobe, greeting me with a glass of orange juice, which was
indispensible, sane, and freshly squeezed.

I told her it was saving my life.

"Great," she said. "So let's cook breakfast and put it back to
normal."

Vicki led me to the pots and pans, where the demons of the
night seemed to vanish with the sound of cracking eggs and the
smell of perking coffee. Vicki had a gift for consolation. Friends.
It felt like friends. We didn't know it yet, but Vicki and I had
much in common. For one thing, we were absorbed in a
common adversary: Mel — and we were living in a common
jeopardy. We must have sensed that somehow. That morning,
over the sizzling bacon, we treated each other with the kindness
of those who would soon be needing it. We began to be buddies.

In which spirit, Vicki commandeered Mel's van and drove

with me into the Springs town common, where I was to have
my rendezvous with the realtor brokering the dream house.
The Springs town common is hardly a common at all, just as
the Springs is hardly a town. It is a bit of green that would be
almost indistinguishable from an open field, were it not marked
by a clapboard community house at one end. You can peer in
its windows, and see its piano, its little elevated stage, its flag.
Outside, there is a set of monkey bars. Near them, a rough
diamond for baseball. Near that, the Veteran's Monument.
Across the road by one side of the green sward, a church. Across
the road at the other, the Springs L.I., N.Y. Volunteer Fire
Department, where on the cement sidewalk in front, the chairs
of summer already had been set out, for the guys to tilt and talk
and drink beer among their playing dogs, waiting for disaster.

We pulled up behind a parked Falcon in front of the
community house. The driver's door was hooked open; the
agency lady stuck out her legs and sunned herself in the spring
light.

"So *you* are the lucky couple," she cooed when we walked up
to her car.

Confusion. "Oh hi — but no, no!" I burst out. "*We're* not the
couple."

Vicki laughed.

"I mean this lady isn't . . . Vicki here is just a friend who's
come along."

I blushed. "Oh, I see," said the lady.

"The real couple is . . . is me . . . me and my girlfriend.
Another lady. Not . . . not . . ."

"Yes, yes, I see," the woman said.

Vicki laughed again.

Then the woman pointed across the street and I looked
where she pointed. I loved what I saw from that moment on.
The house Mel had found stood just across the street from the
community house behind a privet hedge and within the green
serenity of an American country pastoral. It was a white
wooden farmhouse with a wrap-around porch, reached by a

gravel driveway that led past the Hopperesque inclined plane of its cellar doors and then dwindled to nothing in the coolness of pines and apple trees and a back yard that seemed to go back forever. "The apple trees will be blossoming any time now," the woman said as she led us through the hedge and around to the back. I pictured fluttering canvas chairs in the yard. "You know how spring just rushes in and *happens*."

Then she conducted Vicki and me through the back screen door, which slammed behind us with the welcoming immemorial American bang.

Except for a newish white Westinghouse fridge, every detail of the country kitchen seemed unchanged since the days of Franklin Roosevelt. There was a kitchen work table with an enameled steel top and a honeycomb of drawers and latched cabinets below. There was a creamy breadbox, and a pantry with dark unpainted shelves in back for storing stewed tomatoes and dilly beans. From the linen cabinet came the smell of Rinso white, and the scrolled backs of the cream-colored wooden kitchen chairs where completed with little flower decals.

I wanted to move in then and there. There were four bedrooms upstairs, and as we glanced through them I assigned each its role. The master bedroom was for Nancy and me. Now we were going to have a bedroom, a shared bedroom, for us. A bedroom that *meant* something. The room right beside the master bedroom would be my study. There, looking out its dormer windows, musing on playing children and plain thinking townfolk in their community house, I was going to complete my analysis of high esthetic perversity. There I would finish *The Bachelors' Bride*. To a small bedroom in the back, with a not quite full-sized — three-quarter bed — I consigned Cullen Crine. That left us a spare for guests. Wonderful guests. The play-husband had found his play-domain.

I proceeded to explore every single corner of the place, while Vicki gave my enthusiasm the slip and went to sit contemplating the May sunlight from a dusty wicker chair out on that front wrap-around porch. She parked one foot on the railing and stared out into the American space.

This house was going to be my escape. I inspected the furnace, peering through the murk at the water heater and lawn mower. This house was going to be my lucidity. Let Mel live in his madness over there above the bay. This was the place where my sanity and strength were going to gather and be restored.

I strode out onto that porch purring over the place's perfection. "This house, this *house*," I said, coming up behind Vicki and leaning on the yielding wicker back.

"You like?" Vicki twisted to smile up.

"I love, I *love*." Then I glanced up, and over the privet hedge, out in the intersection near the church, I had a sudden glimpse of trouble in paradise, and it made me gasp.

Perched like fantasy's assassin on an idling motorcycle forty feet from the community house sat Jeffrey Hastings, looking angry. Here! *Et in arcadia the male ego*, as invasive and premonitory as Cocteau's deathriders in *Orpheus*. Jeffrey had stopped in the intersection in front of the church, pausing with one booted foot on the tarmac while his engine, like his anger, idled and spat. Jeffrey must have been riding hard; in spite of the mild chill, he was in a heavy sweat, and he'd pulled off his crash helmet to swab the moisture from his forehead and eyes with a loose scarf around his neck. Now his head was turning; he was about to look directly at Vicki and me standing behind her, there on the idyllic porch.

"Hey," Vicki asked. "You know that guy?" She had felt my shock of surprise through the wicker.

"You mean the guy on the motorcycle?"

Jeffrey almost had seen us. "That's right," Vicki said.

For some reason I thought I had to lie. "Uh — I'm not sure. Just vaguely. I think . . . think he may be familiar."

Jeffrey's eyes now connected directly with ours, and the moment they did, he held perfectly still. He stared without surprise. His fineboned face was uninflected by any expression except the unflinching steadiness of his rejected fury. He did not look away, and he did not give the hint of any recognition, apart from the inflexible stare. He did give his handlebar accelerators a couple of small nervous spurts of gas.

I had to do something. I lifted one uncertain hand from the wicker and gave a little wave. It was a wave Jeffrey did not return. I could not quite tell whether it was Vicki or me who more deeply held his attention. Then, still staring, he clipped his helmet onto his head and snapped the buckle to.

"Who *is* it?" Vicki asked, her curiosity stirred. "He's a spook." She gave another glance at the intruder, her face a little twisted between curiosity and distaste.

"Just a guy," I lied again. "I can't even think of his name."

Then Jeffrey put the Harley in gear and roared away.

On the drive back to Mel's house I decided to come clean on the Three Mile Harbor Road.

"Vicki," I said as we made the turn, "you know I cannot tell a lie. Or maybe I just can't carry off a lie. Anyway, back at the house, I lied."

"You *did* ? Jason! A boy like you? A professor? Telling lies?"

"Not lies, Vicki. Just one lie. One teeny-weeny little lie."

"Uh-huh?"

"Except that the teeny-weeny little lie isn't really so very unimportant."

"You're kidding." Curious now, Vicki dropped the merry mockery in her voice. "What's so important about the mean spooky guy on the motorcycle?"

"You guessed! You knew all along?"

"Knew you were lying about that guy? Oh come *on*, Jason. Believe me, you are a lousy liar. Take it from a pro. You stink. Of *course* I knew. I just didn't give a damn. Not until now."

We were coming to the little dirt turn-off that led to Mel's big house on the strand. Vicki pulled the van into it with a fine fast aggressive competence. "So tell me. Who's Mr. Mystery Macho?"

"Well, it's Jeffrey Hastings. The guy on the motorcycle was Jeffrey Hastings."

"Ahhhhh-*so*." Vicki soaked up the intricate shock in silence. We glided beneath the budding trees. "I should have guessed," she murmured as if to herself. "I should have felt it, deep down, the second I laid eyes on that one." She was gently braking as the van pulled up to Mel's drive. She pulled the van around, out of sight, into the obscurity of a grove behind the Porsche.

"So that's the guy," she said, "who makes my boyfriend crazy."

The engine died.

Seymour and Iva Kaplan were waiting for us inside the big house (Mel still was sulking in his studio, probably drinking while he contrived his dissociations), and the Kaplans were shining with joy. I'd begun the morning trying to kid myself into thinking this would be a splendid day. But for Seymour and Iva, a splendid day was exactly what it had turned out to be.

"Kiss me!" cried Iva. "As of today, Seymour and I are rich and housed, both. First of all, Seymour and I just put down our money on the house that Mel found for us out here, and that house is perfect. Believe me, the best we've ever had. Second, we have what to put down because your cockamamie girlfriend," Iva wagged a pudgy finger in my face, "has managed to sell two — count them, two, *two*! — of Seymour's best paintings to this man Cotter who is coming to dinner here tonight. And she sold them without discounts! Do you appreciate fully what that means? Full value? No discount?"

"To sell at all," murmured Seymour. "To sell at all."

"All right, all right, Seymour. I agree — sell at all. But you know we've never once in your life sold a picture at full price." Then Iva clapped her hand over her mouth. "Me and my mouth," she said. "Shouldn't say that so loud."

"Well, congratulations," and I kissed them both. Seymour blushed and beamed.

"Tonight," Iva crowed, "tonight is a red letter night. Tonight is the beginning of great things. This night, Seymour, I tell you," and once again Iva was wagging her finger, though at her husband now, "this night may look to you like a mound of steamed mussels. But I am telling you that underneath its quiet and unassuming surface, this is night number one of the big time."

The celebratory party began to gather around five o'clock, when Nancy and Cullen Crine rolled into Mel's driveway in the leased Renault that was to become, along with Vicki and the hydra of Marcel Duchamp's awesome and mean-spirited mind, my summer's real companion. Certainly that companion did not turn out to be the Nancy Hopkins, who carried in her triumph with the offhand grace of a guest carrying in the gift of a bottle of wine. Cullen greeted Vicki with a great big kiss. It was like a meeting in a mirror.

Mel remained invisible while we foregathered, and I bubbled with enthusiasm for the house on the Springs town common — bubbled, a bit off-key, as I soon enough discovered, when Nancy, Cullen and I piled into the new Renault for a further look at the find.

"I guess it's OK," Nancy remarked, without enthusiasm, once I had finished guiding them through the play-husband's play-domain.

"Don't you *like* it?" Nancy's dry little blink of indifference before my delight had caught me entirely off guard.

"I like it fine, Jason," Nancy said, using a tone that gently emphasized her wide spirit of tolerance. "It's nice. It is a nice, temporary, little summer place."

"Well, of course it is temporary, but —" Deflation left me candid. "Gosh, I thought it was just great. The ideal place for us. I was so thrilled."

Nancy permitted herself a wan smile.

"Mel's house is great," Cullen chimed in. "This house, on

the other hand, is nice. Besides, Jason, I have a suspicion that this house matters a bit more to you than to . . . *us*."

A sigh like something from a punctured tire sizzled out of me. I sank back against the wall. "Us?" The word faltered from my lips.

So Cullen explained himself while Nancy surveyed, with an air of bland contempt, the kitchen I had found so irresistibly the kitchen of innocence and its dreams. "Remember, Jason darling, that you are the one who will be living here all the time, slugging away at your endless scholarship. It is perfectly natural that you would want a nice homey little place where nobody would want to disturb you." Nancy's eyes seemed fixed, in disgust, on the breadbox.

Now I groaned and threw up my exasperated hands.

"Whereas we, on the other hand — Nancy and I — have no choice but to stay stuck in the big glamorous city, making real money. We'll just be coming out here now and then to . . . escape."

I was no longer leaning against the wall. "Well, that is just wonderful. And here I'd been deluding myself with the thought that some kind of enthusiasm might exist here, that maybe the two of us . . . excuse me, I mean the three of us. . . ."

"Oh now, Jason," Nancy interrupted, "don't get huffy and touchy."

"Heaven forbid," I said.

"The house is fine. We're taking it, aren't we? So calm down." She kissed me on the cheek.

But I did not calm down. I remained touchy, very touchy, through the rest of the evening. I was sufficiently touchy, in fact, to pick a fight, quite gratuitously, with Tom Cotter — Mel's main guest that night, and apparently his new confidant; the Kaplan's benefactor; and though I had not yet grasped the secret, my new, and my final, rival.

Especially back in those halcyon days — while ignoring his first wife, and not yet married to his second — Tom Cotter exuded the immaculate air of an easy, virile confidence. He carried himself with the beautifully brushed look of a man who has forgotten what it means to deny himself anything because of money. Mind you, I have always liked Tom. I liked him then. I like him now. He even (especially then) rather fascinated me, with that look of careless self-confidence. It even occurred to me — back in those days when almost any man looked to me more real than *me* — that Tom Cotter might be in on some secret that, if only I could guess it, might even lend *me* some of that easy attractive glow.

Except that it was not the relaxed mystery of Tom Cotter's confident glow I tried to plum that night over our pretty supper of steamed mussels and Caesar Salad. As we gathered around the big round table in Mel's kitchen — the Kaplans ebullient; Mel, back from the studio, watchful and untalkative, always at Vicki's side, touching her, brushing against her, his arm draped around her, wishing to look exactly like a man at ease with the woman at his side — I was busy behind the mask of banal politeness, waiting, watching, as events revealed, for a fight.

I got my fight about three-quarters of the way through the meal. Because of my dissertation, there had been early in the evening some perfunctory discussion of Duchamp, and Tom had expressed polite interest, gently letting me know along the way that though he was a businessman, Marcel Duchamp posed no mystery for him. In fact, Tom may have had in mind the mirthful sage of autism and indeterminacy — of art as the refusal to speak — when he raised the name of Elizabeth Jarrett. I did not then know — I should have sensed it, I suppose — that before my time, and above all before going on to establish her independence by becoming a rising star in a new generation of minimalist artists, Elizabeth Jarrett had been a charter member of The Bunch. And almost certainly had been one of Mel's girlfriends in those lost, epochal, early days. I had been vaguely aware that some minor scandal had attached itself to Jarrett's name at the Venice Biennale a few months before, but I barely paid attention to it until the moment over that Caesar salad and abundantly flowing white wine, it leapt forward as the catalyst for fury.

"Speaking of Duchamp, did you hear about this awful business Liz Jarrett went through at the Biennale?" Tom asked. Mel muttered some sulky sound of recognition, but the question seemed to have been directed toward me.

"I had heard something about it, vaguely."

"Well there was a lot of noise about it back at the Biennale, especially talk about censorship. Elizabeth even got a petition sent around, and I signed the thing, because I really do think it is a case of censorship."

"I absolutely agree," Nancy chimed in. "I signed that petition too."

"It sounds like quite an event," said I. "What's all the excitement about?"

"Well," Tom continued — and was that a malign little smile of provocation I caught on his manly lips? "I never actually saw Liz's piece, but it seems that what she had done was a piece which included — uh. . . ." he looked for the ideal expression, "a *human* participant."

"Oh," I answered in a slight, clipped voice. I really must have sensed what was going on beneath the surface, somehow. My hostility was taking shape very fast. "A human participant?"

"Yeah. Liz went into the slums of Venice to a section where there are lots of Italians with Down's Syndrome. You know, Mongoloids? And she paid the family of one of these kids to be part of the piece, take part in the art."

"Really," I said dryly. "Participate how? Doing what?"

"Just sitting there. In a glass case." That was a sly smile, I was sure of it.

"I see. And I take it somebody objected to this procedure?"

"Right. There was a huge hue and cry all over the place about how inhuman it was, and the protests got to the directors of the Biennale. They made Liz back off. They refused to let her exhibit the piece."

"The *piece*," I said. I no longer was waiting for the fight to form in my mind. "So they wouldn't let her exhibit her Duchampian found object," I said. "In its glass cage. And everybody is all in an uproar about censorship."

A glance to the place across the round table where my girlfriend sat with a fork demurely poised in a mussel shell, showed how magically the cold tone in my voice was making her features harden. I was not sure I cared.

"Well," I continued. "I wish somebody would have asked me to sign this petition. That would have been an interesting moment for us all." I sipped some more of the white wine, which in its abundance seemed to have entirely relieved my hangover of the night before.

"You don't give the impression of much enthusiasm," Tom said.

"I would," I went on, "have absolutely refused to have anything to do with it. In any form."

"But an artist, a good artist, was prevented from mounting the work she had in mind. In a major exhibition."

"And you genuinely think of that as censorship?"

"Sure I do," said Tom, very gently, very smoothly.

"I think censorship is a completely false issue. To prevent the exploitation of an unfortunate human being who is not able to defend himself by some rich, fifth-rate American publicity-hound trying to make herself look interesting. No, I do not think it is censorship. I think it is elementary decency." I vaguely noticed that for the first time in the evening, I had Mel's undivided attention. It must have been a willed unknowing that kept me from seeing how Jarrett was part of Mel's apparatus, but it was working. Mel was listening, most intently, to every word I said. His arm may have been draped loosely across Vicki's shoulders, but he was all ears, all eyes, for me. "As a matter of fact," I continued, "I think it is an intellectual and, if I may say so, spiritual disgrace even to raise the word censorship in such a context. And then to defend it with the name of Duchamp is worse." (In fact, I knew there was nothing unlikely about it at all; Duchamp might well have loved it. I could hear the old man's laughter, his unending mordant delight. I also glimpsed the bewildered face of the exhibited idiot child). "I think it is a disgrace." Tom continued very elegantly to ignore that I was in effect accusing him — and Nancy — of having slipped into intellectual and spiritual disgrace. "The thought of it is sinister. There is this child — a girl? a boy?"

"Don't know," Tom answered, entirely unruffled.

"This child, probably not capable of understanding what is happening, put into a glass box for all our marvellously accomplished *and* privileged — let's *not* forget privileged — friends to pass by and think advanced thoughts? They should have kicked her out of the Biennale. I would have seen it happen with a song in my heart."

"Don't you think that's going a bit far?" — ah, those of us in art's most radical tradition must never go too far — "after all, the family was paid. Probably what was for them quite a lot." The businessman would eventually get back to business.

"Paid? Well, that's just wonderful. There's good old American generosity at work. I have an even better idea. The next time Elizabeth Jarrett wants to assist some poor Italian family with an afflicted kid, let her just plain write a check. There's a work of art for you. Let her put the cancelled check behind glass. Then we can all go parading by and think superior, subtle thoughts."

Tom now surveyed the silenced table with a look of suave triumph. "Well," said he, "I guess Liz succeeded at one thing." Tom's smile, suddenly, reminded me of Mel's. Mel's last night. "Provocation is as provocation does."

The bastard was right. I, who flattered myself on my intellectual elevation above the issues, had been provoked. And this very bourgeois businessman was the one who'd done it. Meanwhile, I was ruining the Kaplan's party. I was

embarrassing these people. My friends. I was falling for
something. From far across the sea, Elizabeth Jarrett (aided by
Cotter) had tapped my knee with her tiny mean shrewd little
Duchampian hammer, and my boring knee had produced its
boring jerk. They tricked me into expressing the emotion dada
most delighted to mock: outrage. I wasn't commenting on it
any more. I was manifesting it. I was furious and making a fool
of myself. Babbling on about cancelled checks behind glass.

Yet I reeled on, weakly. "I protest," I insisted. "I protest
against the plain indecency of it. Against the almost imperialist
exploitation by this rich American. I don't care if Jarrett isn't
really rich. She is rich and privileged in their eyes. Raiding the
slums for this hurt child! I protest against the humiliation, the
shared humiliation, degradation, between spectator and
spectacle. Oh, it's Duchamp all right. Duchamp all over. The
high art of high misunderstanding? The esthetic of confounded
pieties? Fine. I even will admit it is the basis of something like
great art. Sometimes." Mel was now deep in his listening
silence. He sat in his chair and seemed to have condensed into a
somewhat smaller presence when I glanced at him. "But the
essence of this thing is more than the mere esthetics of
misunderstanding, more than the esthetics of confounded
pieties. It is humiliation. Humiliation for the poor kid behind
the glass. That's the most obvious. Humiliation even if he can't
grasp what is happening to him. But then there's the
humiliation for all those people who look at the kid, and that's
just as important. There is an incredibly demeaned position
they've been put in, looking at this thing. Trying to keep up
their sophistication by not noticing . . . the contempt, the
contempt behind what's being offered to them. The contempt . . .
for us all."

I fell silent. I felt like a creature stupefied, driven and derided
by feelings I couldn't name.

"Well, I for one am with Jason." It was Iva's voice. Good old
Iva. "I think it is one hundred percent sick and nasty. I
wouldn't know about censorship, I'm not smart enough for

that. But I don't go for this putting kids in boxes. What can I say? I've known Liz for years. She'd do worse than that to get on the cover of *Artforum*."

Dear, good, smart Iva. There I sat, fouling their celebration. There she sat, taking my side against their patron. Not ordinary probity. Not ordinary nerve.

Mel had been listening in absolute silence. His eyelids half lowered, hooded half by drink, half by anger, I am sure. Seymour was twiddling the stem of his wineglass, waiting, wishing, for other things. I was ruining everything.

Whereupon Tom Cotter, without missing a beat, changed the subject to his absent wife Elaine, and that tiresome but tumultuous aspect of the social life in East Hampton over which she presided. It was a shrewd and ever so gently downbeat release from our dilemma. Nancy listened to his every word with interest.

Strange to say, the first person to excuse herself that night was Vicki, who kissed first the top of Mel's head, then his lips, then vanished upstairs. He made no move to follow. Nancy was next, after an effusive goodbye to Tom and the promise of a visit the next day to discuss details. Tom did not linger long after her departure, and once Tom Cotter was on his feet, so were Seymour and Iva. They all left together, it seemed, happily.

That left me among the ruins of the mussel shells with Mel. I sat again at my desolated place, troubled by the damage I might have done. Mel got up and went to the refrigerator, after yet another bottle of wine. He slipped the Orvieto between his knees, and his eyes still full on me, pulled the cork with a sudden yank. When he got to the table he poured me a refill.

Then he leaned forward a little. He drew up close to me. "Well, Jason, that was quite a little speech you gave us tonight." His dark eyes were on me. "A little like the speech you gave us last night." There was something . . . unduly tender in his voice. It was quite unsettling.

"It is hard for you to let things happen, isn't it?" As he spoke, he was near enough so I could feel his breath against my skin. I wondered if it was the rejected lover speaking to me, or if it was his mockery. The question raised a sickened, scared feeling inside me. The room, it occurred to me, seemed to have been cleared of everyone except us as if for some purpose. It was as though everyone had left us there to continue our obscure battle with one another. "You just can't let things be free, can you? That's too much for your intellectual's sense of power. You don't know how to play. You know how to explain. You can explain a lot. You think — everything. But you can't play. You talk about freedom — you make theories about freedom, but you don't know anything about it. You explain. You explain — all in order to hold the world still. All in order to hold meaning still. All in order to keep things from happening."

The smile on Mel's face was frighteningly near. Now he laid his hand on my hand. "What you are, Jason, is explanation as . . . composition. As stillness. As dying." Mel's smile now was a sweet, sickeningly sweet, and plainly mocking thing.

"But you can't control . . . *me*. Can you, Jason?"

I wanted to pull my hand out from under his, but could not bring myself to make the move. "I've never wanted to control you, Mel. Never. I don't know where you get that idea."

"You understand a lot, don't you?"

Mel was lightly brushing the back of my hand with his thumb. "You don't miss a thing, right?" The movie-star eyes had filled with a mocking merriment and contempt. I was swimming in mortification.

"I try to understand things. I don't know if I succeed. Obviously I don't. You. Myself."

"You are going to explain all this someday, aren't you? All of it. You are going to explain it all some day." The contemptuous smile curled too near me. "Won't you, Jason?"

At last I pulled my hand away. "I don't know, Mel. Right now I think I don't understand anything. Nothing at all. Please, just let me free."

Then, without another glance at him, I pushed myself away from the table and was on my way to the door to the deck, once again in flight. When I was outdoors, it slammed shut on his laughter.

I was out under the immense arcana of stars, thinking *the son of a bitch. I hate him. I'll always hate him. How much insult and shit does he think he can hand out? How low do I have to sink just because I've admired him?*

I started down the long snaking flight of steps, careful in the unlit darkness, my head alive with the slow beating of hurt rage, shivering against the weather.

When I reached the beach itself, I shoved my fists into my pockets and locked into my angry impotent reverie, I once again made my way to the water's edge. There by the edge of that unmoving black water, so alive in its silence, I held tight again the insult and hurt. It seemed all that watchful darkness might somehow absorb it all.

"Hi there neighbor."

The voice startled me completely. I jumped and glanced about wildly in the dark, really afraid, trying to find the unknown voice.

"Who's there?"

"Just me, Jason. Nobody but me."

It was Cullen. He came stepping out of the dark, shaking back the blond hair, wearing a light white jacket and a smile that seemed to come from deep inside, radiating from some private amusement all his own.

"*Christ*, Cullen, but you scared the shit out of me. I had no idea you were down here."

"Mmmmmm," he said, maintaining that private smile.

"I just assumed you'd gone to bed like everybody else."

"Mmmmmmmmmm."

"I had no idea," I went on, "that anybody around here shared my solitary tastes." With that, Cullen looked at me rather sharply, and his smile disappeared. "I mean — solitary walks on the beach."

He took a couple of steps forward. He'd been down here sitting in the dark, hearing the muffled sounds of Mel and me talk, our voices drifting down from the kitchen window.

"So tell me," Cullen asked. "What other solitary tastes do you have, besides walking on the beaches?"

"Oh, I don't know," I said. "Despair." It just slipped out. "Despair is a solitary taste, I guess."

Cullen expressed not the slightest surprise. He nodded gently with what seemed entire comprehension. The wind caught the flawlessly cut blond hair as it blew in the night air.

He understood. Too well. Too well. Did he know about last night? Was it his idea?

He tilted his head. "Well, don't."

"Don't what?" Cullen stepped up as close to me as Mel had been a few minutes before.

"Despair." He was very near.

Before I could answer he reached out and gripped the back of my neck and pulled me toward him in a heavy pass, driving a raunchy tonguing kiss against my mouth. I remember feeling his lips still speaking as he kissed me, his clean-shaven but bristly male face crawling against mine, repeating, "don't . . . don't . . . despair . . . don't . . . ." His hands were at my crotch, one knee was driving between my legs, his mouth was all over my mouth, all over my face. I breathed the vodka-splashed breath, and everything around me was streaming into the hungry, drunken, frightening eroticism.

"Don't," I said.

I pulled back and away. "Hey, come on, Cullen . . . *please* . . ." and I pushed him away. "Hey, come *on* . . ." And then he reeled back a couple of steps in the classic movement backward of the spurned. He pulled his hair from his eyes and said, the words very distinct with anger: "I just thought you might like to try something — a little less *solitary*, Jason."

I had darted one worried glance back across the dunes at the house — the bedroom windows. Cullen caught the gesture in an instant. "Oh, don't worry, honey, everybody's asleep. Don't panic about your precious little reputation."

I caught the accusation; cowardice. "I'll tell you frankly that I wouldn't mind being asleep myself right now," I said, "*if* you don't mind."

"Why should I mind," Cullen snapped in return. "Sleeping is a nice solitary thing to do. Just like hiding in a nice solitary little closet."

"Why do you say that," I said, wounded. "Why?"

"I don't think you like love much," Cullen said, staring at me. "I think if you liked loving more you'd do more of it." He stared at me with desolate gaze. *What did he know about last night? Of whom was he speaking?* His voice now assumed a rather commanding cutting edge. "Go on in to sleep."

"OK, I'm going in." I shoved my hands into my back pockets. My breath had returned to normal. The wetness of Cullen's mouth was still on my face and I hesitated for some reason to wipe it dry before I was out of sight.

"Are you coming in?"

He answered without any hesitation. "No, not yet. I will stay out here a while." It seemed Cullen's tastes were even more solitary than mine.

"All right," I said. "See you tomorrow."

"See you tomorrow." He spoke gently. It was not at all unfriendly.

"G'night." I turned and began walking back.

Then he called after me, "Hey, Jason," and I glanced back. "Don't despair," he said.

I responded with a little strangulated snort of hurt laughter. I pulled my right hand free and waved him a little goodbye wave, as if with the small back and forth movement of my fingertips I were trying to erase a small chalkmark of secret feeling from the blackboard of the black water, black sky. As I turned to start back up the long wooden stairs I could hear him repeat it. "Don't despair, Jason. Be careful. And don't despair."

I left the kitchen lights burning and went upstairs, down the empty hall to our room.

Inside, Nancy was asleep, or pretending to be. I stepped in on tiptoes and didn't even query the darkness with a half-whispered, "Nan?" Instead I found my way in the dark, feeling for a chair beside the bed where I undressed as quietly as I could. I was conscious only of the night sounds of my movements, the rustle and slide of my clothes as I took them off, the brush of cotton against my skin as I stepped out of my underwear.

Very carefully, I lifted back the covers of the bed and creaked into my side. There we lay: I on my back, Nancy on her side, her back turned to me. Rather than whisper, "Nancy?" I lay instead perfectly still, and then rolled onto my side, pressed my fingers between my knees, and lay looking, in the dark, at her hair on the pillow and the shape of her bare shoulder. I was certain she was awake.

I pulled my hands free and then I kissed her hair. She let me. Then I kissed the back of her head, and her neck, and she let me. There was some odd anonymity at work. Not once did I kiss her mouth. Not once did either of us say a single word. Not once did I even think of turning on a light. I moved directly to her breasts, nuzzling and tonguing. I felt a slow, silent, oddly focused kind of love. Her hands were on my back. Step by slow worldless step, carefully, anonymously, and as it were, terminally, we made love in the dark.

chapter 14

Nancy and I struggled on, at least in name, almost until Labor Day.

We even managed to have a couple of times that looked like good times in the Springs house. At first. The first week I was there, Nancy dutifully followed me out on Saturday night, and we played a bit. We were alone together. Our housemate Cullen Crine couldn't make it. It helped that the Hamptons party season was not yet rolling that early in May. We had time on our hands. It made us edgy. That made the rich randy old heterosexuality come rolling back, as if for old times' sake. We ravened through the house. We bounced all over the master bedroom. We violated Cullen's bed. We romped through the makeshift study. There were no curtains up in the living room, but we didn't care. Oh, it was almost like love again.

Except it wasn't. In the post coital sadness, the sad thing that kept beating in the brain was the end, the end, the end. Then Nancy went back to the city and the real darling of my every day was my clattering typewriter. I had fixed up the study in the country solitude with all my notes, my slides, my somber annotated rows of tomes liberated for the summer from the Institute Library. There we were together, me and Duchamp. It turned out that Cullen spent more weekends under our roof than Nancy ever did. He had the impetuous habit of showing up without calling. Often he'd creep into the house very late, long after I, alone in the master bedroom, had fallen into my word-weary sleep. The next morning I would find him in the kitchen, sometimes sweet-talking some trick over the bacon and eggs.

But usually it was just me and the grey ghost. I would have been desperately lonely if my sometime temptress Vicki had not been just as lonely as I. Mel left Vicki alone too much. Mel had told me he thought of Vicki as a fantasy. Perhaps. Certainly, he did not attend to her life apart from him. He wanted to be moved, touched, excited, brought to life by Vicki. But he did not want to live with her. When she was not touching him in some interesting way, he wanted her to flicker out of existence.

And that is when she would call me.

We spent a lot of time on the beach, and at first Mel even sometimes tagged along. It was easier when he didn't. Strolling with that celebrity into so celebrity-conscious a space as Asparagus Beach could be trying. Since we were three, we would take the van or my — I mean, our — Renault. On the ride over, Mel would be relatively relaxed, but everything would change as we pulled into the beach parking lot, and the master prepared for the ordeal of recognition. He'd descend from the back seat like a spy dropped behind enemy lines. Out would come the dark glasses. He'd wrap a towel around his neck as if for disguise and clutch his beach bag as if it were a shield. Then, shaded eyes downward, he hunched over as if trying to make himself smaller for our trudge toward the water, down the gauntlet of his visibility. The game was to absolutely ignore absolutely any sign of recognition from anybody — unless of course the glance flashed our way was from a Cotter or Castelli, which Mel managed somehow never to miss. Meanwhile, all his efforts to pass unnoticed only made him more visible. Which, I concluded, was more or less the idea.

"So, Jason," Vicki said to me one afternoon. "Tell me about

Duchamp. I don't know anything about him, you know." Mel
was along that day. The surf rushed toward us and was
scooped back into its own tumult.

"You should ask Mel about that," I said. "Mel's the one who
knew the man, probably as well as any person of his generation.
He's Duchamp's heir. That's my theory."

"Oh no, you're the big expert," Mel countered, his tone a
shade less amicable than I might have liked. "So far as I'm
concerned, Marcel is . . . Marcel has disappeared. I never think
about Marcel. I've forgotten Marcel. It's Marcel *disparu*. As for
this crap about being the heir, I don't know what you're talking
about. Heir? Bullshit. You and I have had a couple of chats
about Duchamp. So what? But you're the big intellectual. The
art historian. You're the professional rememberer. I am a
forgetter. I'm leaving all the remembering to you."

Then, while I was stung inside, he finished off by favoring me
with a smile. I paused long enough to get that stinging under
control, and then I said, "that's a very interesting remark Mel.
Not that I'm exactly clear about what it is supposed to mean
. . ."

"It doesn't mean anything more than it says. You're the guy
who's so hung up on meaning. All I mean is that art isn't made
with thinking. And it isn't made with words. Ideas."

"Not even Duchamp's art? Not the most cerebral art of all?"

Mel shrugged the loaded question off. Then: "No. Not even
Duchamp. Not really. Of course, a person thinks. You can't
help thinking. And some people like Marcel are a lot better at it
than some others. But none of us can help thinking. Art comes
from something else."

"Such as?"

He paused, as if annoyed because I was rising to his bait.

"Such as doing something with the thinking. *Doing*
something."

"But surely you mean doing something in plastic terms,
something against the tenor of all that involuntary thinking?"

"Yeah. Well, those are just words. But yeah, if you insist.

Yeah, against the thinking. Definitely. Against whatever it is you're dealing with. The art comes from whatever you do against whatever it is you're dealing with."

Vicki leaned forward and waved her hand in our faces. "Hey, you guys, I'm the one that asked the question! Remember? Here I am. So quit being snotty with each other and explain Duchamp. I don't want to hear from Mel. You tell me, Jason."

Mel subsided.

"There's a lot to tell," I said.

"Yeah, OK. Let's make it easy. Like what are you writing about now? I mean, were you writing about Duchamp this very morning?"

"Of course I was. Every bloody day."

"So what were you writing?"

"This morning? Well this morning was a long section on Duchamp and women."

"Ah-ha!" Vicki pounced on the word as if it were her victory. "I knew we'd get down to Old Duchamp with the girls, eh?"

"Well, Vicki, let's put it more formally. More in dissertationese. Let's say Duchamp and Woman."

"Ah, Woman!"

"With a capital W."

"So how does the capital W work?"

"Well, for example, I am writing about Duchamp and the classic female nude. Duchamp and virginity. Duchamp and the muse — since the muse is supposed to be female. Duchamp in drag, Duchamp and transvestism. Duchamp and the whole cult of capital-W 'Woman', in fact."

"Cult. What a word. Cult." Vicki tongued it laciviously, brought it two tones deeper as she dwelt on it. "The cult . . . of woooh-man." Then she simpered, large eyed, at Mel. "Mel, is 'cult' some sort of dirty word?"

Mel answered with a pleased little smirk. "Not unless you make it that way," he said. He was enjoying this little lesson. So far.

"I bet. So, *cult* . . ." Vicki fingered the hot dry sand, musing, maybe, on how that might be done. "Cult," she mused on. "Cut. Then Killed. Then *culte*." (Her French 'u' was flawless). "Then — cunt. See. I knew I could follow through. I know the whole conjugation. Didn't think I did, didja?"

She poked Mel in the chest and laughed.

"You know a lot, Vicki. I know that."

"But seriously, Jason." She leaned back a bit. "What do you really mean? The cult of woman? Teach me."

"Well," said I, professorial on command, "during the romantic movement, and particularly during the mid-nineteenth century — when modernism begins plainly to emerge from romanticism — all the arts began to show increasingly self-conscious insistence not merely on the artist's relation to his feelings in general, but to his quite specifically — quite *realistically* — erotic feelings above all, as opposed to the generally ecstatic emotion that so interested earlier romantics. We hear less about nightingales and more about lust. And the lust is quite exactly specified. A new description of desire, therefore a new description of women — Woman — begins to emerge. This takes various forms in various arts, but in the art of painting such classic crypto-erotic themes as the artist with his model, woman as muse, the myth of Pygmalion, a bare-breasted Liberty leading the people, and the rest of it, assume a newly disassociated, explicitly sexual look. The classroom examples are Manet's *Olympia* or *Déjeuner sur L'Herbe*." (And there were the three of us, two boys and a girl, clustered together half-naked in our swimsuits.) "Anyway, as modernist painting proceeds from, let's say, Manet, this concern grows more explicitly evident. In the popular mind, *and* elsewhere, the question of modernism and pornography become linked. They will remain so for a hundred years. Take response to Manet, or the obscenity trial of *Madame Bovary* — the avant-garde starts to smack of libertinage. Think of Baudelaire with his mistress Jeanne Duval. Think, in the twentieth century, of Molly Bloom.

"Actually, this transposed, but shared, obsession with the

role of woman as the object of desire may be the principal link between romanticism and modernism. Quite obviously, once the iconography of Catholicism's cult of woman begins to recede — all those Virgins and mothers-and-child and Magdalenes and pietas — the romantics see sexual desire less as a source of pain, or as a temptation to sin, or as a snare and a delusion, or the subject of renunciation and elevation, and more as . . . simply, *the* life force. OK? OK. The modernists continue in that tradition. Just as much as the romantics, they assert eros as *the* life force, the privileged subject of art. By the time you reach mid-century, Picasso's whole *life* is chronicled in terms of his wives and mistresses. You know the Dora Maar period. The Jacqueline Roque period. Et cetera. *Except* — except that the modernists refuse to play along with what they see as romantic naivete on the subject. They get raunchy about it. Rough. Ironic. Remember the standard classic of cubism is a group portrait of some whores. With animal masks. And a nasty, jeering title . . . *'Les Demoiselles'* . . . We have come a long way from Ingres and *Le Bain Turc* . . . Not to mention, say, a *Judgement of Paris*. In fact, a response to the romantic cult of woman is a principal wellspring of all modernist irony, that irony which stands at the heart of modernism. And *that* is an irony of which Marcel Duchamp" — my professorial forefinger now rose in the hot beach air — "is the most radical practitioner of the twentieth century, and *which*," (my triumphant breath was going to carry me to the point of periphrasistic strangulation) "is the whole subject of *The Bride*."

Vicki took me in with a steady look. "So that," she concluded, "is the cult of woman." She chomped her gum. "Wow." Then, reflecting, Vicki tilted her head to the right. "Women don't have a lot to say about it, do they?"

"A strong point," said I.

"But you are the *center* of it," Mel said, flicking some sand in his fantasy's direction. "You! Just you!" Mel began to crawl toward Vicki lobster-like, across the beach blanket. "You are

the object and center of all desire! All aspiration! All *meaning!*"
He tossed a beach bag at her, which she batted aside with a
smile.

"Big deal," Vicki said. She was giving Mel the eye.

Mel continued to crawl toward her. "Don't you understand,
my sweet tender young thing? You, *you* are the picnic on the
grass!"

"Wow," Vicki said.

Arching over the picnic basket, Mel twirled the imaginary
moustaches on his lubricious lips. "You, my scrumptious
lovely, are the maid of modernist irony." Mel ran his lips across
Vicki's sun-tanned shoulders. "How does *that* feel?"

"It feels," Vicki replied, cringing from the mouth nibbling
her neck, "funny peculiar. Not funny ha-ha."

"What!" cried Mel. "Can you possibly suggest that you do
not *wish* to be the maid of modernist irony?"

"I wish to know what the hell you are talking about." She
pushed her paramour back into the sand.

"You do? The anxious object wants to become the reflexive
object?"

"Well, at least this reflexive sex-object has a question or two
for you, Mr Art."

"Such as?"

"Such as, before you told Jason you always work against the
given."

"So? So what is your question, my little Miss Given?"

"Cute. My question is does that mean you work against me.
Against women. Against Woman, in your art."

"Smart question, Miss Given."

"And I have another one, this time for Jason."

"Yes?"

"Did Duchamp love women? Did he hate them? Now wait.
Don't tell me. I bet I already know the answer. It is both?"

"Both."

"See," said Vicki, simpering at her genius. "I know you
guys."

She didn't know us well enough to keep Mel. As June deepened, Mel joined Vicki and me less and less often on our outings surfside. Now of course it's well known that Mel was sinking into his final depression. But on the scene, I didn't have enough clarity to name the problem so simply. I was aware, vaguely, that Mel's work was going nowhere. I sensed he was stuck. In the years since then, I've often thought that perhaps my little beachside lecturette on the cult of woman may have touched a more tender spot than I knew. Consider Mel's famous remark (*I* made it famous; he made it to me in the great days): "The first rush in my work is always sexual. I know the piece is done when the desire is gone." It's true. Dworkin's art can be seen as a consideration of the mystery of arousal. It was deeply perplexing to him, and deep inside him. How does the mind turn on to what it sees? How does it make the world come alive? He pursued metaphors for the flesh. The imagined flesh, of course. That was his bride. And when he lost touch with her, he sank down, depressively, into himself.

He also was sinking away from me. I had certainly gathered that I was growing less grata by the week, and that the role his depression had assigned me was the unlovely and unwelcome role of the assassin intellect. But I did my best to avoid thinking clearly about why both my hero *and* my girlfriend seemed never to spend any time in my life anymore. I made up a batch of feeble rationalizations and let the bell jar of absorption in work sink down over me. When the weekend would roll around with again no invitation from the big house and with a call from Nancy with the pretext for staying in town, I would pout. But I accepted the excuses and softened them in a cloud of vagary that did not really want to be disturbed. I didn't *really* lack for company. I was comforted by my country solitude. With the green of the town common in front of my desk, and the silence of an unshared bedroom behind, I navigated through Duchamp and the mockery of desire.

Meanwhile, Vicki remained my pal on Asparagus Beach. As June moved toward July, I began to pick up hints of trouble for

Vicki with Mel. She was never — well, almost never — indiscreet about him, until one afternoon the rough edge of truth and temper made its appearance, briefly. We were at our usual spot on our usual blanket.

"So," Vicki queried a little irritably, "is Nancy coming out this Saturday or are you going to be batching it this weekend just like you did last one? Boy, you have a lot of fun."

"Well," I replied, marshalling the rationalizations, "it does look like Nancy won't be able to make it. It seems some honchos from the Houston Museum are in town and Nancy wants to spend as much time as she can with them. She says, *says*, she might bring them all out on Sunday. You know, to meet Mel. But even that looks iffy."

"Mmmmmm." Vicki considered it. "Well, let me clue you in about one detail. I'd be amazed if the Mel part of it comes to anything. Because the genius," Vicki had taken to referring to Mel as the genius, sometimes affectionately, sometimes not, "the genius is not in a very charming mood. He hasn't been in a long time. And it is really getting to be a drag."

Vicki played in the sand with petulant little digging movements, funneling it, hot and dry, from hand to hand. "So listen, Jason, what's the matter between Nancy and you? Don't you *want* to see each other?"

"Sure, sure we want to."

"Well, why don't you?"

"Well, I think it is just a matter of logistics."

"Logistics!" Her tone was deep with disbelief. Then she lay back on the blanket, removed her dark glasses and closed her eyes, as if for a sun bath. The scent of Coppertone drifted my way. I was hurting a bit from her question. I listened to the roll of the surf, the crying gulls, the talking, shouting voices around us, miniturized, tiny in the intimate, hot, immense beach air.

"All I want," Vicki muttered, "is to be brown and be—au—ti—ful."

So she was. She was very brown. Very beautiful.

I closed my eyes and the sun beat down on us, making bursts

of yellow and orange behind my eyelids. More gulls. A juddering engine out on the water. "And I'll tell you something else I want," Vicki muttered. Then the next sentence was very loud and clear. "I want *not* to go back to that god-*damn* house."

That made me open my eyes. Vicki had pulled herself into a sitting position and was staring at me as she shaded her eyes with her hand.

"You don't want *what??*" I sat up too. "You don't want to go where?"

"You heard me." Vicki clipped on her dark glasses again. "I don't want to go back to Mel's god-*damned* house. You heard right. But . . . forget I said it. Just forget it. I promised myself I would never say it."

She looked out at the sea.

"But you did say it."

Silence.

"So, what's wrong?"

"Oh, it just gets to be a little much sometimes."

"You had a fight."

More silence.

"Tell papa."

"Oh, shit," Vicki leaned back a bit. "You know, Jason, this relationship with Mel started out being really kind of wonderful. Beautiful, in a way. I know we got kind of flaky with you that night. Nothing personal. You know? But it *was* wonderful. He was this guy, and he was so delighted, and so excited with me when we first got together. And what happened between us was so passionate and so hot. And I was all of a sudden part of his life. And he was teaching me all about art, and he seemed to love doing that, and then there was the Springs and Saint Maarten's, and then Europe, and it was all first class, and all so interesting, and all so much fun. And it was . . ." she caught herself a moment . . . "it was tender. I know you saw us flakey, but it was tender. There was something there. Really. Because I know Mel had been down very, very low after Jeffrey Hastings and the winter and all. When he met me, he was in a very depressed state. He had been in a slump, and all of a sudden I was the person who was bringing him out of that slump. And that's a great feeling, Jason. You know? The feeling that somebody is just turning around toward great things thanks to you? That you are the saving grace? You know, you're the reason the new day looks great. I mean, I made Mel want to go waltzing around the whole world. He just couldn't wait to rush off and buy the tickets to Berlin."

"Sounds like a pretty nice feeling, Vicki."

"It was a pretty nice feeling. And I have some more news for you, Papa. It is *gone. Fi-ni-to.* Just gone."

Vicki took off her glasses and then, with the flat of her bunched fingers, wiped away the tears that had begun. Sweet, cynical Vicki. Then she put the glasses back on and returned her gaze to the high wide North Atlantic inane.

"And I can also tell you that when that feeling goes away, what fills up the space it leaves behind is real shit. I used to be the woman that made the genius' day great. Well, bully. Now I'm the one that turns it into a mound of crap. So that's another feeling I have gotten out of this relationship. A little less nice."

There was silence, except for the tiny voices of the beach and the slow surf, distant, near. A couple passed by us, and their chatting voices came clear. There were two or three sailboats on the grey-blue sea, very far out, very still, and near the horizon line, a real ship.

"I try to bring it back, of course. I try to get it back where we were. Make the old feelings come back. But it seems I never get it right. They don't come back. The sex — I just don't like the sex anymore. It isn't fun anymore. And it used to be so great. Plus he drinks. God, how he drinks. He didn't drink like that before, did he?"

"Well, sometimes. Quite a lot. Yeah."

"Well, he's doing it again. And then sometimes he talks and talks, and it is so *boring,* and so self-*absorbed.* And at first he was so interesting. Or else he holes up in that damn studio, where he doesn't even work. Just putters. Or he mopes around the house, which isn't even a house. It's just a museum with a kitchen. And he doesn't talk to me at all. Of course, he gets all lovey-dovey when other people are around, except there are never people around anymore, because the genius doesn't want to be bothered with people. You've noticed you're never invited anymore?"

"Well, yeah. I have."

"I've got news. Neither is anybody else."

She seemed to be concentrating on that distant real ship.

"I watch a lot of TV these days, Jason. A *whole* lot of TV."

Then she pulled the glasses off again, and I saw the tears running down her face. The silent crying broke into sobs as I waded through the sand on my knees and laid my arm across her shaking shoulders.

"It's like he doesn't even care if I feel bad. Like I don't count at all. And sometimes he makes me feel *so* bad."

"He's a selfish son of a bitch," I muttered, squeezing her shoulders, my knees off balance in the sinking sand.

"I *try*. I really *try* to make it great between us. It's just that everything always ends up turned against me."

"I know, honey. I know. He's a stinking louse. He doesn't deserve you." I was fumbling for a beach towel. I shook the sand out of it and tried to daub her eyes.

"I try to make everything nice. And what happens?"

"He's a schmuck. Here you are — the one *good* thing that's happened to Mel all this year. And he wrecks it."

"I *know*," Vicki said. She had now taken charge of the towel herself. "Shit," she said. "I need to blow my nose."

A long rummage in her beach bag seemed to console her. Just as she produced a large wad of tissues, a couple I did not know — I think part of Elaine Cotter's bunch — were coming toward us waving.

"Well, look who's here," Vicki said, snorting into the wad. She was brightening through her sniffle as everybody said hello. "How am I? What does it look like? I'm crying in my beer. But I'm done with that now," she said. "Sit down, sit

down, there's lots of sand. You know my friend Jason?"
She sniffled. It was over.

By the time July peeked through the ocean haze, I could sense
that more was happening in Vicki's life than nasty withdrawal
symptoms of Mel's affection, and too many hours in front of
TV. I noticed that Vicki's mood seemed to improve right
around the time she became less available for our times on the
beach. A full-length Hamptons summer, after all, is anything
but a socially isolating experience. Celebrity Beach grew ever
more crowded. Vicki could not ignore that there were a great
many more rich and famous men in the ten mile radius than her
sullen genius. Mel had needed a fantasy to lift him from his
depression. One man's fantasy is not so deep and secret that it
may not be another's. I guess without ever quite knowing how
or why, Vicki had that summer embarked on a kind of career.
From then on, Vicki would be more or less always in some
liaison with somebody of either sex who, though invariably
glamorous, invariably a name, seemed to need a fantasy, too.

Invitations of course came into the big house all the time, and
that July, unless they perhaps touched his unfailing business
sense, Mel usually ignored them. But Vicki was not asleep at
the switch. She began to accept, all on her own. It was a simple
expedient, and it enabled Vicki to carry her downy beauty onto
some of the fancier decks of the summer colony. Opportunities
for the opportunist must have abounded. Meanwhile, on those
same decks, Cullen Crine, soul brother and opportunist
supreme, must have now and then secretly flashed her the wink
of his subtle and consoling approval. Go to it, kid.

What Mel knew about all this, or conjured up in his
paranoiac fancies, I cannot say. I saw him less and less. When
Mel called, it was usually because Nancy chanced to be
spending one of her rare weekends in residence. When I went to
the big house it was almost always to see Vicki. Mel often did
not even emerge from the studio to say hello. I was still invited
to the rare party, though sometimes Mel barely said hello.

Something less than friendliness emanated from the house on the strand. I was left alone more than ever, there with my nattering bride.

chapter 15

The destroyed are destructive. Jeffrey Hastings spent the entire summer in the Hamptons that year only to be near Mel, and the truth is that his obsession with Mel had by then reached almost the level of an erotic mania. My melodramatic little frisson at the first sight of him in May had not been in any way misplaced. Jeffrey became that summer the absent presence in all our lives. His disaster had made him ominously patient. He was on the long, bitter watch. Against Mel. Against me too, for that matter. Even in his absence he was destructive. I very much suspect that much of Mel's final paranoia about me derives from a morbid absorption in Jeffrey, and I still burn with fury when I reflect that Jeffrey was probably a witness to my final humiliation at Mel's hands.

That event took place at the last of those too long, too wine-soaked seafood dinners around Mel's round table. When the meal was over, somebody suggested a late-night swim in the sound.

It must have been Iva Kaplan — she was the one who seemed most to enjoy it. We all went down to the beach below Mel's house, swathed in darkness, and stripped off our clothes to swim in that black cool water, suitless. Vicki and Mel, Seymour and Iva, and me. Nancy wasn't there that night. But then she was never there. We splashed and played, barely able to see one another under the huge starry night. The picture lingers in my mind like a passage I cannot explain in an otherwise perfectly lucid work, an inexplicable crux in some dour bacchanal of Cezanne. But we played, and I had no idea that Mel, among all our bathers, was playing so very joylessly, or that his rage against me was so very near the breaking point. Still less did I have any idea why.

Cullen was the one who saw Jeffrey, because out of some unexpected modesty Cullen had lingered behind, upstairs in the house, and so it was Cullen who saw Jeffrey standing and staring into the house of his exclusion, there in the front door. "He must have been surprised to see me," Cullen told me later, "but he didn't seem surprised. Well, he probably was too high to register any particular emotion. He just stood there in the door, looking in. Without one little word. Dead silent. So, I thought I had to say *some*thing, so I said, 'here to join the party, Jeffrey?' and of course he didn't answer, he just gave me a kind of sneer. So I just finished up. I just said, 'sorry Jeffrey, but there's nobody here but me. They've all gone down to the beach to swim.' Then, still without a single word, he backed away and I watched his form dissolve behind the screen door. For a second I thought I was hallucinating, but no, it was the real Jeffrey all right, and I suppose he took my advice and went around and down to the beach. But then nobody mentioned it when you all came back upstairs, and then came your little set-to with the masterpiece maker, and I decided that perhaps we all had had enough fun for the evening. So I just didn't mention it." Cullen gave me his sinister little smile. "Until now."

"*Feeeeeeeel* your way!" Vicki called out as we made our way down the unlit wooden steps. "*Feeeeeeeel* your way."

"Mel, are you a millionaire or are you a millionaire? You can't own a flashlight? Something to show the way?" It was Iva. "Oh no, that would be normal."

"Look at that night," Seymour said. "Just look at it . . ."

"Seymour, do me a favor and don't crack your head open."
Mel came following, and ominously silent.

The rocky little beach lay naked under the night, pathless, comfortless, infirm in dark languor, still, except where salt runlets splashed into the low tidal pool and seabirds, disturbed by our splashing, flitted up from their margins with questioning cries.

Squinting a bit, I could see Iva, dumpy in the darkness, tossing off clothes as one might toss off shadows. Nearer me, Seymour in silhouette unbuttoned his jeans and breathed deep. Then came a sudden splash. "Perfect!" Iva shouted from beyond the shoreline. "This water is *perfect!*" I had gotten my own clothes off, after worrying about the immodest moment. Behind me, near the staircase landing, I could see Mel, only a dark form prying off his shoes, heel to toe. Vicki seemed already naked.

"*Seymour!*" Iva shouted, as a wing of sprayed white water rose in the dark, "you *splashed* me!" And then came a cataclysm of a water fight between husband and wife. I slowly started into the bay, tiptoeing more and more prancingly as the inching water rose in a cold tickle up my thighs toward my crotch.

I heard Vicki plunge in behind me, and I glanced back to see Mel out waist-deep staring after her, hugging his biceps as if trying to contain some uncontrollable trembling. He dipped his hand into the black water and swabbed wet salty fingers across his lips, and Vicki called out "Come on, Mel! Jump! Jump!" The watcher sank on one hip, while I took my dive, and the sticky evening was swept away in one brave crash of coolness. I surfaced, rolled into my steady backstroke and looked up as I moved out at the immeasurably high unmoving order of the stars above. "Jump!" Vicki was calling, more faintly, "Come *onnn*, Mel. *Jump!*" As I pushed farther out, I saw the house above us, the deck and kitchen windows bright, the open door lit. A surge of fatuous tenderness passed through me.

Peace, I thought. *I feel peace.*

Peace! With all that rage gathering in the dark.

I swam.

I supposed myself to be the first one out of the water — and the next to come wading up from the deep was Seymour, who lurched toward me across the pebbles, peering and dripping. "Jason. That you? Feels great, doesn't it? Can you see the towels and stuff?" As I bent to hand Seymour a towel I noticed I had not, in fact, been the first out. It had been Mel, who had reached shore before us all and who now stood on the darkest part of the beach, in jeans but no shirt, staring in silence at the rest of us, clutching himself, shivering against imagined cold.

Seymour spotted him. "Hey Dworkin, that you?"

"It's me," Mel answered, his voice like death. It was frightening.

"*Seymour!*" It was Iva calling from the water. "How come you're going *in*? I *love* this!"

"Because I've had it, that's why," Seymour yelled. "Come on *in*, Iva, you can't swim all night."

"But," Vicki called, "This feels sooooo *sen*sual, and sooooo *great*. I could stay out forever."

"Yeah," Iva called back. "Well, the *men* are going in. Can't take it."

I heard Seymour's low laugh. "Iva," he muttered, bemused, but he was peering in the direction of Vicki's voice, waiting for her to come up naked from the sea. He had just a hint of an erection, which made him dry off fast and hustle into his clothes.

Mel stood in the background, silent, his crazy anger growing.

Out of the water, Vicki did not dress, but exhibitionistically wrapped herself in a big beach towel and began to squeeze her hair. As we started back up the stairs toward the house again, Mel stepped aside, letting everybody pass before him, silent, his eyes wide.

When Vicki put her arms around him and kissed him, he stayed as wooden as a cigar-store Indian. "Oh," Vicki murmured, "not in the mood, eh?" She laughed. He stayed silent until we climbed toward the light upstairs.

Mel's first move back in the kitchen was to fill his glass with bourbon once again. Cullen sauntered out from the main room without mentioning Jeffrey. There was a roomful of banality about how nice it, the swimming, had been. I too said how nice it had been. Then with painful effort, as if it were insuperably difficult to speak, Mel said, "I didn't think it was so great. I had a shitty time."

The statement *seemed* to be addressed to me.

Iva's smile faded. Vicki, who had been toweling her hair, still wrapped in the beach sheet, held still, pure apprehension.

Now Mel looked directly at me, addressed me directly. "I don't like the company," he said. "There is a certain kind of person I don't want to be around anymore."

"I'm sorry about that Mel," I said.

"Sorry," Mel muttered. "I bet you are."

Iva was in the fray. "Mel Dworkin, what is the *matter* with you?" Mel ignored her, and knocked back another slug of liquor. It was as though he and I were the only people in the room.

"I mean, I'm as sorry as I can be about a swim on a beach." I was trying to sound calm.

"You've had a pretty nice free ride off of my life, haven't you?" His eyebrows lifted in drunken, questioning fury. "My life. My work. My friends? Right, my friends. Not yours. Mine. And my dealer? My mind? Maybe my girlfriend?"

"What?" I was astounded.

"*Mel!*" Vicki's cry was likewise ignored.

"You have been a very busy boy with everything I have, haven't you? Meddling with it? Getting stuff from it? Lots of stuff. Trying to make it all yours."

I was moving my head back and forth in dumbfounded denial. Who, what, had planted all this in Mel's mind?

"Who the fuck asked you to worm your way into my life, anyway?"

When at last I was able to speak, my voice sounded to me small, cold, distant, lost. "I thought you did, Mel."

"Why are you here alone tonight? Why are you here always alone and hovering around, hovering around me? What is it you are trying to sneak away with? What is it you are trying to filch from my life? You parasite. You death's head. Hanging around all the time. With your theories. Don't you have your own life?"

Seymour had pulled himself up to full stature. He and Iva were darting glances back and forth, and Iva was shaking her hand in a quite unconcealed gesture of: *Be careful. No. No.* Cullen had pulled into the safety of the background, and had become all eyes.

"I think I have my own life," I said softly. "I don't think I am trying to steal anything from you. It really isn't true, Mel."

"Don't you tell me what's true and not true, you wordy little creep. I am sick of listening to you. Let's see if you can do something besides talk. Talk and worm your way out."

With his open hand, Mel gave my chest a little push.

"Hey, come on Mel. . . ."

"Leech! *Parasite!*" His first blow came fast, and even after that first shove it was an absolute surprise. It was just one fast smack to the side of my face. Then a belt at the ribs in my right side and my arms went involuntarily up, followed by flailing, a windmill of enraged Mel's arms flailing and mine were up, merely to protect myself. He was shouting incoherently until, in sudden surprise, a cold douse of water came splashing over us both. Next I saw Iva tossing aside the plastic basin she'd filled at the sink, so she could wedge herself in between us as Seymour came up on Mel from behind and pinned his arms in a plain full nelson. Iva did the talking.

"*MEL-DWORKIN-HAVE-YOU-GONE-OUT-OF-YOUR-MIND?*"

Whereupon she delivered one solid interrupting slap across his face.

Mel teetered back, still pinned by Seymour. Sick, Seymour

Kaplan is approximately five times stronger than Mel Dworkin at the top of his form. That, and the slap, and the splash, helped bring Mel back. His eyes softened, changed.

Iva did not let up. *"NOW-WILL-YOU-STOP-ACTING-LIKE-A-CRAZY-MAN?"* All of the Bronx was talking to Mel, and it was *very* fast, and *very* loud.

Mel seemed about to say something, but Iva did not surrender her advantage.

"OR-DO-YOU-WANT-MORE-WATER-IN-YOUR-FACE?"

Mel groaned.

"You should groan," Iva hollered, just a shade more softly. "Now apologize. And hold him, Seymour." Seymour held him, tight. "You apologize to Jason right now, and you stop acting like an asshole. All right?"

"I'm sorry. I'm sorry, Jason," Mel mumbled, still held, hangdog. On the word "sorry" Seymour loosened him a little. "I'm sorry," Mel repeated. That set him free. "I had too much. I'm sorry, I just had too much to drink."

"Fucking 'A' you had too much to drink," Iva snapped. "You're a *disgrace*. Now you get up to bed and you sleep it off before you do something else to make me sick."

"I . . . I . . . I'm sorry. I am."

"Good," Iva said. *"Be* sorry. And go to bed." As Mel turned to leave the room, he moved toward his glass and the bourbon bottle. But Iva was right there.

"Mel Dworkin don't you DARE touch that glass. Don't you touch it. Or I'll smack you again, I swear I will."

"I'm sorry."

"Good," Iva finished.

Mel left the room.

The moment he vanished Iva turned and did a little spin around as if set free. A low sick groan came from Vicki. Then Iva went to Seymour and began to hug him, while Seymour shook his disapproving head.

As for me, I still was standing exactly where I had been standing when he hit me. I had not yet said a single word. I felt

around me a lostness I cannot name. It seemed to me I was . . .
elsewhere. But I knew I had to leave the place where I was. I
knew I had to be alone. And quickly.

"Excuse me," I said at last, perhaps not quite audibly, or to
anybody. There was a little washup bathroom off the kitchen,
and I started walking toward it. I remember hearing without
understanding Iva's voice behind me, then Seymour's. I
remember passing Cullen, who said nothing as I went by. I
remember pulling the door closed behind me. I remember the
tremor in my hands as I tried to get the hook of the door into the
eye. I did not want to do anything at all until I was safely locked
in. My trembling hand made the lock shake loose repeatedly,
but at last it was safely in place. Then my shoulder went against
the cool bathroom wall and I began slowly to slide down to the
floor. And then, when I was on my knees, my grief came tearing
out of me and I began to wail.

interlude

"Have you always wanted to do this?" I murmured. In my tiny bedroom on Perry Street, Vicki and I nestled together and fit almost too nicely. "I always have," I continued. "Ever since the time we met in Cullen's apartment."

In a week Vicki would be leaving New York, returning to Europe. The disorder and abandon of her first grief now seemed over. Above us, bare footsteps crossed my bedroom ceiling. Cullen had not yet moved out of Perry Street, although he would soon enough, on the argosy that would end in his ownership of Mel's Mercer Street loft.

"Does Cullen know you're here?" I asked.

Vicki shook her head, no. "Not yet. I'll surprise him later."

"And tell him all," I murmured.

"Maybe," Vicki answered, merry music. She kissed me on the cheek. "You know, I made it a point to wrap up all the loose ends before I leave for Europe."

"Thanks so much," I said. "So flattering to be a loose end. And wrapped up."

"Now, Jason."

Vicki thought for a while, her arms thrown back on the pillow.

"You want to know the last time I saw him?"

"Who, Mel? I already know the last time you saw him. You said he called you up and you had dinner together in . . ."

"No, no, no." Vicki shook her head. "That story was a lie. I made it up. I had to have some sort of story to tell people, and I didn't think I could tell the real story. It was too bizarre. I made up the dinner together in Montauk. It never happened. The real story was just so . . . so weird."

"Really?"

"I saw Mel three days before he died, and it was just the two of us out at the big house, all alone. It is true I'd already moved out, and I told myself I had left Mel Dworkin behind, forever. It is just that I hadn't. But I was living with my friend Elly out near Amagansett, and sometimes I would stay over with other people, too."

"You mean, people like Jeffrey Hastings."

Vicki did not blench in the least. "Yeah, I spent a lot of nights with Jeffrey. Poor Jeffrey." She turned to look at me directly. "Listen, Jason, tell me the truth. Do you think it was murder? Really? In your heart of hearts?"

"I honestly do not know. In my heart of hearts, I do not know. I can't imagine anybody does know. I think it could have been murder. It's possible. I think Jeffrey hated Mel that much."

"See," Vicki insisted, "I don't think that at all. I don't think Jeffrey hated Mel at all. Just the opposite. The only thing poor Jeffrey wanted in the whole world was to have his friendship with Mel back. That's why I was so special for him. So magical. The way he touched me. Looked at me. It was his way of getting back. That was what made him so fascinating. You know something? Jeffrey Hastings was the gentlest man I ever have been with. Ever. He touched me like I was a baby. I was his link to Mel, and I can tell you it was not hate he was acting out. I was really some sort of magical being and it was terribly important to him that every move be right."

Vicki paused.

"Oh God, if I talk any more about this I'll start crying again.

I promised myself, no more crying. Not until I get back to Europe."

"So you have got a whole tearless week to go."

"And I'll make it, too. I'm through crying over those men. God, I can't wait to get out of this damn country. Get free of this grief. It's a new life I need, Jason. You've no idea how much I need it. It is going to be Rome. I love Rome. I want to see Rome and stop seeing death."

Vicki closed her eyes. She was so gentle and beautiful there beside me, that I could not speak. And she was leaving in a week. Once again it was fall outside the Perry Street windows. Winter would be coming, very soon.

"Anyway," I said at last. "You were talking about the last time you saw Mel."

She left her reverie. "Right. Well, I was seeing Jeffrey, and what happened was that Jeffrey awakened all my old feelings for Mel. Of course, I knew perfectly well I was a kind of human link between them. That's why I got to know Jeffrey in the first place. Jeffrey was really a sweet guy. And he was no murderer. But I was there because of Mel, not him. And of course, the thing was that Jeffrey always took me back to Mel, and that is how I came to go out to the big house that one last time.

"See, Mel never really believed I was going to leave him. He always assumed I was going to come back. He always said so. He saw himself as waiting for me. But in my own mind it was fi-neet-o. So I was seeing other guys. And they were interesting. And they were not all penniless out-of-work studio assistants."

"I bet they weren't."

"Jason, don't be snide." Vicki bestowed one of her more knowing little smiles on me. "I was just a girl looking around. And then I discovered that Jeffrey was really getting to me, and I decided that was really because of Mel, and one night when I was all alone at Elly's I realized that I hadn't got over Mel at all. That was why I was so hung up on Jeffrey. I'd gotten into the surrogate game. With his friend. Well, his friend-enemy. And my feelings were showing me that there was some sort of unfinished business between Mel and me. And that night, I decided I was going to finish the business. On a bicycle!"

"Why a bicycle? What are you talking about?"

"Well, see, Elly had gone off to some party in her car, and I was stuck at her place with absolutely no wheels. But I was there, and my head was just full of what I had to do. I knew I absolutely had to see Mel. But there was this bicycle in Elly's backyard. And so I didn't call or anything, I just went into the backyard, grabbed the bike, kicked up the kickstand and off I went, thinking it isn't much, but it is transportation. I was feeling a little crazy last August, Jason. Believe me. Pitch dark, and there I was on the bike."

And now her smile was so simple and sweet. Vicki was very pleased with this little tale. I had to smile back at her.

"So I started pedaling in the pitch dark with this little headlight run by a tire generator? Back to the Springs. Right over the railroad tracks, the whole trip."

She paused.

"You want to know a little secret about women?"

"Sure I do. I need all the inside information I can get."

"OK. There is this terrific turn-on for women. Well, for me at least."

"Mmmmmmmmm?"

"Men asleep. Looking at men asleep."

"Hmmmmmm?"

"Right. I don't know why. So . . . I pedaled all the way to the Springs, past your place. I sailed right by. A little farther, and I stopped to rest, then I went pedaling on, scared to death, because cars came roaring past and here I was on this rickety little nothing bike, wearing this navy blue sweatshirt and jeans and only that little wavering headlight flickering down to nothing and dying out.

"Do you want some of this, Jason?" Vicki had picked up what was left of the joint she'd smoked during our foreplay, laying in a saucer. She lit it.

"Finally I pulled up by the gateposts, *soaking* from the heat. I pedaled down the driveway and there were lights. I thought, oh thank God, he is home. And then I realized I didn't have my keys. They were at Elly's. So I banged. And banged. No answer. I started yelling at the top of my voice. Mel! Mel! Nothing.

"I went to the studio door. Locked. The deck's door. Locked. Well, I thought, I *know* he is here. The car is here. Maybe he's dead. Oh help. It seems awful to say it now, doesn't it? I was afraid he'd died. Well, anyway, then I remembered about the downstairs bedroom where the lock was broken on a long window. So I went around and stood on tiptoes to look into the place. Lo and behold, there was Mel, asleep on the bed inside. He looked, just out. And I kept knocking on the window and calling, and then I realized that he really had passed out. And I hate to tell you, Jason, that was not so unusual. Mel passing out. Once it happened, there was no waking him. But luckily, he had left the window open. So I just got my tomboy going and I climbed in. It was nothing. I dropped into that bedroom in a second.

"The lights were on everywhere, and Mel was sprawling on the bed face down in his underwear. There I was breathing hard, like a second-story man."

Vicki took another long toke. "I haven't told anybody this before. I mean except Cullen. Cullen's different . . .

"Well, here goes. Mel was dead to the world. I yelled, *Mel!* Really loud. He didn't even move in the bed. Of course, I could see he was *breathing* and everything. He was on his stomach. Alive. Mel had this really, really *nice* back. And that cute little ass. So, he was alive. But I came over and looked closely at him. *Mel?* Then I knelt down by the bed and tried to shake him. I took his shoulder, and it was nice and warm, and I shook his shoulder hard. He was dead to the world. I had seen him like that lots.

"So I stood up and I thought, all right, fuck you. And I went out into the kitchen thinking, at least it's just like I have the whole place to myself. Nice. Nice. And there was this open bottle of wine, *naturally*. And I poured myself a glass, and then at the kitchen table I had this thought. I can stay here and he'll find me here tomorrow. That'll be cute. Besides, he's so cute when he's asleep. I wonder what he'll think? And then I sat still, and I looked at the window and thought, OK, I'm going to go get in beside him and when he wakes up there will be this surprise. I was calming down a little, but I was tired. So I took the glass and went back into the bedroom and there he was. I came in on tiptoes, because I felt a little funny, a little scared, you know?

"Boy dolls. He was just like this big boy doll in the bed. See? So. I thought maybe turn off the main light, leave on just the bedlamp. So I did. And I climbed into the bed beside him, and I thought, well now. I turned and looked at him. His mouth was open a little. I liked to look at the way his eyes were closed. The fringe of his black eyelashes. And then I reached out with my index finger and I ran my finger down the skin of his face, like it was the skin of a balloon. He didn't move at all. Then I rolled over on my stomach and looked at him some more. He really was just this boy doll. And *sweet*.

"So I said loud, Mel? Mel? I started to shake him a *lot*, but nothing happened. Like he just moved a little and then I decided, very innocent of course, that I was just going to get undressed and go to sleep beside him, because drunk or no he was nice and warm and everything. First, I'd look at him a little more. Then I would go to sleep. And so I got up and took off my stuff and got back into bed with him. Hi there, Mel, I said to him, since I was sure he wouldn't wake up and hear me. You're just a big baby doll, aren't you? You are just dead to the world, aren't you, pussycat. Then I got daring and I slipped my hand under his underpants and copped a little feel. Well, he just lay there. It was *fun*." As if to prove her daring, Vicki demonstrated with a quick squeeze on me. "You *sure* you don't want some grass?" She relit her toy. "It was just the beginning," she said.

"So. How do you like *that*, Mr Professor Phillips? I bet *that* strikes fear into your male heart. Like the old myth of the succubus, draining away your precious bodily fluids in the night."

"Oh Lord, I'm scared, I'm *scared*."

"It was *fun*," said Vicki, slipping onto her back. "I mean, first, all I did was sort of hug him, and then I thought, why not kiss him? He won't wake up. And sort of play with his hair and stuff? Well at first it was really kind of funny, because he did wake up a little bit. I mean he *moved*, like he wanted to be left alone. But I kept right on, and there were special parts of his body — like, see, Mel had this mole on his hip. It was really disgusting, and I never knew why he didn't go and get some electrolysis or something, but no. And so I was looking at it and touching it and I tasted it with my tongue and stuff. And then the funny thing is that I kept right on hugging him, and he changed. He rolled back toward me, and then he was sort of still asleep . . ."

"You mean he woke up?"

"No. *Noooo*. That's the *thing*. That was the really funny thing about it, because he did *not* wake up really. But he grabbed me, and he gave me this kiss, it was with his mouth wide open, you know. And it was this really *passionate* kiss."

"Tongue kissing?"

"Well, kind of. I thought to myself, Well, well, *well, in vino veritas*. Here is somebody who has been *so* cold lately. So turned off. And now here *in vino veritas*. In dreams begin whatever it is. *He loves me*, I thought. *He's passed out but he loves me*. And then I copped another feel and, lo and behold, guess who was getting a little bit stirred *up*, a little *stiff* down there? That's right, sweetie, that was our little Mel."

"You're kidding."

"I am not kidding. Like I was really getting kind of excited, you know, so I just thought, OK, Mr Mel, this is it. So I just slipped off his underwear and my own too, and he was sort of stirring and mumbling but he was not awake at all, and then I rolled him onto his back and . . ."

"Vicki, you are not going to tell me that you really made love with Mel unconscious?"

She looked at me in a sparkle of triumph, nodding to me, yes, she was telling me precisely that.

"And he never woke up? Not once?"

She shook her head no, to tell me precisely that.

"And you did it all? And he came? He had an orgasm?"

She shook her head, yes.

"And did you?"

"Oh yes. Oh yes."

She was looking at me with a dry secret pleasure.

"That's quite a story," I said. "What happened when he woke up in the morning and found you there?"

"Mel? He was hung over. As usual. He thought I'd come home."

"Yes, but did he remember anything about what had happened the night before?"

She shook her head, no.

PART 4

chapter 16

Mel was on the phone the next day with some vague apology, but nothing helped. The heart of our friendship was broken, and although we talked on the telephone in a desultory way a few more times, we never saw each other again after that dreadful night. The friendship of my youth was over.

Meanwhile, the approaching end with Nancy gathered force. As the summer deepened, she had been on the scene less and less, and as time went on, when she did arrive she would arrive late, or irritably, or needing to leave early. She would call from the city with the last minute news that she just had — it could *not* be helped — to fly to Houston, or L.A., or Minneapolis, or who knew where for the weekend. Then, a bit before that last encounter with Mel, Nancy explained that she was absolutely forced, she had no choice whatsoever, but to spend the first two weeks of August in Europe.

"Europe!" I wailed in despair, like a fool.

"Jason, I have tried and *tried* to get out of this."

Ten days later, on one of my increasingly rare beach dates with Vicki, I learned the truth.

"Jason," she said to me as we baked. "You know that something is going on with Nancy, don't you? I mean, you have figured out that much, I hope."

I had been pouring some sand through my fingers. I stopped,

and my whole body was held still by the solid grip of the inevitable.

"Something? Something going on with Nancy? Well, I *guess* I'm pretty aware of what's happening with Nancy."

"Jason, be serious. You *guess* you are aware? Or you know you're aware?"

"Sure I know. Of course, I know."

"You want to know something, Jason. I don't think you know this about what's going on. Tell me what you know. Just lay it out, right here. Let's take a look. For real."

"About . . . about what?"

"Jason, why play dumb? What does dumbness get you?"

"Well, all right, if you are going to needle me all afternoon, I suppose I can say that since Nancy is never here, I guess I draw some conclusions."

"Uh-huh. Like what? What conclusions?"

"Well, I understand that relationships don't go on forever. You were just telling me you were thinking about moving out of the big house."

"Jason. Don't get mad. Just because we're talking about you for a change. Which let's do. You. Not me."

"OK, since you insist, I admit it. I don't know what the hell she is up to." I bent forward, thinking I might play with the sand a bit more. "Besides. I've been scared to ask."

"*I* know what's going on," Vicki said. Her tone really was very gentle, very kind. "You want to ask me?"

"I know she is in Europe on business for the gallery. It was an unavoidable trip."

"Do you want to ask me who she's with?"

I didn't answer. I played with the sand.

"She's with Tom Cotter."

I knew it! I knew it! I knew it! The unctious bastard!

I said nothing. But I did stop pouring the sand.

"That's who she's in Europe with. Tom. It's not a business trip."

"Well," I said at last. "That doesn't surprise me."

"It shouldn't surprise you."

"So. All those times when Nancy stayed in New York, that was with Tom?"

"Uh-huh."

"And is this liaison very widely known about?"

"Wide enough. Cullen knows, of course. Which means, as I assume you assume, that a pretty long list of other people also know. Seymour and Iva know. And now you know."

"Now I know."

"I was beginning to feel a little shitty, walking around and seeing you and all, and knowing you did not know."

"Thanks Vicki," I said. I leaned over and kissed her on the lips. Then I lingered near, covering my pain with a joke. "Thank God Mel can't see us now. He'd *really* have something to hit me for."

"Fuck Mel," Vicki murmured back.

Riding home in the Porsche, I thought, *leave. Just get the hell out of here, get out of the Springs.* My place in New York was sublet; but I thought, *who cares, find someplace, anyplace.*

Vicki drove while I rolled my head on the back of the passenger seat, seeing the high North Shore sky slide past above us. "Vicki," I moaned, disingenuous with pain, "I *partly* feel terrible, but I also feel *good*. True, this feels terrible. But this is also positive. Positive in a weird way. But positive."

My head lolled in the unconsoling luxury of the soft seat leather as I maundered on. "I've seen it coming. Seen it. Now at last I am free. Free."

She shifted up as we reached the turn-off by the IGA. Vicki darted me a disbelieving glance. "Why even *try* to fight Cotter's twenty million? Why fight for something that hasn't made me happy? This is a positive thing, not a negative thing. Who cares? I'm free."

Vicki banked through a curve.

"What would *you* do, Vicki?" I asked over the whine of shifting gears as we spun down the tunnel of green. "What *are* you doing?" Thinking, *Two rejected lovers. That's why we have been summer buddies.*

"Me?" Vicki said. We had pulled up outside the house on the town common. The superb engine was idling with such elegance that Vicki could answer in something like a whisper. "Pretend you know what you want . . ." She paused and gave me the strange, hard compassion of her eyes. "*Play.*"

The engine idled: I had to go inside: Vicki to drive back to Mel's. I wanted to grip her wrist. *Vicki, don't leave. Stay. You see what I don't see. Help me.* I wanted to say: *Let's go off to some silly seafood restaurant and bitch about our unloving paramours. Let's play.*

I didn't. Instead I leaned over, kissed her downy cheek, and said, "Vicki, thanks for the truth. I don't love it," I opened the car door, "but I can live with it." Then I stepped out and waved, wanly, as she drove away.

My recollection of the rest of that night, alone in the house, remains a blur of unmanaged emotions punctuated by a set of absolutely precise images. Inside, I climbed the stairs and went to my study, dumped my bookbag. I flopped onto the daybed I'd set up in there and tossed in the jetsom of my thoughts for half an hour, trying, pretending to have the escape of a nap. At last I gave up and sat up, deciding on a walk. I went to the study window and glanced down. On the steps of the community house, two of the local women stood talking. One wore an apron. She gossiped with her hands folded over her belly, under the cloth.

It was nearing sunset.

The half-conscious intention of my walk was to wander to exhaustion, during which time I proposed not to think about It or Her. I wanted the beat of my footsteps to pound all that to bits. Feeling and not feeling, thinking and not thinking, I started walking the three miles to the beach. The promenade seemed to go on and on. I stopped only once in those three miles. The place, I remember, was near a horse farm. Twilight was forming. Two boys were leading some horses into the barn. I ignored them. I stood very still.

My humiliation had caught up with me. It held me still. I stood with folded arms for perhaps two minutes, struggling. Two minutes is a rather long time to stand alone on a country road, struggling.

I went walking on. At last I reached the embankment that runs along the beach above that part of Gardiner's Bay. My memory of all this remains quite precise. The access road down to the water was another half-mile away. I didn't bother to go to it. I merely climbed over a guard rail crusted with road grime and let myself slide down the high bank, dislodging sand and little clattering rocks from the crumbly slope as I skittered down. Then I was on the beach, and I had a whole new endlessness to stroll along, thinking it good to be so decisively alone, walking by the verge. I scooped up some sea water and let it stream down my face, tasting the salt. Then I began to walk again until, at last, all that trudging had made my legs begin to ache. Darkness was closing down now. I remember a roadside phone booth up above the embankment; an aluminum booth, isolated, glazed with road dust and grime. It was lit in the dusk, an electric outpost on the desolate ground. I remember being troubled by two voices, a man's and a woman's. I never saw the couple, but they seemed at any moment about to intrude on my precious hurt solitude. I imagined them helping each other down the crumbly bank, giggling lovers, slipping a bit, reaching the water and, like me, expecting to be alone. Ah, but that pastoral couple was *not* alone. I was there. There with my disappointment, my skulking hands stuffed into my jeans pockets.

I saw a house high above on a point. For five self-pitying minutes I mistook its lights for Mel's. *I hate him*, I thought, *I hate them. I hate them all.* I realized I was quite mistaken. Those were not lights from Mel's house after all. It was a house I had never seen before. It was large; every room was lit up. My uncertainty darkened. No, I thought, Mel must be further down the beach.

So I walked further toward where I supposed it to be, telling myself how much I did not want to see it or him or any of them, hating him and everyone. Then, suddenly, there were the real lights at Mel's. I had almost reached his point, his beach, his steps, what I was so insistently refusing. Perhaps fifty yards from Mel's beach, almost there, and almost not, I sat on a rock, and there I rested, and there I grieved, under his auspices, as it were.

chapter 17

The next day, swarming with the unmanaged emotions of rejection, I wrote the central, clinching, and finest chapter of *The Bachelors' Bride* in one sustained, totally concentrated and unfootnoted rage of emotional evasion. Every triumphant second of that day's work was illuminated by wretchedness, and by 5:18 that afternoon the whole thing was written and revised, from first sentence to last, notes and citations excluded.

Then that evening I found my consolation in the arms of Cullen Crine. It was something he'd been waiting for.

But then, so had I.

By the time Cullen arrived from the city that evening, I had the whole thing secretly planned, though since I never quite consciously thought through what the whole thing might be, I kept the secret even, partly, from myself. Instead, I rode the day-long crest of my wave of energy and insight. Explicit awareness went no further than calling Cullen in the city and suggesting we have dinner together in a seafood joint we knew out on the Sunrise Highway. Cullen surprised me by saying yes, and a bit more of the whole thing slipped, veiled, into my mind's eye view. I stared at it, shimmering and alluring, before banishing the notion from my hyperactive brain.

Cullen pulled in on the seven o'clock train, and I met him on the platform. I was leaning against a post in the summery

evening light, positively glowing with my exhausted rapture of
misery and triumph; there was the high publicity and high chic
of *le tout* New York stepping onto the platform of its
more-of-the-same Oceanside. Elsewhere. As the golden boy
made his descent from the hissing, sagging, benumbed old
L.I.R.R. car, a bit more of my secret agenda flickered into view.

"Cullen," I said, "congratulate me. You are looking at the
happiest, desperately unhappy man you've ever *seen*."

"OK. Congratulations," Cullen said. The crowd around us
was thinning into its BMW's.

"We might as well start the evening by finding out if you
know already that I know already," I said as we settled into our
much more modest little Renault. "You know — that Vicki has
told me all about Nancy."

"I know everything," Cullen said simply.

"Foolish of me even to ask," I started the engine. "Well, I am
dealing with the tragedy in a funny way. I am completely
wretched, and yet I am here to tell you that in spite of my
misery, or maybe even because of my misery, I have put in
today at the typewriter the best day of work I have ever done,
anywhere, any time. Isn't that strange? I feel great. And yet I
could burst into tears at the same time."

"Well," Cullen said. "It sounds like we have a brand-new
Jason on our hands."

I gave the beauty a glance as we pulled out of the parking lot.

We had gins and tonic in the backyard. Cullen sipped his drink,
his shirt open, loose at the collar, his summer whites spotted
with sweat. "I guess," I continued, "that I *should* be unhappy."
I was getting increasingly worked up, watching Cullen relax.
"What I am feeling is an excited unhappiness. A liberated
unhappiness. It comes as a big surprise, but I quite
unexpectedly seem to be free."

"Well," said Cullen. "You are a blank slate."

"A new, unhappy, brilliant blank slate."

"So what do you plan to do with all that freedom?" Cullen

sat there in easy succulent splendor, one knee lifted. I was getting clearer about what I thought I might do.

"Don't know," said I.

Cullen intuited the moment with exact precision. "Sounds to me," he said, "like an ideal time to do all sorts of new things."

"Like what?" I was all bright eagerness.

"Well, for example, you might try coming out of the closet."

I was promptly defensive. "That assumes," I said with hardened voice, draining my g & t, "that a closet is where I find myself. I know perfectly well you've always thought that's where I live. I know you think my relation with Nancy never was real. I mean — you never thought it was real, even when it was real."

"Lots of fairies can get it up for girls," Cullen said gently, tonguing the rim of his glass a bit.

"I know you think it was all inauthentic. I remember that night on the beach."

"I remember a night when you followed me all the way to a gay bar over by the docks. Back when it was supposed to be so very real with Nancy."

"So you *did* see me that night."

"I see a lot of things, Jason."

"OK. So what else do you see?"

"What else? I see you looking at life as if it were a tragedy, except it's a tragedy where you can't figure out your part. That's a lousy dreary way to live, Jason. You ought to learn better how to play."

"Damn. It seems everybody is singing the same tune these days. Play, play, play."

"Maybe everybody's right. Who's the other singer?"

"About play? My other adviser? Paranoiac, vicious, jealous Mel. Always so full of fun. Such a playful guy."

"Oh him. Well, he's crazy. A great artist. But crazy."

"Oh, cut it out, Cullen. Stop playing the company man. I am sick to death of people excusing that sullen bully just because he is such a great artist. He's certainly been sweet to your friend

Vicki lately, hasn't he? I cared about that man. I put him and
his fucking great art right in the center of my life. I let him
permeate my whole being. And now Mel has turned around
and transformed every good feeling I ever had for him into
something that feels sick and vile. Admiration. Excitement.
Friendship. You'd think he'd welcome them. I don't even know
where to hide those feelings anymore. I don't know. I must
have served that secretive mind of his in some secretive way.
Now that it's finished, I'm made to feel like some sort of sick,
corrupt thing and, to boot, told to run off and play. Sorry. I am
touchy about that word these days."

"You sound," Cullen said, "like an angry lover."

"OK. I'll accept that. I am an angry lover. Not that it ever
was physical." I was very anxious to clarify that point. "But it's
a lot like being a rejected lover. He's a son of a bitch. I can
understand Jeffrey Hastings and all the other people he's used
up and thrown away. Understand how they hate him."

I was surprising myself as I spoke.

"Well, anyway," I continued, "today I played the typewriter
as I never have played it before. Today was a gift from the muse
of play. No mean cracks about closets can take that away. And
Mel Dworkin can't take it away, either."

"Who wants to take it away? What do you say we go have our
seafood specials?"

And off we drove.

We had not left the subject behind. At the restaurant, over a
fresh set of gins and tonic, waiting for our deep fried platters, I
pushed forward, not caring, and quite incapable of disting-
uishing between curiosity and seduction. My curiosity was set
loose, for the first time, from the constraints I had set on it from
the beginning.

"Cullen, tell me why you can't simply accept the plain
simple possibility that somebody can be really and truly
bisexual?"

Cullen rolled his eyes. "Bisexual. Here we go. I will answer that not-very-interesting question only if you answer one of my questions first."

"OK."

"How come we are having this conversation for the very first time now? Tonight of all nights?"

"OK," I admitted, "That's a good question. And I suppose the answer has to be that I always have felt guarded until now. You're so close to Nancy. I didn't want to cross wires. You're so close to her I was jealous, except maybe sometimes it was hard to tell . . ." I took a breath, "which of you I was jealous of. You. Her. Both. I just wanted to keep things orderly and sensible and sane. Is that so terrible?"

"No," Cullen said. "There's nothing terrible about it. But it does sound like a very accurate description of a closet."

"OK. OK."

Our seafood had arrived.

"Only now you have to answer my uninteresting question about believing in bisexuality."

"Well, belief." Cullen sank back in his seat and gave me a very seductive look. "I could say, that I do accept it. I could be gracious and vague and let it pass. That's what everybody is supposed to do. The only problem is that that's a lie. A nice lie, maybe. But bisexuality is a lie, Jason. I have been listening to people talk about it my whole life long, and I never have known a single case, anywhere or anyhow, where it was anything except a flat out plain and simple lie. Nothing but cover. Every single time."

"Including tonight."

"Including, I am afraid, tonight."

"Are you so very sure? So sure you can see that easily into the center of my life?"

"I see *that* much. I saw it the first minute I met you. I always know when somebody is gay. It's the first thing I see, and I'm never wrong. We know each other. You know that I wasn't wrong with you. Was I?"

"I don't . . . I don't try to hide . . . that side of . . . myself. I just don't understand why you can't accept that bisexuality might be . . . real. Not hypocrisy. Real."

He leaned back and gave more twilight again, while I charged ahead. "This is one of the things I most resent," I said, "about this new sexual scene shaping up around us. I hate, *hate*, this mindless impulse to politicize every emotion, the way every feeling has to be hardened into instant ideology. I mean, just because a person has a little . . . *tendency* in a certain direction, everybody bangs away on some agitprop line about Hypocrisy and Coming Out Of Closets and Accepting Your Own Nature and Facing The Truth and all that . . . damn *Cant!*"

"*Cant!*" The echo of that word, shouting through the dining room, made me suddenly stop, holding my breath in mortification. Cullen looked on with an amused little smile. "I mean . . . I mean . . . I don't mean to imply it's cant for *everybody* . . . I believe in the *truth*. I don't advocate repression . . . or *denial* or anything . . ."

A merciful waiter rescued me with our meal and Cullen tossed back the forelock in delicate triumph. . . . The twilight of the eyes was full on me. In an all but invisible movement of his lips as he lifted his fork, Cullen blew me an almost imperceptible kiss.

I assumed no more grand positions. The meal was over quickly enough, and as we left there was no hint of our going anywhere but straight back to the house on the square. As I drove from the restaurant we said almost nothing; I simply sensed Cullen near me in the passenger seat. At the house, I pulled the car particularly far back into the drive, deep amid some trees at the rear of the lot. I killed the engine and turned out the lights. Then I reached out in the dark and quite clumsily touched Cullen on the shoulder. He merely sat looking at me, saying, doing nothing. Awkward though it was, I let my hand linger on his shoulder long enough for us to both be sure.

"Here we are," I said at last.

"Here we are."

My hand wandered to his face, caressing. He simply watched

while he let this happen. Then we got out of the car. There was a gentle slamming of doors. When Cullen came walking around from the passenger side, I was waiting for him. I put my arms around him and kissed him in a long, open-mouthed kiss of passion. There is a moment in which the swarm of pre-sexual anxiety is suddenly transformed and becomes the silk of eros. Under the big elm tree, kissing another man, I thought, my mouth on his mouth, *can anybody see?* As my body flooded; my hands were all over his back, fingers trying to hold, feel, more. *Let them*, I thought. *Let them see.* I opened my eyes and saw Cullen's eyes open, taking me in, close-up. When I pulled back, Cullen's hand fluttered to my crotch. For some reason I'd thought of Cullen as unlike me, delicate, compact. Now, pressed against me, his body was interestingly like my own.

"I think we'd better go inside."

In the kitchen, I extracted a bottle of Orvieto from the fridge, pulled open the drawer beside the ancient summer sink, and rummaged for a corkscrew amid the teaballs and pinking shears and skewers. I tore away the lead foil, drove in the corkscrew, put the bottle between my knees and yanked the cork with a flourish.

Cullen drank vodka, not wine.

"But to go back to our conversation in the restaurant," I said. "Do you really think I am a hypocrite, just because I'm bisexual?"

"Oh, that *word!*" Cullen groaned. "*Bisexual!*" He spat it out.

"You really think people can't desire both sexes?"

"I think so-called bisexuality is nothing but a way to fight against what you want. I think it's a scared, lying way of holding back. I think it's a *word.*"

I was silent a moment. "And . . . you know what I want?"

"I know *exactly* what you want," he said.

"Not words," I said.

"Not words."

Upstairs, we went straight to my study — where I had worked

so brilliantly during the day — and there I learned in intimacy Cullen's almost depthless appetite for a) alcohol, and b) sodomy. His sexuality was almost uncannily passive. Wordless, he stood near me as I began to unbutton his shirt. "Let me," I said, in a whisper. "Please, let me." He did. Cullen stood completely still as I slowly undid the buttons, pulled the shirt loose, and let it drop to the floor. His naked torso. Now I could look. Look in the absolute way I'd never dare on the beach.

My mouth began to move across his naked shoulders. "Beautiful," I murmured. "Beautiful."

The word excited me.

Cullen wished to be adored. Suddenly, I had found the wish to adore. Adore at long last in some entirely unguarded fashion. Free. I kissed his neck and shoulders and the brown boyish nipples, wide as half-dollars, and, adored, he watched me from the distance of his passivity, his eyes coolly open, his head tilted slightly back, the forelock dangling. He wanted to watch my excitement happen: his face remained expressionless, safe, in the distance of his narcissism. He watched me watch him.

"Beautiful," I said again, moving down his body. "Beautiful."

I now find myself rather interested in my almost incantatory use of this word, in the way I kept saying it over and over again, as if it encoded everything illicit in our excitement. I suppose this comes partly from the mild sense of transgression provoked by using the word "beautiful" to describe a man. But there was more to it than that. Somehow the word stirred something deep and frightening in me. *Beautiful.* At one moment, I thought I might almost choke on what those syllables awakened in me. I felt myself slipping into something secret, dangerous, private beyond describing. For me, that stirred, dangerous, secret thing constitutes the one true difference between my homosexual and my heterosexual lovemaking. It was frightening; it was exciting; it was deep in a dissociated privacy which was part of my soul. I suppose Cullen would have called it my truth, or rather, Truth.

Yet even that deep, secret excitement had its double side. I think it worth noting how for all its strangeness, what we did found expression in the most classical gestures of eros; *mutatis homosexualis mutandis*. As we tumbled into it, I continued to describe my mystery with *the* most ordinary word in the entire erotic vocabulary. *Beautiful, beautiful, beautiful.* In truth, ours was a quite ordinary swoon, though it drew me into the depths. I suspect even Aschenbach, as he entered the forbidden, isolating extenuations of his last vision of desire, must have realized that there was also something in his ecstasy of adoration just a bit ordinary, just a shade banal.

"Please," I said. "Please let me strip you down."

Inch by self-exciting inch, I loosened the belt, slid down the pants, saving the downward slide of the shorts for last. All through this ritual, Cullen's arms hung limp at his sides, the vodka glass dangling from one hand. He now had an erection, and it was enthusiastic enough in its somber, ignored, poking rigidity. But otherwise, as Cullen grew more and more excited, he became more and more loose and pliant.

I had stripped him bare.

Beautiful, I groaned, blinded by the vision.

A certain amount of elementary but essential equipment was called for what next transpired. However simple, that equipment was not to be found in "our" medicine chest. Luckily, Cullen travelled with a fully equipped flight bag. His paraphernalia included a silver hip flask filled with vodka; several giant economy size tubes of lubricant; and the amyl nitrate that in those days still was sold in illegal ampules called poppers, items which played a central role in Cullen's sex life and of course none at all in Nancy's and mine. Still naked, still beautiful, Cullen padded down the hall — I loved watching him walk — and returned from his cubicle, equipped.

We went on and on. Everything that Cullen's suspicions possibly could have intuited since we'd met was now performed in the summer swelter. We did much that men can do with women, and much that they can't. Cullen remained utterly,

enchantingly passive throughout; I felt, coursing out onto that
tender corrupt boyish passivity, all the bitterness that was
mixed in my capacity for excitement and delight. We slipped in
each other's sweat; the musty sheets of the daybed were soaked,
reeking in KY; again and again I drove down on top of those
. . . those *beautiful* fineboned shoulders. Again and again I
heard it, the same shrieking outcry that used to wake me at 4
a.m. on Perry Street, a cry almost like the wail of some creature
hurled over the abyss; a cry that contained all the hurt violence,
all the anger, all the rage I had felt in Cullen's cold person the
first night I met him, that hard contained energy I sensed
lurking in the passive twilight of his watchful and calculating
eyes.

Against all this was the counter-rhythm of the hip-flask and
the drugs, that steady resorting at every pause for breath, to the
swig of the secret drinker; or, high in his excitement, the burst of
a popper and then the sucking sound of Cullen inhaling, as the
drug drove him deep into the vascular ooze. It was something I
first had suspected that first night of the summer, when I had
come upon Cullen on Mel's beach in the night chill, the night
Cullen had admonished me not to despair. I watched him
drink, there in the warm tangled sexual nakedness beside me,
then he hit a popper again and then, just as I always had
wanted him to, grind the perfect beauty of that face against
mine, reeking with the chemical smell. I experienced, among
other things, a simple sense of Cullen's own despair as he
indulged the luxuries of his self-obliteration; I sensed his
yearning to shatter the ego, a yearning more angry and violent
than any I ever had seen before, but which was nonetheless
only one more configuration of that sublime sundering of the
ego that orgasm brings to everyone, and which makes its joy at
once the most profound and evanescent of all the moral lessons
taught by the flesh.

My new path to passion was quickly detoured. I'd ended our
debauch that night by dragging Cullen to bed in the master

bedroom, the room that once had glowed for me as the sanctum of my heterosexuality. I'd pulled him to sleep after me, reeling and sated, and we both slept at last, deep and in each other's warmth. But when I surfaced from the numb dreamless state that had ended all that tumult, I recognized with a small hollow start that he was gone. I was alone.

"I sleep better in my own bed," Cullen explained when I found him in the kitchen. He seemed miraculously restored from all of last night's ravishings, both physical and chemical, and was coolly finishing a breakfast for one. His tone was not exactly love-struck.

"That's a disappointment," I said. "It's been so long since I've slept beside anybody in that bed, I would have liked waking up with somebody. Even with this hangover. Are you sure," I asked with what I hoped was a saucy turn of my eyebrow, "that you don't want to try the big bedroom again tonight?"

Cullen was sure. Despite my fantasy that we had discovered a new and wonderful level of intensity together, Cullen's views to the contrary seemed remarkably clear.

"I am sure," Cullen dryly pointed out, "that sleeping in my boss' bed with my boss' boyfriend is not the shrewdest idea I can think of."

"Well then, I'll sleep in *your* bed." I tossed away the privilege of the master bedroom without a second thought. "Besides, Cullen, remember I am Nancy's former boyfriend. *Former* boyfriend. Our relation is ancient history. . . . Well, almost ancient history."

"You may recall," Cullen said, "that my bed, which you chose for me, is very narrow. I think we had better stick with what we have."

Cullen was not particularly loving during the afternoon either. Around two o'clock, he announced he was going out. He assumed I'd be working.

"Oh no, no," said I, ever eager, in spite of the prevailing chill. "After a day and a night like yesterday's I feel completely free to play all day today. I'm free, free as air. Who are you planning to see?"

Most uninvitingly, Cullen gave me the names.

"They sound fascinating." My smile was wobbling just a tad.

"They aren't. I can see you'd like to come and ordinarily I'd ask you, but today I don't think that is a good idea at all."

That took care of the smile. "OK," I said. "Whatever you like. Just one little question. Is the problem that I've through some indiscretion picked up a major disease? Maybe I made myself highly infectious doing something I shouldn't with somebody?"

"But," Cullen insisted, "you don't know these people."

"I don't know of any law that says I can never meet new people, no matter what."

"Not these new people. They are close to the gallery."

"So? So am I close to the gallery. It turns out I'm close to it in more ways than one."

"Oh, you're close all right."

"Cullen, don't be cryptic."

"OK, I'll be uncryptic." Cullen tossed back the forelock. "I live on a salary. I'd like to keep it. You may be Nancy's former boyfriend, but she is my permanent employer. Is that clear? And after that I am going back to New York. It was *fun*."

There it was. When Cullen crept out of my bed in that bleary dawn, he had done so because the politician in him had retaken control of his thinking. Cullen had loved many things about the night that had passed between us. He loved the sex. He loved having the goods on me. He loved, I have no doubt, acting on a long-standing fantasy about Nancy. He loved our little dirty secret.

But fun was fun. In one roaring night, he had accomplished everything he wanted to accomplish with me. Career compromise, on the other hand, was forever.

chapter 18

Nancy stayed on in Europe one forthrightly faithless week longer than she'd planned. I was informed of her extended stay by a picture postcard (it was Duchamp's moustached Mona Lisa) on which the message space was dense with a tiny scribble that packed into a very small area a very large number of fibs. The real message came through the scrawl clearly. We were minutes from midnight.

And so I tacked the moustached Mona Lisa to the window above my desk and worked through the long unpeopled days in front of the clattering machine, busy with the task of scholarship, while the shuttlecock of my unconscious darted back and forth, following its own secret rhythm, reweaving the rent fabric of my ego. By day's end I was drained, though physically charged.

I needed some way to work off all those words and feelings. I developed the habit of repeating the long walk to the beach I'd taken that first night I'd learned Nancy was jilting me. When evening came close enough for the typewriter to set me free, I'd set out wearing sandals, shorts and a long-sleeved shirt as protection against the mosquitoes, walking myself almost to weariness. When I'd reach the beach, I'd climb over the guard rail and slide down the embankment to the water. Then I'd sit in the sand while the darkness came on down, bringing my mind to rest in silence in front of that blackening tidal water.

That was where I saw Jeffrey Hastings for the last time. I had reached the water again, and dusk had begun to fall. The shrieking gulls were squabbling over their evening meal. I had slipped off my sandals and was walking in the froth, letting the tide river over my feet.

"Well, as I live and breathe," It was a voice that came from up on the bank, above me. "If it isn't Jason Phillips, all by his lonesome."

Jeffrey.

Finally!

That was my first response. *Finally.* The encounter at the heart of this wretched summer had come round at last. I did not feel fear; I didn't even feel surprise. I was struck by a certain shock, but it was only the classic shock of recognition, something between spotting a friend in a crowd and the moment when the dream delivers the horror it has had, all along, in store.

"Jeffrey? Is that you?"

Jeffrey had been crouching in the sand like a gargoyle halfway up the bank, perched there with his cigarette and his resentments.

"Yeah, it's me. Me watching you."

Then he stood up with a creak of leather and denim and amid a clatter of gravel and stones, came scooping down toward me, his arms out for balance like a surfer's. He flicked his cigarette butt into the sea.

"Well, hello Jeffrey." I held out my hand when he came close enough, but with one dismissive glance he refused it. I decided to go on. "So we meet again."

"We meet again. Too bad, I bet. Sort of thing that bothers you, I bet."

"That's not true at all Jeffrey. Why on earth would it bother me?"

"Well, I guess you figured you'd gotten rid of me way back last winter. I guess you and that whole gang around Dworkin

figured you'd aced me out, once and for all." Jeffrey was, oddly
enough, smiling as he made these accusations. His manner was
so paradoxically friendly, almost confidential, that when I
answered I was half-smiling myself.

"Jeffrey, that just isn't true. It is simply not the case. You and
I may have had our troubles. . . ."

"*Troubles!* You wanted me out of Mercer Street the very first
day you laid eyes on me, that day when you sat there sounding
off about your theories. You took one look at me and you
decided I had to go. Then, when trouble came, all you guys just
rubbed it in against me. You made everything worse. You had
everything you wanted at last."

"You are so wrong. I don't even know where to begin.
Jeffrey, in case you are interested, you ought to know that I
have never once had a discussion with Mel Dworkin on the
subject of you, not once, not one word, since the day you tore up
the *Quick Dreams*. Want to know why? Because Mel would never
have stood for it. He was too loyal to talk about you, and he was
also too hurt. Did you ever think that maybe you had
something to do with what happened last winter?"

"I *explained* about those prints," Jeffrey said petulantly.
"Dworkin never would have cared about those prints at all. He
didn't give a damn about them. There wouldn't have been a
problem if you all hadn't been there to poison his mind against
me."

"That's not the way I remember it, Jeff."

"You remember it the way you want to remember it."

"All right, I'm not going to argue with you. All I can say is
that this version of events simply isn't true. The reality, as a
matter of fact, is much more favorable to us both than you seem
to grasp. But if you insist, the story is all yours. Have it your
way."

"My way is the true way."

"Well, if it's any satisfaction to you, Jeffrey, the friendship is
all over between me and Mel. He's turned against me. I'm out
of The Bunch, and it was a lot more violent than anything that

ever happened to you. You'll also be delighted to hear that he has turned against me in exactly the way you always wanted him to. Everything you used to hate about me, he hates about me now. It's almost as if he kicked me out to satisfy you."

Jeffrey nodded in recognition of our common plight. "Everybody goes," he said. "Everybody goes."

"Jeffrey, will you please explain something to me? Just what in hell did you find so terrible about me? Why was it so impossible for us to get along?"

"I just don't like your kind." Jeffrey had crammed his hands into his pockets. "Filling everybody's head with your answers. You and your fucking answers. You think you have them all, don't you?"

"In truth I don't think I've got the answers to much of anything these days. I don't know what went wrong with Mel. I don't even know what went wrong with you."

This felt like an unexpected moment of intimacy, and it managed sufficiently to invade Jeffrey's mood that I saw an impulse to relent against me warring with his anger and paranoia. I could see it happening on his forehead, in his eyes. Then he said, "I'm still alive. I'm still alive, but I've lost something. It was a great thing I lost, and it was knowing Mel that made me lose it. See, I started out my life with a talent, with a promise, with something inside me that you . . . *you* could never possibly understand. But it was there inside me, and if things had gone right I might have done things . . . I . . . I . . . I could have been *twice* the artist, *twice* the man he is. It was all there inside me, and it was just waiting to happen, to come out and show itself. Except that nobody could see it at first. Nobody except Mel. He saw it. He saw it real clear. Real clear."

"That's true," I said. The dusk was falling rapidly now. "Mel was always a believer in your talent."

"That's right. I know it. Because there was something inside me. It was . . . it was a sacred thing. And Dworkin was the very person ever to see it completely clearly. Besides me, of course."

"Of course," I said. "Of course, you saw it first."

"That's right. But then, once Mel had seen what I had, I made a mistake. Just a dumb mistake. But a serious one."

"Yes?"

"My mistake was that I trusted him. Not that that was so bad to do, because it wasn't Mel's fault that things went wrong. Not his personal fault. It was his position. See, I had this thing inside me that the world should have seen. But it is a big mistake to trust somebody who is already famous. Somebody who the world has already seen, like they should have seen me. But instead, I said to myself, this guy understands how to do it as an artist. I said, there's a guy who really knows how to live. I said to myself, this guy knows all the short cuts, all the coolest ways. All of them. He's got the magic, and magic rubs off. Do it the way he does it. Let him show you how."

Jeffrey lit another cigarette.

"So that is what I did. And that was my mistake. I came to him with my life, and I took my life and I just handed it over to him. Just like a little kid. Just like some trusting little kid. I would have given him anything, so I gave him my life."

"And that was your mistake."

"That was my mistake. I figured if I gave him my life it would come back with the magic rubbed off onto it. It would come back turned into something great. Then I found out that's not how it worked. I found out that when I gave him my life, I had just plain given my life away."

"And so," I murmured, "'you tried to take it back."

Jeffrey did not reply.

"But Jeffrey," I insisted, "that's not something you can't retrieve. You can get your life back. All you need to do is walk away. Just turn your back on the bastard. Forget it. Shake the sand from your feet, chalk it up to experience. The minute you don't care anymore, your life will come back. Right away."

"Me? Oh, don't you worry about me. I've got my life back. That's all the past. It's all mine now."

"But I don't think you have, Jeffrey. You're not really free yet. You can't get him out of your sights. You can't get him out of your head."

Jeffrey ignored this remark. "He's all finished with that blond girl, you know. What's her name?"

"Vicki."

"Yeah. Vicki. It's all over with her. She hates his guts. I know all about it. She's finished with him."

"That's what I've heard. I've heard it's over. That's right."

"See, I want revenge. I look at the life I could have had and I want revenge. Otherwise, I get this hollow feeling. Otherwise, I get so I'm not sure . . . Forget it. Somebody like you never could understand."

"Are you so sure of that, Jeffrey? I've been hurt myself. I'm pretty annoyed with that passive egomaniac myself."

"You can't understand me. I have to choose one or the other. You don't understand revenge. Either it's revenge or . . . or I stop feeling real. Real."

So strange. This conversation surely ranks among the most sinister and alarming I have ever had. Yet I felt quite calm. I felt no fear at all.

"Jeffrey, what do you mean when you say that lack of revenge makes you feel not real?"

"I've got feelings you can't understand. You never were mixed up with him like I was. But even so — maybe you do. Maybe you can see some of it. All of us — see, we're just pieces. Nothing but broken-up pieces of the same broken-up man."

I ignored this last little bit of paranoiac mysticism. My attention was addressed to something quite different. "Revenge," I insisted. "How do you plan on pulling off this revenge you say you have got to have?"

Now it was Jeffrey's turn to laugh. "You? You think I'm so crazy that I'd tell you? Forget it. You just keep those critic's eyes of yours open. You just watch, Mr Mind. You'll see. Just remember that things aren't necessarily over just because they look like they're over. . . ."

Jeffrey pulled back to light another cigarette, and then he

turned to leave, having said too much perhaps. In any case he left without one more word. He climbed the crumbling embankment, sand and stones tumbling down after his climb. When he reached the crest of the bank, he stepped over the guard rail and called back. "So don't count Jeffrey Hastings out quite yet. Jeffrey Hastings is very much around. Jeffrey Hastings is here."

He climbed onto his motorcycle and the headlight was lit. "You'll be seeing me again, Jason Phillips, and sooner than you think. You'll be seeing *me!*" He bounced on the jump start, once, twice, and then he roared away.

That night, I slept in "our" bedroom, dreaming dreams that were turbulent with images borrowed, without disguise, from my waking hours. Hour after night hour, lived life and dreamed dream mingled in an odd tossing urgency. Restlessly asleep, still standing on that beach, my sandals still dangling from my hand, I shouted into a transatlantic telephone, frightened, trying to reach Nancy, wherever she was, whoever she was with, trying urgently, urgently to warn her, she *had* to be warned, that the thief had been restored; that Jeffrey was back, intent upon doing damage, damage to *her.* Oh, I tried, I tried, but all my night-phone connections turned out to be terribly bad. Sometimes in the crackling dream I seemed to have reached her, and then moments later I had not. But I *tried* to reach her. I *tried* to protect her. Against him. Him.

I woke. It still was deep night. I lay still while the old farmhouse around me creaked. When I got up for the bathroom, I refused to touch the lights, trying to keep the sleep closed up within my mind. All of us, pieces of the same broken man, The Bunch were waiting for me, there at the nether edge of somnolence. Their quarrel, my quarrel was desperately close to the surface of thought. Nancy was among them, Vicki was among them, I heard Cullen Crine's laughter and I felt the brush of his flesh. Mel was shouting something to me I could not hear. Nancy was in danger, Jeffrey was murderous, and the telephone wire was humming with distance, unreachable distance. . . .

"Jason." It was Duchamp. "You are being a very foolish young man. You should stop."

"*How?*" I cried out, I didn't care if he saw my pain. Let him see. "How? *HOW?*"

Once again, I woke to the old man's laughter, staring.

I hid my sense of urgency in the days to come.

Ten days later, Nancy was back from her European adventure, and late on the afternoon of her first day back, she called the Springs from New York. After a guarded hello, she told me how Cullen had told her that I knew the story with Tom, and she wanted me to know that she was glad I knew. And so we talked our way through the erotic endgame. It took a bit of long distance time, from Nancy's first "there's something I feel I should say," to her final "I truly hope this has not been painful for you, Jason." As the call came to an end, Nancy told me she intended to spend the rest of the summer in the city, and I told her I felt it was only fair, with my apartment sublet, that I stay on in the Springs house. She immediately agreed.

We were nearing the end. "I'm sorry, Jason. We *have* had a good time, but I guess good things end. I'm sorry. Really, I am."

"We all have our necessities," I said, playing the gentleman. "So we follow them. We did have a good time, and now I guess we are ending it," I lied on, "more or less without pain." I was, in fact, in some considerable pain. "By the way," I added, "my dissertation is almost done."

"Oh, that's wonderful, *wonderful!*" Nancy gurgled, "Oh, congratulations. I just can't *wait* to read it."

"Well, I'll be very anxious to know what you think."

"Truly, I hope this has not been too painful for you, Jason. I just don't know what made us slide apart."

"Belief," I said, quickly, hardly thinking, the word jumping forward, cryptic, a surprise. "Belief and lack of belief."

Moments later, that sudden word crumbled again into its mystery and became inexplicable even to me as I cradled the phone. Our little midnight, solemn, predicted, mechanical in the circle of its turn, had struck at last.

chapter 19

The ending begins with a plume of smoke.

Not the summery, sumptuous, delicious wood smoke, capable of making the whole heavy opulence of the August air suddenly delicate and clear. No. This was a smudging plume of acrid industrial chemistry released and rising high, straight into the unmoving humid empyrean of mid-morning, August 23, 1970, lifting and spreading the stink of burning rubber. I was in my bedroom study, utterly absorbed — it was something like an ecstasy of intellectual attention — in writing the synthetic final chapter of *The Bachelors' Bride*: "Duchamp and the Dispositions of Language."

Then I looked up, looked across the comforting green of the common, the kids, the white clapboard, the sleeping dogs, and I saw it. Smoke. Smoke. Smoke at the very moment the tower siren started to wail. This siren was located on the roof of the Springs, L.I.N.Y. Volunteer Fire Department, visible across the green. It began its scream as it had all summer, with a low, soft, excitable awakening murmur that tightened up and upward until the ear-splitting shriek could be heard by every gasoline station attendant and civic-minded tough guy in town, who instantly dropped everything and came racing to the firehouse of their excitement, and to the rescue. I watched the smoke hover, almost still in the distant perspective. It was nasty-looking; thin, high, visible from perhaps three miles away, hovering in the pellucid blue. Relieved for a moment from the Duchamp-dream, I twirled a pencil between my fingers, thinking how even these country emergencies have their bucolic side. I watched the Fire Department's Irish setter yelping as the stalwarts came tearing up in their Chevrolets. Then the garage door was rising on the revving, precious, red machine, and soon the guys arrived, and the clanging engine roared away. With an indifferent final glance at the smoke, I returned to a parenthetical consideration of the *Étant Donnée*.

That smoke was rising from Jeffrey Hastings' motorcycle, on fire at the bottom of a ravine— a gravel pit, really — near a little stand of woods about four miles from Springs. Of course, the fire volunteers had no idea whose it was; they found only a burning machine abandoned, a ruin of blackened metal, its fenders twisted by the fire, the last smoking carbonized bits of rubber in its tires dripping off the rims in smoldering, bubbling strings. The guys blasted it all with their foam, and then extinguished a little brushfire, nothing serious, set by the exploded gas tank, a few yards beyond the gravelly ravine. It was over in twenty minutes.

Nothing more was discovered about the anonymous burnt Harley Davidson until around one that afternoon, when a sobbing but sullen eleven-year-old boy, accompanied by his tight-lipped parents, was admitted to the hospital in South Hampton with a nasty burn on his right arm. In due course, while his arm was buried in a stainless steel pan under a cascade of ice cubes, he made his confession. Early that morning, he and a band of four or five eleven-year-olds had been tooling around the countryside on their bikes, and they had chanced to find, neatly parked on the shoulder of a rather remote beach road, a motorcycle. Of course they immediately dismounted, needing to check out any such find. It was a fully equipped cycle, all ready to go. It had a full tank of gas. Its keys hung there irresistibly. The machine was still wet, chrome and rubber and glossy maroon enamel beaded with dew.

The boys spent half an hour snooping and tinkering — and scouting the area for the owner, scared of his possible return. But, after half an hour, he did not return. So they set about playing a bit more in earnest. Experiments with starting the engine took another five or ten minutes, until with a grand splutter and blast, the ignition worked. A further twenty minutes was absorbed in boyish fiddling with the mystery of the gears, always in fear that the owner might be coming back. At last, two of the braver kids climbed onto the seat and made the machine lurch forward a few feet. Then a few yards. And then, daring all, two of the nerviest got it to chug out onto the road, while the others hopped on their bikes and wildly raced along behind.

It is perhaps miraculous that the boys managed to get the outsized machine as far down the road as they did. They managed to ride the Harley a full eight miles into the more remote unpaved back roads around Springs, always figuring they were safer from the avenging owner in unpaved obscurity. All seemed well, until near a ravine they hit a soft shoulder. There was a skid. Like an animal enraged in an emergency, the Harley flung the two boys from its back in effortless fury and then pitched over the edge, rolling, its engine in a gear-torn squeal as it bounced downward. Then it stopped. And died.

Trouble for small boys. One precocious rider had cracked a rib when he hit the gravel. He first ignored, then secretly nursed his pain until a full two days later, when aspirin and lying no longer sufficed, he broke his silence in tears. Of course, the boys immediately had gathered around the wrecked object, debating whether just to run, or whether to try somehow to get the thing upright again.

This discussion was punctuated with much fruitless tugging and heaving, during which one boy happened to notice the smell of gasoline spreading, growing stronger. The likely explanation is that in the cycle's slide into the pit, the gas tank lost its cap or somehow was torn open. This worried the boys all the more. In the days to come, silence and confession were the subjects of fierce disputation among them; they endlessly debated, over their parents' telephones, the meaning of treason. Who did and said what to whom was fruitlessly contested. In any case, it seems one of the boys, his identity still unknown, in a momentary flicker of perversity, apparently without one word to his companions, slid his hand into his pocket, extracted a wooden kitchen match, and striking it against a brass rivet on his jeans, tossed it onto the wreck.

It was about twenty-five minutes later that I looked up, saw that streak of black smoke, and the siren began its wail.

"See, what I don't get," said a Suffolk County cop to his sergeant, after they had called in the motorcycle serial number to Albany, "what *I* don't get is why the guy parks on a nowhere road and leaves his *keys* behind, unless he thought he was coming right back, like in a second or two, then he didn't. You know how those guys think about their bikes. Why would he leave it there?"

Guided by an eleven-year-old who was given his first ride ever in a patrol car, the cop drove to the place above the embankment where the boys had discovered the machine that morning.

The patrolman climbed down the embankment toward the water's edge. The afternoon beach light was dazzling, and the cop extracted his dark glasses from his shirt pocket. Fifty feet from where he stood, a little crowd of shouting August swimmers were being made nervous by the sight of a uniform. This was not an authorized public beach. Not that the cop cared. He'd gone to all the illegal beaches when he was a kid. Still did. He had another concerns. He soon found the unknown thing he was looking for. The tide almost had fingered it out: a clump of damp clothes. Jeffrey's shirt already had been teased into the water, but anchored by his engineer boots, his pants still were on the shore. In his pants was a wallet with I.D.

When someone drowns, the body commonly sinks for several days, and rises to the surface only when decomposition has begun to fill the cadaver with gas. That is not what happened to the body of Jeffrey Hastings. The currents of Gardiner's Bay are tidal, and they can be remarkably brisk. The water gave up Jeffrey's body, naked and battered by the rocks, about two miles downshore from that pile of his abandoned clothes.

I suppose most beachcombers are prepared for the bare foot to sink into . . . something, the squishy sickening remains the infantile sea drools on its bib: a jellyfish, a dead porgy, puffed with rot. Still . . . As the tide receded, a woman had jettisoned her shoes to rock-hop down the shallows, peering for shells. She suddenly stopped in fear and held very still for several very long seconds before she feebly called to the man behind her. When he ignored her, the cries became *very* loud. He trotted to her side, still smiling. Both stared, taking in the thing. Then they embraced, and a second later clambered as fast as they could up the embankment, scattering rocks and sand until they regained the road. As it happened, a roadside telephone booth was on the crown of the bank, and from that booth they placed a call for help. The cops arrived within ten minutes. Though of course they still lacked formal identification, two and two were put together. The natural assumptions were made.

Word spread fast. By four o'clock that afternoon I was at the height of my culminating excitement, in the final pages of "Duchamp and the Dispositions of Language." I remember the very page that was in the machine when I glanced down to see Iva in the Kaplans' battered pink VW, chugging into the drive, her face fixed in a frown that even from the second floor I knew meant business. And interruption. I loved Iva dearly, but I did not love interruption. She pulled her roseate wreck around to the back of the house and came in through the kitchen screen door, without (being Iva) knocking. I heard it slam.

"Jason," Iva yelled up from the foot of the stairs. Rolling my eyes, I rocked back and forth in a small seated dance of annoyance. "What *is* it, Iva, I'm busy. I'm *working*, in my study."

"I *know* you're working. Come on down. We've got trouble."

I tossed down my pencil with a wistful last glance at the interrupted page. I would not see it again for a week.

In the kitchen, Iva was rigid when I kissed her. She didn't smile when I made a wisecrack about her and her trouble.

"Don't joke, Jason. Jeffrey Hastings drowned last night. It's all over town."

"Oh—my—*God*."

Remembering Jeffrey's tirade, I instantly thought of suicide. So in the end all that fury had been turned against himself. So that revenge he thought so essential had found its true object.

We sat down together at the kitchen table, and Iva did not flinch even a little when I asked if she thought Jeffrey had killed himself.

"I don't know," she answered. "Could be. I don't know."

She proceeded to recount the story then spreading through East Hampton.

"Somebody," Iva announced, "has got to tell Mel about this."

Iva was right. For a moment, I did not answer. Jeffrey had been so obsessively certain that we were in an irresoluble rivalry for Mel's friendship; so sure we never could both be Mel's friends; so convinced that our mutual contempt never could be arbitrated by one man. Now something else had done the arbitrating, and I had . . . won. *Won!* A false triumph in a false encounter over a false choice, but there it was before me: Triumph — solemn, small, vile. *I* was about to inform Mel that Jeffrey was dead, very possibly a suicide. I, the theoretician, had outlived the doomed clown of male energy, the thief who'd marauded on Mel's ebullient strut, the enraged other self who'd torn up his quick dreams. I had survived the rivalry we'd all invented. Yet hadn't Jeffrey been the one — crazy, drug-smashed, self-destroyed, and vengeful — who'd seen our communality?

"Do we call him," I asked Iva, "or do we go out there?"

"We go out there," she said. "Now."

As we drove out in her VW, I noticed my hand trembling in my lap.

When we reached Mel's place, the Porsche sat magnificent in its customary shade to the side of the traffic circle, so it seemed Mel was home. We had heard, of course, that the sulking Vicki was gone from the house. She had been staying with a girlfriend named Elly and proclaiming It over. On the other hand, Vicki was Vicki; Mel insisted she would come back, and Iva and I certainly would not have been shocked to see her, creamy in her white shorts, stepping out all smiles at the front door.

When Mel didn't answer the doorbell, we began to shout around. The pine woods around the house echoed with a pelting of *Mel! Mel! Hey Mel!* The house stood open. Iva trotted back to the parked VW and leaned on the horn for a few penetrating blasts. Nothing. *Mel!* Nothing but the house, the Porsche, and the hot, dog-day air. "Try around on the water side," Iva said, scanning the house with her squint.

I walked around the building, and reached the bayside of the house, the deck and stairs.

Jeffrey dead.

The light of late afternoon had begun to slant across the water, and the tide was sliding out. I stood still, quiet, glad to be alone, out of Iva's sight. Images of the emergency were taking shape in my head. I stood on that lawn and realized that something inside me was indeed exultant with this news, that I was gaping with a kind of fascinated fury at the notion of Jeffrey's sulking, hulking self-destructiveness, completing itself at last, going down, down — ah, it did please an evil side of my heart. So much for his superior manhood. Down, down, and the thought of those last desperate moments of that terrified suffocating mind, the bursting lungs and the blaze of internal mindlight, as the synapses blew in life's last fighting instincts before sinking into the extinguishing drowned dark — there, in that evil hour, I felt a throb of pleasure at the thought of it. *Jeffrey dead.* A suicide.

Immediately, sentimentality came rushing in to cover my impulses; it hurried play at penance: I felt a sudden surge of terrible sadness for poor Jeffrey. Poor drowned suicidal Jeffrey. Poor, sad, mind-blasted, failed, lost boy. He to whom I had mattered. Too much.

"Mel!" I called out over the water. "Hey *Mel!*"

There was nobody below on the beach. I walked to the deck entrance.

Inside, Iva had taken a can of beer from the refrigerator. "Well, he's not in the house, and he's not in the studio, and he's not outside, so it looks like he's not here."

"So?" I asked.

"So maybe somebody beat us to it, maybe took him back to town in their car."

"So?"

"So, I guess, leave a note and head back to town."

Iva had just begun to write a note for Mel on the butcher-block table when the phone rang. I picked it up. It was Seymour, who skipped the pleasantries and asked for his wife. I handed her the receiver, and Iva stood stiffly by the wall phone while her husband explained to her that a second body had been discovered, not on the same beach as Jeffrey; three miles at least from the point where Jeffrey had been found in Springs; near Noyak. Seymour then told her that thus far no positive identification had been made, and so there might, *might* still be reason to hope, but just the same, half of East Hampton was absolutely wild with the rumor that it was Mel.

Precisely what happened is unknown.

Mel and Jeffrey were together that night. That much is clear. They were spotted slightly before midnight in an all-night roadhouse about two miles from Sag Harbor, drinking together in the murky half-light of a small beery booth in the rear of a tavern beneath a Miller Hi-Life sign. It seems nobody but the bartender spoke to them, but a young woman from Manhattan who had been drinking with the locals at the bar, did spot the celebrity in the room. She felt the frisson of fame. He was in the place for about an hour. While he sat there with Jeffrey, the girl tried to catch his eye, feigning a trip to the ladies' room to stroll as close as she could to their dark walnut bar, turning at the bar to stare at them, straight on. But she could not catch his eye. The famous man leaned forward, hunched over his glass of bourbon, listening. His argumentative friend, swigging beer, was being loud and angry. They had no eyes for her.

Back in the busy art-bars of the sixties, there was a little sexual trick that Mel used to call "leaving his card." When he saw a woman he liked, he would make a point of looking her over, very conspicuously, just once, and then ignoring her, just as conspicuously, for the rest of the evening. Then, just before he left, he'd ask the bartender for some scrap of paper, scribble on it, and ask the bartender to slip it to the lucky girl, timing the delivery exactly to coincide with Mel getting up and sauntering, the most famous person in the room, out the door. The message would read:

DWORKIN

18 BOND STREET

MIDNIGHT

But not this midnight. The girl could not distract the two men from each other. She remembered only that the friend was the one who seemed to be doing all the talking, and that it had been an argument. Mel and Jeffrey left the bar, apparently, a little after one o'clock, their faces still concentrated in their quarrel, their voices subdued in anger.

They left the roadhouse parking lot on Jeffrey's Harley, and proceeded, whatever their intended destination, to the same beach along the great Peconic Bay where I had encountered Jeffrey a week or so before, and for the last time. It is what happened on that beach that remains a mystery.

Let us suppose that Jeffrey stopped his motorcycle there, and somehow got Mel down to the water, for the express purpose of killing him. It is possible. We know that both bodies were found with bruises and scratches about the head and shoulders made not by rocks but by some sort of physical altercation. Mel was especially battered: he had been hit, hard, and repeatedly. That is the strongest evidence for Jeffrey as a killer. In addition, but less reliably, a local motorist did report that while driving home late on the beach drive, he had heard two men shouting at each other in what he'd assumed was a quarrel. Unfortunately, when questioned he was vague about where, and when he tried to lead police to the spot he got it all wrong. Still, it is possible.

Then there is a final known fact to be taken into account. Mel's body was discovered fully clothed. Jeffrey Hasting's body, on the other hand, had been stripped bare.

So what happened?

If it really was murder, if Jeffrey really did in the end exact the revenge he claimed that I should keep my eyes open for, Mr Mind — I suspect he took Mel to that beach intentionally, and perhaps in a way in that his paranoid thinking, was linked to me. He stopped the Harley, perhaps without explanation, and there on the embankment the quarrel continued. They shouted at one another, and it is possibly then that the motorist heard their voices. More likely they already were down by the shore. There the quarrel came to blows, and they scuffled, grappled together. Mel was hit several times. It is possible that he was even knocked unconscious, or I suppose it is also possible that he was held underwater until he lost consciousness. He might even have been held under there at the water's edge until he was dead.

That is when Jeffrey would have stripped off his clothes. Why? Because he was about to swim, far out, from shore.

Jeffrey's next task would have been to make this event seem, if not accidental, at least inexplicable. And so, naked now, he waded out into the black, still water, dragging Mel's inert body after him, pulling it out, half-floating, half-sinking, his grip digging into the soaked clothes. The late August moon would have been large, and very full. Jeffrey would have pulled the body until at last he reached his depth, his toes deep in the tidal ooze. Then, still hoping to pull Mel even further out from shore, he would have struck out swimming, pulling the body behind him in some unmanageable version of a lifesaver's backstroke.

How exactly he ran into trouble is impossible to say. But it is obvious that he managed to pull Mel's unconscious, perhaps already dead, body far enough out to be caught in the rivering and overpowering tidal currents. It is conceivable that Mel even regained conciousness, and began to struggle for his life again. We know only that nobody could resist such a current, and that it swept them, killer and killed, in different directions. We do not even know certainly which of them, killer or killed, was the first to die.

Possible. It is all quite possible.

Or perhaps the reality is some act of violence that rumor and fantasy have not been able to contrive.

Or on the other hand, their deaths may have been quite innocent, both of them. A matter of accident, pure and simple.

Let us say, for example, that the reason they stopped the Harley by that beach where I'd talked to Jeffrey was not at all that it had been selected as the site of vengeance, but simply because on a sweltering hot night, after a lot of drinking, one of them wanted to cool off with a dip. That is entirely possible, even likely. For one thing, it affords a much more sensible explanation for Jeffrey's state of undress than the murder theory, and at least as strong an explanation for how they both found themselves in the tidal currents.

When they got down to the water, it was Jeffrey, not Mel, who wanted the swim, and so he slipped off his clothes while Mel sat by the water and waited, and once he had laid all his clothes in a neat pile beside a rock, Jeffrey waded out into the black water, moving slowly, quietly. The only sound would have been the small splashing against his legs and made by his trailing hands, as he moved out and the cold water line tickled up his skin.

Mel would have watched him go out. He would have been able, beneath that August moon, to keep his eye on Jeffrey until he was quite far out — at least until he reached the end of the shallows and sank down into his stroke. Even after Jeffrey was mainly in the water, Mel would quite possibly have been able to see the movements of his arms.

At least until Jeffrey reached the tidal current. Then the trouble would have begun. Of course, the current would have completely outpulled Jeffrey's stroke. And Jeffrey almost certainly would have struggled against it, rather than surrendering himself to the element. Very likely, he would have struggled against it at first in silence, before he really grasped just how dire his situation really was. Then his fear must have started mounting, very rapidly, toward panic.

A shout in the night, suddenly.

A second shout.

When Mel grasped what was happening, he must have shouted back, often, and loud, trying to pinpoint where the cries were coming from. These may well have been what our uncertain passing motorist heard. Jeffrey may have raised his arms, he may have splashed, hoping to show Mel where he was, and as Mel recognized the emergency, and recognized it late, he may have supposed he had no time. He kicked off his shoes and ran crashing headlong into the water, without so much as pulling off his turtleneck. He himself would have been dealing with sudden fear, swimming as hard as he could, out toward that thrashing, shouting spot in the still, black water. He was not much of a swimmer, and as he went, his jeans amd that damned turtleneck must have grown heavier and heavier. Until, inevitably, he swam directly into the same tidal current that had overwhelmed his friend.

By the time Mel reached him in the water, Jeffrey would have already gone down, perhaps several times. He would by then have been swallowing water; he was certainly by then entirely a creature of his terror. Mel knew next to nothing about lifesaving holds, lifesaving technique, and so he probably went about things in precisely the wrong, instinctive, way. This consists in simply attempting to grab ahold of the drowning man in the naive effort to hold him up, keep him from sinking again.

What he would have grasped would have been merely flailing, fighting arms, violent with terror's great strength. And as a creature of his terror, Jeffrey would have responded in precisely the wrong, instinctive way, which would have been simply to grab ahold of Mel and attempt, in absolute futility, to climb up out of the water, using Mel as a kind of impossible ladder.

That was probably when the blows found on the bodies of both men were struck — as they grappled together there in desperation, as they fought together, as they went down together and died together, separated and swept in different directions only after death in the wild embrace that had come with that final furious battle royal of rescue.

chapter 20

And so Nancy Hopkins and I were brought together for our third, terminal, reconciliation. She pulled into the Springs with Cullen at nine o'clock that night, at the end of a demon drive from town in a car they'd rented as soon as I called with the news, driving straight to the house on the common. I was waiting for them, and at the screen door in a second when I heard the car crunch into the drive. Without closing the door behind her, Nancy jumped from the passenger seat and came across the lawn toward me in a stumble of unhappiness. We embraced. She wept, in soft, soundless sobs. Cullen slid out of the driver's seat and quietly closed the door she'd left gaping.

The news of Mel's death had gone public while Nancy and Cullen still were on the road, carried both on the local evening news programs in New York, and as a short flash on two of the three national networks at 7. The *Times* was not yet out: It would hit the streets, with its front page story, at 11. The phone must have been ringing off the wall in Mel's empty loft on Mercer Street; in the big house, Seymour and Iva were immured, like two beings besieged, inside the circle of publicity. When Nancy and Cullen and I pulled up in the rented car, automobiles were double-parked for half a mile outside Mel's driveway; other rubberneckers crawled by, hoping to see something, anything, that was part of the news. It was like a country fourth of July, with TV lights as the fireworks. Down at the house, the flattening glare of the camera-crews' arc-lights scooped spoon-shaped pools of brilliance against the walls, and as we approached, people frankly broke the distance of decency, stooping without embarrassment to peer zoo-like at us as we crawled down the drive. I remember faces crowding in the car windows as we moved.

The press had been primed but put off by Seymour and Iva. Nancy gave cool, quite properly evasive answers to the eight or ten shouted questions about suspicious circumstances. All the great public saw were a few dark tilting seconds of the three of us wedging our way into the house.

"Thank *God!*" Iva moaned when at last we closed the door on them, and she embraced us all.

The emergency made us a team. The next three days were work: Iva and I drove and talked and arranged, picked up important people at airports and deposited them here and there; Cullen, Seymour and Nancy handled an unendingly ringing phone and negotiated what are called "the arrangements," planning the famous-person funeral in the little country arcadia of the Springs' famous-person potter's field. The question of seating and its higher snobberies, for all the friends and pseudo-friends the famous collect, took on positively Proustian dimensions. Cullen and Nancy and I sat at the butcher-block table, sorting out the social game, sharing, rather sweetly, the cynical black comedy of it all. Mel's telephone in Springs was unlisted, but to hang up was to have the thing ring again. Cullen, Iva and I took turns fielding those hundreds of people, half of them in tears, each with something terribly urgent to do or say. Nancy agreed to a press conference the second day at three o'clock. We worked out a schedule for the rest of that day's time, which included two meetings with lawyers and one with the mortician — and (not the least incidentally), our first encounter with Marilyn Dworkin, a woman who has remained in our lives as a permanent, year-in, year-out emergency.

To say that Mel had not been close with his sister understates the case. Not one of us had heard him so much as mention her, ever, even in passing. Nonetheless, she did have Mel's number in Springs and the instant the news hit CBS she was on the telephone, ordering Iva in unlovely and ungrieving tones to meet her at the airport the next day. Before Cronkite had finished reading his short report, Marilyn correctly grasped a major role for her in her millionaire brother's estate. Until that moment, Mel's life and work had been matters to which Marilyn had shown perfect indifference, sustained by mindless philistine scorn. But, like many people shadowed by death, Mel left no will. This understandable but wilful bit of negligence permanently installed the wretched Marilyn in all our lives. It really is very unpleasant to dislike somebody as intensely as I dislike Marilyn Dworkin. But I am a trustee of the estate, which means that several times a year, I am obliged to confront, head-on, the grotesque rapaciousness of that woman, in combination with her imbecile indifference to the integrity or quality of her brother's work. One senses in Marilyn's attitudes toward Mel's estate every possible grotesquerie of a pure mediocrity taking her posthumous revenge on an infinitely superior sibling. Enough. The next day, Iva drove to the airport, and we met the Heiress.

We were all a team except Vicki. Vicki the creamy coquette of the summer dream, now became Vicki the doubly bereaved; Vicki all grief. Oh, those wracking days of Vicki's heavy sobs, filtering down from the second floor of the house on the strand. Widow-like, Vicki had collapsed there in the master bedroom where she and Mel had played such an interesting game, and there she wept, wept without stopping, inconsolable over both the men who had died. She blamed herself, she never would forgive herself, she must have been crazy to be mixed up with Jeffrey Hastings, and why? *Why?* She couldn't even find a reason. She'd only done it to get to Mel, and now he was dead.

Now they both were dead. All she'd wanted was to scare Mel, maybe get revenge — was that it? — make him jealous — just *reach* him; *something*, and now, now they both were dead, and she was to blame, she was sure of that, sure that except for Vicki they would be alive, both alive and here, right this second. Nothing helped. No insistance that it had been an accident; no philosophy about the error of self-reproach. She knew she was the guilty one. It's true, they *both* were crazy, wonderfully crazy, but crazy, and they both had loved *her*. How could it have happened? She spent days prostrate on Mel's double bed, trying to settle her place in the catastrophe.

Vicki wanted Cullen. When he entered the house, she tottered across the kitchen and collapsed in her soul brother's arms. She clung to him. For one whole day she could not let him out of her sight. He would all but carry her up the stairs to the bedroom where she would cry some more and sleep. After an hour or two, she would feel her way down the stairs again and reappear in the kitchen doorway, a grieving ghost, blasted, speechless, looking for Cullen and his improbable consolation. Her need for Cullen seemed odd. He was so much less compassionate with her than any of us, certainly than Iva, even me. Cullen did not grieve. He did not grieve because he had experienced no loss. In the depth of his flawless narcissism — in that ravishing seeming oneness with himself that had made me ache and rage, that once I'd found so beautiful — beautiful Cullen was untouched. Yet in her unstaunchable misery, Vicki turned to him above all, as if instinctively turning to his ungrieving presence, already reaching for the support of the connection that has persisted between them until the present time. Cullen was cold to her grief and guilt. Three days later, at the funeral, it was Cullen, his forelock blown by a little breeze, who stood, arm around her, in the first row, by the grave, as she wept there in the embrace of an enduring *froideur*.

At nine-thirty the morning after Mel was found, Nancy and I

drove together to the Suffolk County Coroner's office for the legal ritual of identifying his body.

The young man who met us at the desk was very correct. He explained with gentle simplicity, and without unction, the relevant facts surrounding the discovery of Mel's body. He told us that an autopsy was to be performed that afternoon, but that the cause of death had been listed tentatively as accidental drowning. He explained the simple procedures of identification, then led us through a plain hospital-like door, into something called the Viewing Room. With its philodendron, its painted cinderblock walls and vinyl-covered furniture, it resembled a motel waiting room. In the wall was a low wide viewing window, completely closed by the solid sheet of a dark green leatherette curtain. The intern asked us to stand before this window; he then let us know that he was about to lift the curtain. He pressed a button; to the hum of a little motor, slowly it went up.

Mel lay on a rolling table a foot or two beyond the glass, his black hair hanging back, his eyes closed, his lips, his face, his hair dry in dry death, dry after all that water. His mouth was just slightly open. Only his face was visible. The rest of his body was draped under a shroud of waxed brown paper stamped: SUFFOLK COUNTY, N.Y. I could see, slightly, our reflections in the glass, three living persons and beyond it death's stillness. I thought: *Do something. Touch her. Take her hand. Say something. Anything.* But I did not.

"Is this your friend?" the young man asked Nancy.

"Yes," Nancy said, not breaking her stare. "Yes, it certainly is." She had begun to tremble a little. By the time she was asked to sign the identifying affidavit a few minutes later, the tremor would shake the pen from her hand. "Yes. That is Mel Dworkin," she said.

"Thank you," the young man said. He pressed the button once again. The curtain lowered and we never saw him again.

The autopsy revealed nothing more. The verdict for both

Jeffrey Hastings and Mel Dworkin stands to this day as death by accidental drowning. The details of the funeral are too well known to rehearse again here. The crowd was very large. Several of Mel's more articulate contemporaries spoke; a group of jazz musicians he used to know from the old days at the Cedar Bar played "Fly Like a Bird to the Mountain." There were two minutes of silence. We stood, and stood still, heads bowed for that long time. The only sounds were the wind, some distant occasional traffic, the hustle and mutter of the camera crews, and the slow, racked sobbing of poor Vicki, held in the arms of her cold companion.

Nancy stayed with Cullen and me in the house on the Springs Village Green. I slept on the daybed in my little study, where the interrupted page of "Duchamp and the Dispositions of Language" remained rolled in the machine. The next day she moved to Mel's house, and from then on Tom was very much in evidence. At the funeral, in the first row, Cullen sat by Vicki, beside them were Iva and Seymour, and next to them, Nancy and Tom Cotter, together in public as a couple for the first time. Nancy and Tom escorted Marilyn Dworkin. I sat alone.

Jeffrey Hastings was buried the day after Mel by his family — who turned out to be gentle middle-class Methodists from Plainsboro, New Jersey. Displaying that capacity for probity and friendship which will make me love them always, Seymour and Iva were up at seven, sputtering down the Sunrise Highway in that dusty pink VW, on the six-hour drive that would get them to the Plainsboro church in time for the service.

Vicki said part of her wanted, wanted desperately, to go, but that she just couldn't face it. It was all too complicated, all too much. She just couldn't.

I suppose it would have been hypocritical for me to attend. And yet I spent the day grieving, I guess; knocking around that house I was about to leave, unable to work, with nobody to call, and in the grip of a melancholy that was new to me.

acknowledgement

The author wishes to thank the copyright holders for permission to quote lyrics from the music of The Supremes.

© 1965 Jobete Music Company, Inc.

Words and music by Eddie Holland, Lamont Dozier, and Brian Holland.

Used by Permission only. All rights reserved. International Copyright Secured.